The Bones of Boulder Creek

By

S. H. McCord

ISBN: 1467932612

ISBN-13: 9781467932615

Library of Congress Control Number: 2011960802

CreateSpace, North Charleston, SC

for Allison

Acknowledgments

I would like to thank the following people for making this a better story than I could have written alone:

Mom, Dad, Joan, Jeff, Sarah Grace, Tory Leigh and Ashleigh for reading a pretty rough first manuscript, and for all of your suggestions for its improvement.

Scotty, Holli, and Tory Leigh for giving me a wealth of ideas and experiences to draw from as I tried to sew together bits and pieces of our lives throughout the story.

Livvy and Anna Claire for their patience, love, and understanding as Daddy spent the summer writing.

But mostly Allison, for listening to the story as it was being written and making it okay for her temperamental writer to follow his dream. I sure do love you.

1

Call Me Nathan

"Call me Nathan." Of course my name isn't Nathan, but Mr. Butler said that an opening like that was one of the most wonderful lines in literary history, and since this is a wonderful story, I thought I'd start it off that way. Nathan was my neighbor, not really a friend, but since we lived so far outside of town, we hung out and played together mostly out of necessity. I'm sorry to say that Nathan was more of a convenient companion to me than a friend, although there were some that did mistake us for friends, including Nathan.

It's hard to know where to even start this story because I've known Nathan ever since the third grade when he moved in with his grandmother to the place next to us out in no man's land. No man's land was really called Cherry Field, which is a laugh because there isn't a single cherry tree in the whole area. It's really no more than a string of twelve houses built in the 1950s in anticipation of a big factory that was supposed to locate nearby. I guess somebody bought property and built a few houses, hoping to make a nice little profit when the factory came. Of course the factory never did come, and so all that was left was a string of twelve houses, too far outside of town for a regular commute, but not far enough to be good for any of the farm families living out in the county.

My father said this made it the best of both worlds, but I think it just made it affordable. If you happened to be taking the scenic route on vacation, and you drove by the neat yards and vegetable gardens cut right out of the pine woods and veils of kudzu on Highway 52, you'd wonder, *Who lives here, and what in the world do they do?* That's Cherry Field, "no man's" land.

For one reason or another, mostly retired people lived in Cherry Field, one younger couple with three little baby girls, Nathan and his grandmother, and me with my "semi-retired" folks. Everybody kept a nice yard and everybody kept a big vegetable garden. You'd think that being so remote would breed a closeness among the families of Cherry Field, but in memory it seems to me that we shared little more than shallow politeness, an occasional favor, a rare visit, but mostly just the call of your name and a wave from the front porch, or a nod and smile at church on Sunday. Of course this could be the imperfect memory of a thirteen-year-old boy or it could just be the kind of people a place like Cherry Field attracted.

So Nathan and I lived in no man's land, waiting every school morning down by the mail boxes on the highway for the county school bus to pick us up and carry us out to East County Elementary. We were the first stop in the morning and the last stop in the afternoon, and we rode a good twenty-five minutes before any other kids were picked up and another twenty-five minutes after the last kids were dropped off in the afternoon. We spent a lot of time on the bus. It seems like there was a dispute between the town of Fair Play and the county as to who was responsible for the education of the Cherry Field kids. We lived pretty much right in the middle of the two school districts, and nobody wanted to spend the money to send a bus twenty-five minutes out of the way every day to pick us up.

I remember when Nathan and I both had the flu in fourth grade. The second morning neither one of us was out at the bus stop my mom got a nasty call from the East County Elementary School principal. After that, my mom had to phone the driver anytime Nathan and I weren't going to catch the bus. This meant when I wasn't going to school, Mom had to call Nathan's grandmother in the wee hours of the morning to find out if Nathan was. This caused a particular problem because Nathan's grandmother was hard of hearing and very used to her own schedule, so more often than not, she didn't answer the phone.

At some point, my mom decided that she wasn't going to walk next door at four o'clock in the morning just to find out if Nathan was going to school, so any time I got sick, she just canceled the bus. I know that sounds a little irresponsible, but Nathan didn't like going to school without me, and I'm sure he was happy to be spared the long ride alone. I don't think his grandmother ever said anything to Mom about any of the spontaneous vacations. I know she wasn't feeble enough to think it was another school holiday. The old lady was probably just glad that someone else took responsibility for making the call to the bus driver, even if it did mean the truancy of her grandson.

Nathan's grandmother was a nice enough old lady, maybe a little worn down from a responsibility that shouldn't have been hers. She had adopted Nathan's mother after her husband died, partially to ease her own loneliness and partially to do a good turn for a child nobody loved. But as sometimes happens, she could never quite reach beyond the wild mistrust that her adopted daughter had learned in the years before, and her fantasy of saving a child became a constant and isolating burden. Late nights, failing grades, boys and men, drugs, alcohol, and even some arrests colored Nathan's mother's life. Seeking to fill the holes in her soul as quickly as possible, she raged against the rules of a family, spewing venom and rejecting the hand of the only one offering true help. When Nathan's mother finally ran away, there was despair at home for a while and then there was peace.

Eighteen months later, Nathan's mother returned home seven months pregnant, full of remorseful promises and seeking forgiveness. Nathan was born two weeks later. When she was feeling a little stronger, his mother walked out the front door, got into a car with a man, and drove away, leaving four-day-old Nathan on the bed to be found by his grandmother when she returned from the store.

Nathan had a couple of postcards and an old leather jacket that his mother sent him in the years before he moved to Cherry Field, but that was it. That was all he had from his mother. I overheard most of the story about Nathan's mom through an open window as my mother talked with Nathan's grandmother on our front porch. They were sipping iced tea when I just wandered into the front room and plopped down in the big brown chair, not intending to eavesdrop. But something they said caught my ear, and that's how I know about Nathan's mom. After that, I was always a little bewildered at Nathan's obvious fondness and love for his mother on the rare occasions he spoke of her.

Nathan and I really didn't talk all that much outside of Cherry Field. Somewhere on that long bus ride to school, he went from being an oddly interesting and entertaining companion to a weird geek that I was ashamed to be seen with. He was even more slightly built than I was, with thick wavy hair, a pasty complexion, and pale freckles. He had a funny gait, almost as if his knees were magnetized and wanted to pull together as he walked. When he ran, his arms flailed about and his knees banged together, making it seem like every bit of his body was moving in a different direction. The sight was so hideous that anyone around would recoil either in disgust or pity. He had a high-pitched shaky, quaky voice that drew mocking mimics nearly every day at school, so Nathan didn't talk much.

Sometimes when the fates cheat us physically, they endow us with gifts of intelligence or academic success to more or less even the score, but not for Nathan. Whenever he was in a regular class at school, we always had two teachers. One was always hovering over him and a few others, making sure that they had written down the homework and had copies of notes. Nathan also took some special ed. classes with only a handful of other students down a special hall at school and at lunch, he always sat with the *special* kids at their table.

I remember watching their group laugh and carry on until a regular kid walked by, and then on perfect cue, they would all go silent like gazelles suspicious of a lion in their midst. I guess I was afraid of the middle school lions as well, and that fear drove me to more regrettable things than simply avoiding Nathan at school. But on the bus ride home, as the students began to thin with every stop, Nathan would transform from an embarrassing geek back into my Cherry Field companion. Although Nathan seemed content that our secret friendship could never manifest until we were finally alone again on the bus, I always felt a tinge of guilt—but not guilt enough. So that's why after all this time I must confess, I was not Nathan's friend.

As I'm remembering all of these things, I realize now that Nathan's story begins for me about the time of the first arrest in the Black Jack Child Murders. The county had seen us all the way through fifth grade and was now sending us to Fair Play Middle School in town, instead of Fielding County Middle School with all of our elementary classmates. It seemed at the time a terrible injustice that Nathan and I should be so easily moved by a previous agreement between the administrators of Fielding County and those of Fair Play, but my parents were accepting and offered no protest on my behalf. For most of us, fate only becomes clear in retrospect, so I will not judge myself for misunderstanding in the moment, but this is where everything changed, and I wish I could look back on it all with a little less shame.

2

Cherry Field Turnaround

There was still a good hour until daylight as I walked across the dew-covered yard and up the front stoop of Nathan's grandmother's house. I pulled open the screen door and lightly tapped on the door.

"Naaathan!" I heard an old woman's voice call inside as the porch light came on. She fumbled with the lock and then pulled the door open. I knew Nathan's grandmother and had seen her thousands of times, but there was always something a little unsettling about her appearance first thing in the morning. Still in her robe, her hollow voice, thin white hair, wrinkled face, and deep-set eyes, all backlit by a dim light somewhere in the house, always made my skin crawl. She looked a lot better after the sun was up. I was always thankful when Nathan answered the door in the morning instead of his grandmother.

"Good morning, Chris," she creaked. "Are you ready for your first day at the new school?"

I looked down at my shoes self-consciously, so that I wouldn't have to look up into her craggily old face. "I'm not really sure, I kind of wish I was going to County," I answered.

"Well, I know, but at least you and Nathan will have each other," she said, just as Nathan emerged at the door with high water pants and his Spiderman backpack from the fourth grade. She gave him a half-hug and rubbed his head. "Good-bye, sugar, have a nice day. And you too, Chris."

"Yes, ma'am," I said as I turned down the front steps and headed across the wet yard with Nathan a couple steps behind.

"You two boys take care of each other!" she sang, watched for a moment, and then closed the door.

I walked a little faster than Nathan's awkward gait could manage, and when I heard him fumble and drop something behind me, I didn't bother to stop or even slow down. I just kept heading straight for the gravel turnaround down by the highway where our new bus would be picking us up. I hated walking through damp grass; my feet were wet and so were the cuffs of my pants, but that's not why I was so agitated. For goodness sakes, we were headed for school—*a new school*—so you'd think Nathan might want to wear some pants that fit and get a backpack that wasn't age appropriate for kindergarten! Being from Cherry Field was going to be bad enough without dressing like a magnet for ridicule. No matter how hard I ignored Nathan at school, I was sure that my Cherry Field association with this goof was going to prevent me from ever really fitting in.

By the time I got to the bus stop, Nathan was a good thirty steps behind me. He was clutching Spiderman in both arms, all out of breath, running like eighty-five ponds of nerve damage. His feet finally hit the crunchy gravel of the turnaround just before the bus's headlights appeared on the highway. We didn't have any time for conversation, so my disgust remained hidden in the predawn darkness. I'm sure Nathan thought I was just preoccupied with not wanting to be late for the bus on our first day, and he was probably thankful that I had set a pace that allowed him to be on time as well.

The bus swung wide onto the gravel followed by the sharp smell of diesel that wafted over us in the early morning air. It rolled a little past where we were standing, so we had to walk up along its yellow side, where "Fair Play Public Schools" was stenciled, to get to the door. The bus hissed and lights came on inside just as the door popped open. "Gooood morning, Cherry Field! I almost didn't see you boys standing there in the dark like that. It would have been a shame to squash you on the first day of school. My name is Bill, boys, and I'll be the one coming to get cha."

I stood at the bottom of the steps just staring at the old driver's face. He certainly was a chipper fellow smiling and smelling of fresh coffee. Unless I had gotten into trouble, our bus driver from the county never said two words to me, so I stood there a little shocked looking up at the old man in the dim bus lights. "C'mon, c'mon, c'mon, let's go, let's go," he said all in one breath, "hop aboard. We got to get it spinning so we won't be late on the first day."

"Yes, sir, good morning," I muttered as I climbed the stairs of the empty bus, meandered a few rows back, tossed my backpack on a seat, and followed it with all my weight and a deep sigh. *Here we go,* I thought.

Nathan had instinctively taken the seat directly behind Bill. He always sat behind the driver on the bus, and it was just better that way. It didn't take too many ear flicks, spit balls, name calling, or any of the other idiotic shenanigans that generally occur on your average school bus ride for Nathan to learn that the safest seat in the house was right behind the driver. That's where he always sat going out to East County, only venturing back into the bus in the afternoon for our solitary ride together after the last students had been dropped off.

I was just an average student, not particularly athletic or strong, so when the bus bullies were having their fun with me, I often thought about sitting up there in the safe seat with Nathan. But I was sure that would have made everything worse. If Nathan and I were ever together around other people, it would have all been much worse, at least for me, I thought.

"Hold on, boys," Bill laughed, "here comes a *tight* turn!" The bus roared and then lurched forward into such a hard left turn that it felt like tires had come off the ground. I heard the gravel spewing, and I slid right off my seat onto my butt in the aisle. My backpack followed, slapping me in the face before I even knew to expect it. Bill thought it was hilarious as he whipped the bus around out onto Highway 52 without even looking and headed toward town for his next stop.

The inside lights popped on. "You okay back there, buddy?" Bill was watching me pick myself up through his big rearview mirror.

"Yes, sir," I said, "I'm fine."

I heard Nathan up front laughing as he retrieved his Spiderman backpack from the stairwell of the bus. "Now that's what I call the *Cherry Field Turnaround!*" Bill bellowed joyfully. Bill pulled that same maneuver any morning he was in an especially good mood. It was a wonder that we never tipped over, and from then on, I made sure to sit on the opposite side of the bus to keep from being slung to the floor.

I leaned my head against the window to let it vibrate my skull and watched the sky begin to lighten as we rolled down the highway. Lulled by the somberness of the early morning and the sound of the road, my mind wandered off, and it wasn't until somebody asked me to scoot over that I noticed that the bus was nearly full.

It was light outside now, and although most of the riders were subdued by the earliness of the first day back, there were a few loud mouths in the back of the bus and some chit-chatty girls sitting a couple of seats in front of me. I'm not particularly outgoing and I don't really meet people all that well, so even though I thought that I recognized some faces from church, I continued to stare out the window until Bill finished the last stops and we rolled into school.

Nathan was one of the first off the bus, and I was glad to see that he didn't wait on me to go inside. I guess he was hoping against hope that Fair Play would be a little better place to be than East County. At least this place was in town, and my dad *had* said that if he needed to be in on business, he would give us a ride home any day that we felt like hanging out at the stores after school.

The halls were crowded. I jostled past a teacher doing her best to direct traffic and answer questions. There was a whir of mass conversation, laughter, and students greeting each other loudly as we pushed through the halls. I finally found my name on a chart paper sign outside my homeroom, went inside, and took a seat.

It became painfully obvious right off the bat that everybody knew somebody and that I was the only one who didn't know anybody. Our teacher gave us our schedules, a bunch of papers for our parents to sign, lockers and locker combinations, instructions about lunch and P.E., and the whole morning routine. When she asked if we had any questions, I did, but since everyone else seemed to understand, I didn't bother to raise my hand. I thought it would be better to figure it out as I went. When the bell rang and we all started to file out, I did hang back a little to show the teacher my schedule and ask which way to go. She pointed me down the hall and to the right for Mr. Butler's first period literacy class. Following her directions, I pushed my way through the crowd, found my room, and sat down, hoping that I was where I was supposed to be.

All of my other teachers that day gave us a syllabus and even a little homework, but not Mr. Butler. He was a big, sweaty man who went on and on about the love of reading and how he had always been a good reader, and that his class was designed to be fun and to help his students develop a *"lifelong love of reading."* He had books stacked on shelves all around the room, and his desk was already cluttered with papers on the first day of school. He paced heavily around the class, asking if anybody else thought the room was too hot.

Mr. Butler talked about how he gave very few tests and quizzes, that his class was a little loose to promote "*the open exchange of thoughts and ideas.*" He talked a lot about his family and told a few stories about going to school in Chicago where he grew up. He seemed a little like a big stuffed character on a preschool television show who really wanted to be pals with the cast of little kids while teaching them about sharing their toys. But even then I knew that adults can't ever really be your friends. Kids do things the kid way and that's something adults neither appreciate nor tolerate. That's just part of being grown. I've always found it a little suspicious when adults make out like they want to be pals with children, and I guess that's why I wasn't a fan of Mr. Butler, even though his class seemed like it was going to be easy.

Mr. Butler had already called roll and was well into his speech about the importance of something, or maybe he was telling a story about a nun, when Nathan walked in late. He had gone to his second period first by accident and was noticeably uneasy about walking into a class that had already begun. Nathan started for the first empty desk he saw.

"Well, well, well, looks like we have a little lost lamb," Mr. Butler announced to the class, keeping his eyes on Nathan. Mr. Butler, obviously trying to amuse us, continued, "And what would your name be, little lamb?"

Nathan, not yet realizing that Mr. Butler had stopped telling his story and was now addressing him, continued to bump through the aisle with his Spiderman backpack, making his way to an empty desk. Mr. Butler looked at his watch, crossed his arms, and tapped his toe in an exaggerated fashion as he waited for Nathan to be seated, drawing chuckles from all of his audience except me. By the time Nathan was settled, Mr. Butler had most of the class laughing openly at his reaction to Nathan's late entry.

Mr. Butler paused a long time. "Are you ready now?" he asked in a sarcastic tone. The class snickered again as Nathan nodded.

"Then would you like to tell me your name?"

"Nathan," responded Nathan in his shaky, quaky voice as he looked nervously around the class, feeling the weight of all our eyes on him.

"Well, Nate," Mr. Butler started, but was immediately interrupted by Nathan.

"My name is Nathan, not Nate and not Nathaniel. It is important to call a person by his name. Call me Nathan." He might have sounded assertive if his voice wasn't so high pitched and quivering when he said it. Even though Nathan was serious, it was hard to take him seriously, and Mr. Butler didn't.

"Well, okay then, *Nathan,*" Mr. Butler laughingly answered, "I was going to say don't feel too bad, because I doubt that you'll be our only *lost lamb* today. So, Nathan, do you have a last name?"

"Of course," Nathan stated flatly.

"And that would be what, Nathan?" Mr. Butler asked, still amusing himself with the discourse.

Nathan, on the other hand, was not amused. His stare got hard and his eyes narrowed. "Lamb," he answered in his broken, quaky voice.

"*Lamb*?" Mr. Butler's voice trailed up, raising his eyebrows nearly to his hairline. The class erupted with laughter, and Mr. Butler howled himself into sweaty tears. When he finally collected himself enough to speak again he said, "Well, I could be wrong, you really may be the only *lost Lamb* that we have today," and he snorted like that was the funniest joke ever told.

I didn't see Nathan again until lunch. We were all supposed to eat with our classes, so he had settled in nicely with his plastic X-Men lunchbox and bag of Fritos at a table full of *Specials.* He looked up and gave me a nonchalant wave as I walked in with my science class. I gave him a quick glance and subtle nod in response, so that no one in the whole cafeteria could have possibly noticed except for Nathan.

I went through the line for my lunch and was sitting alone at a crowded table alive with conversation when I noticed Nathan sitting with his group. He was talking, laughing, saying something, and then everyone around him started laughing too. At that moment he seemed so free among new friends, not sharing any of my fears or insecurities. I was certainly higher on the social food chain than he was, yet he was already coming into his own by lunch on the first day.

A goof with his goofy friends, I tried to tell myself, but it was impossible to be blind to the freedom and ease of his manner. My stomach stirred a little, recognizing now that I was watching a small group of kids forced to endure the rest of us, as we grew out of our own, less visible problems. I turned back to my Sloppy Joe and cold French fries, feeling a tinge of jealousy for the companion that I was always so ready to discard.

All in all it was a pretty typical first day of school. Calling roll, mispronouncing names, assigning seats until the teacher learns who we are, repeating the same rules and procedures over and over in every class, getting our contact information, what we'll be learning, are there any problems, does anyone have any questions, you may talk quietly among yourselves. That's pretty much where we were headed in Ms. Baird and Ms. Addler's social studies class (we all knew that Ms. Baird was the real teacher and Ms. Addler was just there to help the *Specials*) when Nathan appeared late again at the door.

I heard someone whisper something about a *"lost lamb,"* followed by a little snicker, but that was all that accompanied Nathan's late arrival. We all had a sense that Ms. Baird was a no nonsense lady who was wholly intolerant of unsolicited student comment. She was in control and she was not one to be intentionally tested. Ms. Baird confirmed Nathan's name and then checked him off the roll. She issued a stern warning about being to class on time from now on as Ms. Addler helped Nathan find an open desk and made sure that he received all of the papers that had already been handed out. Although the warning about being late had been invited by Nathan, it was addressed to the entire class, and no one thought it was funny.

After Ms. Baird and Ms. Addler's class, we all filed down the hall en masse to the other end of the school for our electives. It must have been an oxymoron that decided to call them electives since most of the classes were mandatory. We all had to take home economics, business, P.E., art, and health at some point during the year. We didn't even get to choose when we were going to take them, which again makes you wonder why they call them electives at all. As it turns out, I had been scheduled for P.E. It didn't really make a whole lot of difference to me, I was just happy the school day was coming to an end and that Nathan wasn't in any of the final classes with me. After more of the *first-day-same* from an old guy we all called "Coach" and the principal's afternoon announcements through crackling speakers, we were released for the bus ride home.

Bill wasn't as eager to greet us on the afternoon ride. He was mostly full of largely ignored commands about facing the front, not changing seats while we were moving, and keeping the noise down. I slid in next to a window followed by a bigger kid who spent the ride turned around talking to the guys in the seat behind ours. Nathan had nested in his usual spot, and I leaned my head against the glass ready to be home. I watched as we passed the stores, the library, and the hospital, as Bill made intermittent stops to release the town kids into their nearby neighborhoods. The bus began to quiet with every stop as some portion of the chatter was left curbside to walk the rest of the way home for a snack and relief from the weight of the day.

It didn't seem terribly long before Nathan and I were left alone on the bus with an odd little girl who seemed as intent on staring out the window as I was. By all regards she was a pretty girl who I would have easily mistaken for one of the popular crowd—if the rebellious dyed red stripe in her hair hadn't given her away. The conformist in me was a little repelled by her open individuality and her big hoop earrings, so I was caught off guard when she noticed my stare, smiled, and asked my name.

"Chris," I answered and turned back to the window without asking hers. I was embarrassed and a little uneasy about tainting myself by association with someone who was so obviously an outsider. I didn't want to be an outsider, so I responded very poorly to the first attempt at conversation anyone had offered me all day. I could feel her watching me, waiting for me to say something more. I offered nothing, so she slid to her feet, hoisted her book bag to her shoulder, and headed up the aisle to sit behind Nathan. I watched as Nathan blushed and squirmed awkwardly in his seat as the cute girl engaged him. Pretty soon they settled in, though, and by the time Bill opened the door to let her off the bus, their conversation appeared very light and natural. She thanked Bill, gave Nathan a quick little wave, and then we left her on the street to head on home by herself.

I was still half watching her through the window when Nathan piped up, "Her name is Halley Kate, she's in our social studies class, you know." Nathan hadn't wasted any time moving back to the seat right in front of mine after we were finally alone on the bus. He had settled in with his back against the bus wall and his legs up across the seat. I guess he never questioned whether or not we would continue our secret homebound routine that had long been established on bus rides home from East County Elementary. I don't know why I did.

"Really," I said, not ready to talk yet, "I don't remember."

"Oh yeah," Nathan half giggled and half snorted, "I stepped right on her purse when I came in. Halley Kate said that I broke her grape lip gloss and it oozed out all over her stuff. You didn't see that? Wow, I could really smell the grape too. Ms. Addler kept looking around like she was trying to catch somebody chewing gum, but there was no gum to be found, because it wasn't gum; it was grape lip gloss. Really, you didn't see that, Chris?"

"No," I droned, "I didn't see any of that. I'm trying to do my best to lay low until I get Fair Play all figured out, so I was trying to pay attention to what Ms. Baird was doing when you walked in." I lied, because after the lost lamb incident, watching Nathan come to social studies late with his arms full of papers and stomping all over people's book bags and purses was simply more than I could bear. I just trained my eyes on Ms. Baird and did my best to ignore the commotion being caused as Nathan fumbled his way to an open seat. Ms. Baird probably thought there was something seriously wrong with me.

"Her name is Halley Kate, huh? That's kind of a funny name."

"Yeah," Nathan grinned, "she says that her dad calls her Halley Cater and sometimes just plain ol' Halley Cat. Nobody else is allowed to call her those names, though, because her dad does it out of love and anybody else would be just poking fun." Nathan stared directly at me when he said that last part about poking fun so that I would understand he was serious about not calling her Halley Cat.

"What's the deal with the red stripe?"

"I don't know, maybe she just wants to be a little different. You know, stand out a little at Fair Play, make a mark or leave people with some way to easily know who she is. She doesn't seem like a hoodlum or anything. She seems real nice." The bus ride was bumpy, so Nathan's voice was a little more jumpy and broken than usual. I think that anyone from the outside looking in or who wasn't used to these bus ride conversations would have found the entire picture quite comical. Two middle school boys bouncing along trying to talk over the noise of the bus; one of them sounding like a high-pitched goose and the other trying to keep it cool and low. We were surely discussing important things.

"You know, Chris," Nathan continued, "I think that you should sit with us some days, you know, after everyone else is off the bus. I think that you and Halley Kate might be friends." Then he said half to himself so that I could just barely hear, "I have a funny feeling about her."

A lot of people talk about having funny feelings about things, and I mostly think they say it because it makes them seem special in some way, like they're deep and connected. Sometimes people hope for things or have a longing for something that will most likely never occur, but by saying that they have a funny feeling, it becomes possible and maybe even fated. I think having a funny feeling is about as common and powerful as blowing out the candles on a cake. So, not thinking too much about it, I chalked up Nathan's funny feeling to puppy love for a Halley Cat.

As the bus rumbled its way toward Cherry Field, our conversation continued about the virtues of red-striped hair and whether or not Nathan's grandmother would allow him to get one. Or maybe, he joked, it would be better if his grandmother got a red stripe instead. If he gave it to her for her birthday, she would have to accept, and just think how great she would look showing up at church on Sunday with a fire engine red stripe right down the middle of her gray head. The thought of it made me laugh like I hadn't laughed all week, and Nathan honked and snorted until tears streamed down his cheeks.

"Yeah! Alright! Thank God!"

Our laughter trailed off as Bill's shouts from the front of the bus caught us a little off guard. We looked up, and Bill was motioning us to the front of the bus. "Hey, boys, hey, boys, they finally got him, they finally got that..." He caught the curse in his mouth before it came out. "They finally caught the guy who's been hurting all them kids." Bill was very excited, almost frantic. He was doing most of his talking as Nathan and I were making our way to the front, so a lot of what he was saying was lost in the noise of the rumbling bus.

I apologized as I slid into the seat behind Bill, "I'm sorry, I couldn't hear what you were saying back there."

Bill patted his portable radio, the one bus drivers aren't supposed to have, and started again, "They just announced that an arrest has been made, and they caught the guy that's been killing all them kids up and down all the little towns. Looks like they're going to charge him in all sixteen murders. It looks like it's all over, boys...*it's all over.*"

I knew something bad had been happening and that they were finding bodies of kids in the woods around a bunch of small towns, but that never really seemed to have anything to do with us. All of that was happening miles away to people we didn't know, so I was kind of surprised that it was so important to my bus driver.

Apparently it was a bigger deal than I thought, because the arrest was all the news would cover, and all the adults would talk about for the next month or two. Everyone with a closet concern was now unveiling it, and they were all relieved that the children of Fair Play and Fielding County were going to be safe. I never knew that we weren't safe, so all of the talk, to me, was just something else that happens in the world of adults.

Bill whipped the bus into the gravel of the Cherry Field turnaround. “Alright, boys, I’ll see you bright and early in the morning. Don’t be late.” He pulled the door open and left us in the wake of his bus after our first day at Fair Play Middle School.

3

Corg

The rest of the week was pretty much more of the same. The weather was still hot and the routine of school left me totally exhausted by Saturday. As usual, my parents insisted that any homework assigned over the weekend be absolutely completed by Saturday evening, so even though I got to sleep in, I still had school work waiting for me on my first day off. It wasn't too bad; a little math, a few pages in social studies, and a short one-page paper about what I did over the summer, and before I knew it, I was sitting on the front steps hoping Dad wouldn't ask me to pull weeds or clean out the garage. There was a comfortable breeze and the sound of the occasional car speeding by down on the highway with passengers that were probably wondering what people did in Cherry Field. It was a good question.

I could see Nathan sitting over in his grandmom's porch swing, sketching away at his pictures. With his tongue sticking out the corner of his mouth, he would shade, shade, shade; pause, look at his work and then scratch and shade some more. I was sure he was drawing another one of his comic superheroes, because that's what he mostly drew, and Nathan was really good at it too. He could easily draw as well as, if not better than, anything I ever saw in comics or in cartoons. It always amazed me that he knew just where to put all of those lines and those shades, so his characters looked so... *real.*

I would love to have been able to draw like that, but Nathan was real strange about it. Even though his bedroom was postered with brilliant sketches of action heroes, fantastic scenes from other worlds, and glorious battles between good and evil, he never let anybody at school know about his talent. Having such a wonderful ability would have given him just a little more to go on at school and would have made him easier to associate with, but anytime he was in art class, he always chose to make an abstract mouse, a fried egg out of clay, or some other stupid thing, instead of sketching anything at all. It always seemed kind of foolish to hear the teachers' criticisms of Nathan's art when they had no idea what wonderful ability lay in his hands. For Nathan's sake, I always wanted to tell, but after being around Nathan, who would have ever believed me?

One of our neighbors cranked a lawn mower, but instead of breaking the silence the whir of the engine only added to it. It's funny, but I have always found the noise of a distant lawn mower a little hypnotic and strangely comforting. I never have liked watching people actually cut the grass, but I've always enjoyed hearing it off in the background somewhere. Maybe it's just the sound of something else happening, or maybe it's the sense that work is being done even if I can't see it, that somehow puts my mind at ease. I'm not sure if it was my boredom or my curiosity of what Nathan was sketching that drew me off my steps to his front porch, but I found myself crossing through the warm grass toward his house as the lawn mower choked and spit out a rock somewhere in the distance.

"Hey, man, what cha doin'?" I called out as I climbed halfway up Nathan's porch steps, turned, and sat down facing the other way. I remember doing that, asking Nathan a question and then turning away before he had the chance to answer. I guess I thought it was cool, but looking back on it now, I think that it was just rude. Nathan, still in his pajamas, slid off the porch swing, padded over in his Iron Man slippers, and sat down on the steps next to me.

"His name is Corg, Corg the Caveman," he whispered as he held up his paper for me to see. "He just came to me this morning."

It's not very often that something takes your breath away, but as my gaze fell on what Nathan had been doing, I let go with a long, deep exhale followed by a low and involuntary, "Wow."

The picture seemed somehow bigger than the paper it was drawn on. There was so much detail that I had a hard time taking it all in, and every moment I stared at Nathan's drawing I seemed to see something new. There was a massive caveman, barefoot, with a tattered loincloth and a bone chain around his neck. His powerful arms were raised high above his head holding a ferocious, snarling lion. There had obviously been a great battle. The muscles in the legs and arms of the caveman had wounds and deep gashes oozing blood that had been slung everywhere in the fight. The caveman, with a tremendous roar, was just about to slam the writhing lion, which was too fierce to be beaten by any other means, into a deep, rocky pit as other lions looked on from the other side.

Then I noticed a neat hedge and low guard rail, and realized that this wasn't a scene from 6,000 BC. Nathan had drawn the battle taking place at a modern-day zoo. There was a little boy in shorts who had fallen down, dropping his big, round lollipop in the grass at the bottom of the picture. His brother, only slightly older, with one arm raised in self-defense, was trying to pull the little boy away to safety. Several adults, including a policeman, were racing down a path toward the great fight, probably arriving in time to do nothing more than console the children and frighten off the victorious caveman.

I must have taken the drawing from Nathan without realizing it. I held the picture in both hands and dove right into its story. "Why is he here?" I asked without looking away.

"They found him in Antarctica and unfroze him," Nathan responded without hesitating. "They wanted to do experiments on him, but he escaped and has been hiding at the zoo because it feels more like home. He can't even talk, he only grunts."

Nathan's work was so wonderful that I couldn't break away. "So he's more like an animal than a real superhero, right? If he's just a brute, and he doesn't know any better, then why would he risk himself to save these children?"

Nathan puffed through his nose a little. "Because he's good, Chris, that's why." I nodded and sat there with Nathan in a solemn moment, gazing over the mighty

Corg as the distant lawn mower scraped and spit out another rock.

"Hey, Chris," Nathan broke the moment by standing and gently pulling Corg away from me, "would you say that I paid attention to detail?" He paused for a second, then turned and headed up the steps to a little table sitting on the porch.

"Yeah, Nathan, you sure do. I mean I wouldn't have thought up half the stuff you put in that picture much less be able to draw it," I answered and followed him up the steps.

"Let me show you something, Chris. Come here and look at this." He picked up a piece of paper, smoothed it out, and laid it back on the little table. "This is one of the first Corg drawings I did this morning…when the idea first came to me. It still looks pretty good for a first draw, huh?" He was half asking me and half telling me as he waved me to his side to look at the picture on the table. With his pencil in hand, he leaned over the drawing and began to tutor me in the art of sketching.

"You see these lines here, Chris, and the shading that's kind of on either side here and here? Well, they have to be exactly like this so Corg's pectorals will match his arms and his torso, giving him that super powerful look that a hero needs to have. You see, Chris," Nathan continued as he began scratch at the old drawing with his pencil, "if I wasn't paying attention, I may have made these lines go like this, and I could have accidently shaded here instead, and if I wasn't focusing, I may have made this loop just a little more, and then there…look at how poor Corg would have come out…if I hadn't been paying attention." Nathan stepped back, concluding his narration at the same time he finished scratching away at the old picture.

I had been watching Nathan more than what he was doing. I was kind of astounded at how nimble and quick his hands moved around the paper, knowing where every line should go without making a single mistake. *How does that work?* I wondered to myself about a kid who was too spazzy to even run across the front yard.

"There," Nathan stated flatly, "that's what attention deficit gets you."

I looked down at Corg, still ferocious, his massive arms and legs laden with muscles, with a wildness in his eyes, his head cocked toward the sky as Nathan had captured him right in the middle of a terrifying howl, and, and... *boobs!* Corg now had superhero Wonder Girl boobs. Nothing dirty, just boobs in sort of a super flashy bikini top.

"Oh maaan, that is sooo wrong," I managed to say right before I coughed up a laugh.

"Yeah," honked Nathan as he stumbled backwards, rolled over, and hit his head on the porch swing, making me laugh even harder. "Poor Corg," Nathan giggled as he picked himself up, "good thing for him that they're wrong about me."

"Good for those zoo kids too," I agreed, looked at the picture, and laughed a little more before Nathan tore it up and put it in the outside trash.

"Now the real question, Nathan," I smiled, still joking, "is... what's *wrong* with *you?*"

I watched as Nathan began to pick up his papers and collect his pencils from around the porch. The smile drifted off his face, and I had the sense with my last attempt at humor, I had gone too far. If I had heard it once, I had heard it a thousand times on any given bus ride home from school. He had gone to the doctor who made him stick out his tongue, checked his ears, and asked him about school. His grandmother repeated to the doctor what his teacher was saying about Nathan's behavior, and presto bango, Nathan left the appointment with four additional letters, ADHD.

"Attention deficit hyperactivity disorder," Nathan said with disgust, "how in the world is any doctor going to look in my ears and tell me I have all that. It was just a set-up, Chris. They should have had Ms. Nichols checked for her ability to teach before they had me stick out my tongue and say that I can't pay attention."

Nathan became increasingly agitated as he continued with his rant over the injustice of his label. "What's so stupid about it is they say that I can't pay attention to anything, when what I really do is pay attention to everything! Things that most people never even notice, I happen to see and wonder about. And when you're wondering about other things, Chris, it can get pretty tough keeping up with the one little thing that everybody else thinks you should be paying attention to! If anything, I have an attention surplus, not an attention deficit! And hyperactivity…"

Nathan's voice started to crack into weird little high-pitched yodels when he got to this part. "Are you kidding me? You know me, Chris, after I sit down in class I try to never get back up again, unless I sneeze or something. I'm always afraid that I'll be stepping on purses or falling over somebody's book bag and hitting my head on the teacher's desk. I'd rather sit there quietly not taking notes or not doing my work than get up in a class full of people and sharpen my pencil or ask to borrow a piece of paper." (Nathan didn't like the way he shook when he sharpened his pencil.) "How's any quack worth a tongue depressor going to see me for two seconds and decide that I'm swinging from the lights at school? How can he just do that Chris? It doesn't help at all." Nathan sighed deeply to collect himself. "They do have me on the disorder part, though, I'm not very well organized, and I lose things all the time."

Nathan didn't say anything more, just piddled around the porch haphazardly stacking papers on the little table just in time for a slight breeze to kick them back off again. We were so far away from school, and after laughing and seeing the masterpiece of Corg I kind of liked Nathan a little better, I'm ashamed to say, the way people like their dogs better after seeing *Old Yeller*. My dad called from across the yard.

"I got to go clean the garage or something, Nathan. I guess I'll see you tomorrow at church. Let us know if you need a lift."

He looked up from what he was doing as I backed down the porch steps. "Grandmom's feeling okay, so I should be alright for a ride. I'll see you tomorrow, Chris."

I held up my arm in a gesture of good-bye and trudged back across the warm grass toward my weekend chores.

4
The Postcard Church

Sunday morning brought Mom's usual scrambled eggs, grits, and bacon before church. Sitting across from Dad at the breakfast table, I stirred my eggs and grits all up together into sort of a yellow and white mash and then crumbled my bacon on top. I knew that Dad disapproved, but because Mom's grandmother was the one who taught me this backwoods country way of eating my breakfast, the ritual was kind of sacred, and my small rebellion always went unchallenged. Her name was Maw Maw, and she was an ancient woman that I really only remember from our visits to the old folks' home. It was always strange for me to see how she ran all over my dad like he was still a little boy, and how either out of respect or reverence, he allowed her to do so, even though it obviously annoyed him. Sitting in the old folks' cafeteria is where Maw Maw made me "coffee milk" and taught me to mix my breakfast, both to the tacit disapproval of Dad.

My mom still talks about that old woman from time to time, and I guess it's the stories she tells that make

Maw Maw more than just a nursing home memory to me. Knowing a little about that old woman in her younger days somehow makes my family seem bigger, more important, and even a little purposed. It's kind of neat to have an ancestral standard, even if you'll never live up to it. I always liked having a hero in the family, particularly one woven in my own mother's memories.

Mom and Dad got up from the breakfast table early, leaving me to halfheartedly scrape the dishes and load the dishwasher before I got dressed for church. I climbed into the backseat of our car and watched as the pines and kudzu went speeding by, finally giving way to houses and then to buildings as we bumped across the railroad tracks and headed on into town. The streets always seemed to move at a slower, more peaceful pace on the Sunday morning drive through Fair Play. We passed the hospital, the Tastee Freeze, B & B Hardware, and the Piggly Wiggly on my side of the car, before turning on to Main Street for the drive into the square.

The Fair Play town square was just like a million others. It was your basic park surrounded by buildings on three sides. There was Charlie's Ice Cream store, Old Sarge's Army Surplus, Reed's Drugstore, a diner, a cloth shop, and a bunch of other little stores that I never went into. About a half-dozen Pullman sleepers and a dining car rested on the abandoned tracks on the far end of the square. They looked pretty cool, really, but I remember there being a big stir over the mayor using town money to buy those old railroad cars. They were supposed to beautify the square and later on be turned into a museum or offices, but in the end, they were only used at Christmas as the place to go to have your picture made with Santa.

Our church sat right on the corner of the Fair Play town square, and the building was so traditional in appearance—sitting on the edge of town with its neat green hedges, its white clapboards, tall steeple, and bell tower—that people actually called it the "Postcard Church." I remember people coming from all over the county to be married at our church. I think that many of them even joined to get the member discount on their wedding fees. And even though it always felt like we should have been there early enough on Sunday mornings to get a space in the church lot, my dad usually had to park at the post office, and we ended up walking two blocks from there.

I wasn't a real big fan of Sunday school, but my dad was insistent that we go every week. "The service is for worship," he'd say, "and Sunday school is where you learn." For me, though, Sunday school was nothing more than taking turns reading a story out of a pamphlet and then discussing it with a bunch of kids who were doing their best to act differently than they did all week. Everyone was simply behaving the way the people immediately around them expected them to behave, just like they did at school. Nobody was ever who they seemed to be on Sunday. So when a popular kid actually spoke to me at church, it meant very little, because I knew that as soon as church was over and we were back at school, that kid wouldn't give me the time of day.

Besides, I didn't like being somebody's Bible story charity case, where they could so easily gain absolution by stooping low enough to speak with the likes of me. So I never liked Sunday school and found myself resenting the inconsistency and hypocrisy that it revealed. In a place where many like me flourished in the brief reprieve of our social status at Fair Play Middle School,

I withdrew and never allowed myself to enjoy the sanctuary and equality that Sunday morning could have provided. I was there to survive, the same way I survived at school.

Sunday school, a place where the judgmental are judged and everyone bends over backwards to be patient with those out on the fringe, was custom made for Nathan. I don't know that he really liked Sunday school as much as he took advantage of it. It was a place where he had a voice and was permitted to ask mostly off-topic questions without a stern reprimand or rippling snickers. He wasn't a "special" at this school, and his teachers couldn't easily shield themselves behind a narrow curriculum and highly defined goals and objectives.

Nathan seemed to think that all of this was very important and paid little attention to the agenda outlined in our Sunday school pamphlets if he didn't regard the topic as worthwhile. He never monopolized any conversation or went off on a rant or anything like that. Nathan just figured as long as he had a representative of the church there who was duty bound to answer his religious questions he would go ahead and ask what he really wanted to know. After all, time was scarce.

The real problem was that his unscripted questions had most of our Sunday school teachers squirming in their seats, earning Nathan a reputation as a pedantic twerp. It's too bad that in the end our teachers were only politely dismissive of him, for if they had considered Nathan a little more closely, they may have seen the innocent irreverence that the truth so dearly loves.

I emerged from a daydream as we wheeled into the post office parking lot to find a spot and got ready for the short trudge across the square. Although my parents talked with each other for the entire walk over, I mostly just watched my feet, only looking up every now and then to avoid bumping into a lamp post or some other unyielding object. As usual, church was crowded and Dad started shaking hands and slapping backs the second we walked in the door. Mom told me to have a good time, that she would see me later in the sanctuary, and off my parents went to whatever class they attended, leaving me to descend the side stairway into the basement where the middle school kids always met.

I was a few minutes late, and as I stepped down from the musty stairwell, I could see that we had already broken out into our groups and Nathan had saved me a seat in our ring of chairs. I made my way over to my spot and sat down as our teacher leaned way over to hand me the pamphlet for the day. The cover had a nice cartoon picture of Jesus sitting with a woman while another woman was in the background doing the dishes. Inside there were a couple of paragraphs, a play skit, and a few discussion questions. As we took turns reading, we learned that the woman with Jesus was another Mary and that the woman doing the dishes was her sister Martha. Apparently Jesus scolded Martha for being too busy making dinner to come in and sit down with him and the other guests. Our teacher certainly toed the line, telling all of us in a near sermon that Martha was nearsighted and thickheaded, and she should have been in the den with Jesus instead of busying herself with mundane daily tasks. It all sounded a little harsh, but that didn't matter, and most of us were eager to join in on the Martha bashing.

The teacher continued to give examples of how we here in Fair Play were like Martha, and how we should all learn from Mary's example. Our teacher nodded in affirmation as we offered our frenzied examples of how to avoid being like stupid ol' Martha. But as the teacher's wife started to chime in support of the derision, I felt Nathan's hand slowly rise, and being that this was Sunday school, he had to be heard no matter what his comment may be.

"Yeess, Nathan," our teacher drew out, rolling his eyes, causing the rest of us to snicker and then fall silent in anticipation of what idiotic thing Nathan might say.

Nathan cocked his head a little, half to me and half to the teacher, and in his shaky, quaky high-pitched voice asked, "Who makes dinner?"

It was kind of funny, but the weight of the question squashed any urge to giggle. As we actually considered what Nathan had asked, all eyes fell back on our teacher, awaiting a sound theological response to a legitimate question.

The teacher made a blowing sound through his nose and then huffed, "What?" as if Nathan's question was hardly worth considering.

Nathan dropped his eyes and then looked up again at the teacher's wife. "I mean, if Jesus was coming to your house for dinner, ma'am, don't you think that you might be really, really busy making sure that everything was just right too?" We all knew the answer to the question, so Nathan didn't wait for her to respond. "It just doesn't feel right to me to sit in a circle in the basement of church talking about how stupid Jesus' friend is for making his supper. I'm pretty sure that Jesus wouldn't like that."

"Wellll, thank you very much, Nathan, for that observation from the backside. That is a very interesting perspective you have there, even though it's not the way the pamphlet teaches us. Let's not think too hard or try to read too much into anything. After all, all we know is what we're told, so let's not make more of it than it is," our Sunday school teacher blustered on as his wife smiled and nodded. "Honey," he finally said, turning to his wife. "Would you like to close us in prayer?" She did, and then we all milled around for a few minutes before heading upstairs to the service.

A lot of kids sat up in the front and center pews during worship. It was kind of a youth group thing that I was never really comfortable enough to join. I mostly sat with my mom and dad in our regular pew a few rows behind Nathan and his grandmother. There were announcements, the choir would sing, I would get up and mouth the words to the required hymns, we would all pray, the Postcard Preacher would start in on his sermon, and I would drift away daydreaming about various disasters that would allow me to save the life of Caroline Golden.

I didn't really know Caroline. She went to school out in the county, attending our church rarely and never coming to Sunday school. She was a tough-looking dirty blonde with a gravelly voice that made me forget how to speak whenever she came near. She and her parents never sat in the same place, and when I finally spotted them in the congregation, I would have to make a conscious effort not to stare too long. Pretty soon I'd be dreaming about robbers, a church fire, an earthquake, or any other disaster I could conjure up that would have me leaping over the backs of the pews to save the life of the fair Caroline Golden. I always ended by carrying her out the front doors of the church to the awe and applause of the townspeople of Fair Play. Her mother would hug me, her father would shake my hand, and Caroline and I would be forever bonded by my single heroic feat.

In the background somewhere I could hear Reverend Lane saying in an overly emphasized voice "No matter what we do, or what we have done, Jesus gives all of us a second chance," but that was pretty much all I got before the closing hymn. God bless Caroline Golden, she really makes a drab sermon truly fly by.

As usual, I waited on the front steps of the church as my parents chit-chatted all the way down the aisle with people they wouldn't see until next Sunday. There was no awe or applause for me outside, just an occasional bump, an "excuse me" or a "have a nice week." Everyone seemed so happy, but I really couldn't tell if the lighter mood was because of church or because church was over.

My parents finally emerged at the top of the stairs, smiling, hugging, and shaking hands as they passed through the crowd. My dad shouldered me a half-hug and my mom gave the back of my head a single stroke as we started off side by side across the square back to the car. They asked me about Sunday school class, but it seemed like too much effort to talk about something that I had only endured, so I didn't have much to say. We piled back into the car, and Mom waved at the people she knew as we wheeled our way out of the parking lot, around the pedestrians, and back out onto the main road. Soon my parents' front seat conversation was lost to me as I let my head rest against the glass, numbing my jaw and tickling my ear as we headed out of town back to the middle of nowhere.

5

The Path to Flat Rock

With chores and homework all completed on Saturday and the Sunday lunch dishes put away, Nathan was my last line of defense against the ever looming boredom of Cherry Field. My relief from the clutches of having absolutely nothing to do was foundational in our association, and although Nathan enjoyed the company, it always seemed to be me seeking him out and never the other way around. I stepped down off the front porch and over to the garage to get my fishing rod before heading across the yard to Nathan's house. I could see that he was sketching out on the front porch again, but I felt sure that he would still want to go with me out to Flat Rock…he always did.

"Hey, man, what cha doing," I called to Nathan as I put my foot on the first porch step and then stopped there.

"Nothing, Grandmom's lying down and told me that I needed to get out of the house awhile. I thought I might draw a little, you want to?" He lifted his pad and pencil in a halfhearted invitation. It was kind of a stupid thing to ask because Nathan and I had only drawn together once when he first moved to Cherry Field. He taught me how to draw a hockey goalie. And that one time, lying on our bellies on his bedroom floor, is when I found out that he was Picasso and I was barely Mr. Stick Figure. I remember at first being in awe and then just being embarrassed, so whenever Nathan asked about drawing after that, I always declined. Besides, I was standing here with a fishing rod in my hand!

"Nah, that's alright. I think I'm going to head out to Flat Rock for a little bit and see if they're biting. You wanna go?"

"Yeah, I'll do that," he grinned as he laid down his pad, tightened his shoes, and pounded down the steps with heavy feet. He was always so noisy.

Nathan had to trot to keep up with me as our pants whipped through the tall grass when we walked up beside Ms. Hall's house. Nathan always liked to walk side by side and he always wanted to talk, which usually left him sweating and out of breath before we even got to the woods. No one ever minded us cutting through their yards as long as we stayed out of the flower beds and walked around the vegetable gardens. So we kept to the stepping stones as we passed by Ms. Hall's rose garden, ducked under her scuppernong arbor (we always helped ourselves to a few), and then went way around the perimeter of her vegetable garden before finding our path to Flat Rock and being swallowed by the woods.

The woods welcomed us as they always did with deep, cool shadows and secrets that whispered through the canopy above. Nathan naturally stopped his chatter to fully bathe in the spell cast by the great trees and thick underbrush as we traipsed along to only the sound of our breath and the rustling leaves at our feet. Cherry Field and Fair Play were so far away and small, and although we would collect those burdens on our way back home, we were free and always seemed more like friends on the path to Flat Rock.

I could hear the familiar roar of the water as we moved away from everything else and closer to our destination. Flat Rock was one giant flat boulder jutting way out into the middle of Boulder Creek. I don't know what the official name of that creek is, but Nathan and I always called it Boulder Creek. Although it was never more than a couple feet deep, the seething water colliding and swirling around the massive rocks could easily sweep you off your feet and send you on a bumpy ride downstream if you weren't careful. The creek seemed to have a spirit of its own, always demanding that we speak up and threatening to trick us into losing track of time. And although the creek often promised arrowheads and gold, it never gave up either, even though we spent long summer days searching for both along its shore. I guess some creeks just love to play with boys.

The climb down to Flat Rock from our side of the creek was a steep one, but it didn't take long to get up or down this part of the bank if you knew what you were doing. Although there was a clear thirty-foot drop down to the flat rock from where we stood at the top of the bank, Nathan and I had stopped being afraid of the climb long ago. We scaled the bank as easily as ever and stepped out onto the big, flat boulder at the bottom. There were high, steep bluffs on our side of the creek, but the banks were low and flat on the far side. It almost seemed like the earth changed levels right here.

The woods that watched from that far side were thicker and veiled in kudzu, unapproachable and forbidden by my parents. Boulder Creek was as far as I was allowed to go in the woods. There was a wide stony beach just downstream from our usual perch on Flat Rock, and Nathan had already slipped off and waded across to hunt for arrowheads. He usually brought back some triangle-shaped rocks that we'd end up skipping across the water before we headed home, and I would cast my spinner into the water for an hour or two thinking of very little.

I hadn't noticed Nathan trudge back through the water with the front of his shirt rolled up into a pouch full of rocks until he dumped them all right next to where I was still sitting.

"Hey, man, don't get me wet! Gah, Nathan, what have you been doing, rolling around on the bank? Look how nasty your shirt is."

"Yeah," Nathan smiled, looking up from his shirt, "I was searching for arrowheads. I think I might have found some too." He put his hands out and tried to pull himself up onto the rock, but he got stuck half way on his belly and had to push himself back down into the creek. He gave me this pitiful look. I hung my head, shaking it a little, and then I got up and gave him a hand out of the water.

"You think any of these are good, Chris?" he asked, pointing to his collection of wet triangles.

"Maybe," I said, fingering through the pile, "but I don't think so. These don't look anything like the one you bought at the souvenir shop. You see, they're too big, they don't have any chip marks in them, and all of their points are as dull as can be."

"Yeah, I see what you mean," Nathan muttered, looking down at his rocks. "Do you think they could be spearheads, Chris?"

I shook my head. "Why do you keep looking for those things, Nathan? Don't you know that you're never going to find what you're looking for? There probably weren't even any Indians around here anyways."

"Oh, I don't believe that, Chris," he said, picking up a triangle rock and trying to skip it across the creek, "because if I was an Indian, I'd bet I'd like to come here."

I reached over and picked up one of Nathan's rocks, stood up, and for the next few minutes we took turns skipping his collection of triangles out across the water. I guess the sound of the creek teased me into thinking about church and, more specifically, rescuing Caroline Golden from some great disaster, so when Nathan's next question broke our silence, it caught me off guard.

"What do you think is on the other side, Chris?"

"Uh, I don't know, maybe a lot of fat little baby angels flying around playing harps, while we stand on a cloud casting a spinner out into the Milky Way." I was trying to be theological as well as poetic.

I could see the tip of a smile that was probably filling the whole back of his head as Nathan considered the possibility of my answer. "No," he said, "I mean, what do you think is on the other side of the creek?"

I'm not very good at laughing at myself, so I felt a little stupid, but that feeling rushed away quickly with the churning water. "I'm sure there are just more woods," I finally answered.

He paused, "Maybe gold," he said, peering into the woods on the far bank.

"Maybe arrowheads," I said, considering the boundary for the first time.

Our voices had almost been too low to hear through the roar of the water around the boulders as we stood on the flat rock a long moment wondering about the other side.

"He's wrong, you know." Nathan broke the silence.

"Who?" I asked, not ready to lose the moment.

"Reverend Lame."

"About what?"

"He said that we all get second chances, but he's wrong."

I turned to look at Nathan, but his eyes were still fixed on the woods beyond the far bank.

"He's wrong," he continued. "We may get forgiveness, but we never get second chances."

6

Dust and Draft

The weeks dragged along making very few memories except for the weight of school and the never ending battle with boredom in Cherry Field. Though I rarely spoke with her myself, it seemed to me that Nathan and Halley Cat had become very comfortable with each other as I watched them talk together even before all the other kids had gotten off the bus. He had a goofy fondness for her, and I could tell that he missed her when she wasn't on the bus ride home, which seemed to be more often than usual. In a way, I guess I resented being Nathan's second choice, although I always knew that I had done that to myself. As the bus hissed and let her out, he would say his geeky good-byes and then stomp back to where I was sitting. I usually took a few minutes to warm up to any conversation.

I guess it was about this time when I discovered that Nathan sometimes went out to Flat Rock without me, which was weird, because I would never go out there alone, not after that one time. I remember Nathan was sick or something and I was doing my best to kill a little of the day, so I wandered on out to the rock. The creek was much louder than usual, and the rocks and the water and the trees all seemed disappointed that I had come by myself. The woods on the far bank threatened to press me right off Flat Rock, and I became so uneasy that I had to leave for home after being out there only a few minutes.

In my haste to scurry back up the bank, I slipped near the top and just barely grabbed on to a root, avoiding a terrible fall to the rocky creek below. It happened in an instant, and I felt the charge of electricity through my muscles as I regained my footing and pulled myself safely to the top. I had been afraid before, but it was in that moment that I also knew that I could be hurt. I got up and ran so fast down the path toward home that from Ms. Hall's back yard, it probably looked like the woods spit me out into her lawn. So the day I went to get Nathan and found out from his grandmother that he was playing in the woods out at "*the flat rock*" all by himself I was stunned, but I didn't go looking for him.

The days seemed ordinary and regimented with only the anxieties of school to break the monotony of my life. I was a modest student and my parents were insistent about me keeping up with school work, so my academics were mostly uneventful and my classes tolerable…except for literacy. Some days sitting in Mr. Butler's class, I longed for a worksheet or for some words to define, but it seemed that my classmates were highly skilled at his distraction, so we rarely did anything but listen to him bluster.

"Alright, class," Mr. Butler bellowed, "today's warm up is on the board, so sit down and get to work so I can see who's here. Gahlee, does anybody else think it's hot in here?"

Mr. Butler, already sweating, paced over to his desk and picked up his clip board from a mountain of papers, but before he could check the roll, he started chatting with a group of girls sitting near the corner. The rest of us shuffled our books, looked for our pencils, shot baskets into the trash with paper wads, talked and laughed with each other while unanimously ignoring the lesson on the board. I glanced over at Nathan, who was looking around the room wide-eyed and grinning from ear to ear, soaking in all of the customary morning mayhem in Mr. Butler's class. Nathan never tossed a paper wad, never shot a spit ball, and never laughed loudly or became disruptive. He just sat there thoroughly enjoying the moment as all of these things were going on around him. Even so, he was usually the first to be punished or sent out to the hall when Mr. Butler would finally assert himself.

"Alright, alright, alright!" Mr. Butler half hollered as he pounded to the front of the room. The class didn't get quiet and Nathan kept smiling. "Okay, okay." Mr. Butler raised his hand. "You guys have had long enough. It is time to start class now." Still the class did not quiet.

"WHAT IS WRONG WITH YOU KIDS? WHAT IS WRONG WITH YOUR PARENTS? ARE YOU BEING RAISED IN A BARN WITH ABSOLUTELY NO RESPECT FOR ANYTHING OR ANYONE?" The voice of the big sweaty man boomed off the walls of the classroom, and it was the volume, not the weight of what he said that temporarily quelled all noise in the class. Nobody cared, and it always seemed like a victory when Mr. Butler would lose it like that. It's kind of funny how the same students that Mr. Butler accused of being raised in a barn were so orderly and worked so diligently in Ms. Baird's class.

The class was quiet, but Mr. Butler continued to glare at Nathan. "Do you think something is funny, Nathaniel?" Mr. Butler demanded.

The smile fell away from Nathan's face, he dropped his eyes and muttered to himself, "My name is Nathan."

"Gooood," Mr. Butler continued, not hearing Nathan's response. "Now, class, how many of you think you know the answer to the warm up?"

I looked up at the board for the first time and quickly read the short paragraph to myself. It was something about a horseman crossing a bridge on Sunday and three days later crossing the same bridge on Sunday again. Mr. Butler wanted to know how this was possible. His eyes gleamed at every incorrect explanation that my classmates offered. The whole thing excited him so that he had us divide up into groups of three or four to work out the problem as he walked around to eavesdrop on our discussions.

My group mostly talked about how Jimmy Malone and Brett Cower had started a rash of "shakings" in the boys' restroom and how Mikey Sullivan had to have his mom bring him a clean pair of pants to school. Even though my group laughed about it, we were all a little fearful that while standing at the urinal, one of Jimmy's henchmen might grab us by the shoulders, give us a few quick shakes, and cause us to bathe ourselves and the wall in a spray of our own pee. We laughed about the "shaking" of poor Mikey, and at the same time, we secretly dreaded crossing paths in the restroom with Jimmy and his crew. As Mr. Butler walked by, our conversation turned back to the horseman and how he could cross the bridge on Sunday.

"So who thinks they have the answer?" Mr. Butler finally asked the class. Even though no one raised their hands, Mr. Butler still solicited a response from each group and then belched a hearty laugh at each incorrect response.

"Looks like you guys aren't quite as smart as your parents think you are," he announced with a fat man's sly smile after the final group had failed to explain the riddle. He plodded to the front of the room grinning, cherry-faced and sweating. He smiled wide and then leaned in to reveal the answer in a whisper, "The horse's name was Sunday." The class groaned, Mr. Butler howled, Nathan smirked and shook his head, and I thought the whole thing was stupid.

"Now that we are all warmed up, we are going to talk about *paradigm shifts.* This will either be a preview or a review depending on whether or not you have been doing the assignments during your silent reading time in class. Who can tell me what a paradigm is...and don't tell me twenty cents."

His last comment obviously amused him as he lumbered back to the front of the room and wrote P-A-R-A-D-I-G-M on the board. Nobody raised a hand, so Mr. Butler went on, "A paradigm is a model, really, a way of looking at something, a way of looking at yourself, and a way of looking at other people. It's kind of an expectation or an understanding of how you fit. As we go through our book we are going to relook at all of that, shift our thinking, and try to develop some solid lifelong habits that will make us more successful students and adults.

I remember when I was a little boy growing up on the streets of Chicago and my uncle had a bakery…"

As Mr. Butler started to settle into a story about a bakery in Chicago, I did the only reasonable thing that a boy who had not yet developed a paradigm to shift could do: I tuned out and started watching a piece of dust float up and down in a drafty corner of the room. The little dust ball floated up along the corner nearly to the ceiling and then drifted out away from the wall to start a long, gentle descent. It fell nearly to the floor before being caught again in the eddy of the floor vent, forcing it back to the corner and up to the ceiling, where it would again make another futile attempt to fall away and escape. I'm not sure if it was the intrigue of the struggle between dust and draft or the dismal lecture droning somewhere in the back of my head that made the whole cycle so remarkable and so mesmerizing.

"Nathan!" Mr. Butler's harsh tone snapped my concentration on the dust ball, and I was again fully aware of the classroom around me. "Nathan! I'm not up here for my health, so I would certainly appreciate it if you would pay attention to what I'm trying to teach you." I guess Nathan had found the focus of something more worthy than Mr. Butler's lecture just like most of the rest of us.

"I am paying attention," Nathan protested as we watched silently.

"Really, Nathaniel?" Mr. Butler smugly clasped his hands across his big belly. "Then why don't you tell the class what the third element of a paradigm shift is."

Nathan paused a long time, and I honestly thought that he wasn't going to reply at all, but Mr. Butler wasn't letting go. He stood there, hands still clasped and staring at Nathan, silently waiting for him to respond.

"Uhhh," Nathan started with his head down and his eyes lowered and then, in his clearest shaky voice, he answered, "*twenty cents*?"

The class erupted into laughter, but not at Nathan's expense this time, and Mr. Butler fumed. Mr. Butler waved his hands and threatened all manner of punishments and extra work until we all finally settled down enough to give him an attentive audience. He wasn't done with Nathan.

"Nathaniel, I thought you said that you were paying attention," Mr. Butler sneered.

"Well, I was kinda looking at that dust over there floating in the corner. You see it?" Several in the class murmured that they had been watching the dust too.

"So," Mr. Butler continued with the cruelty of an embarrassed adult, "you were lying to me; you weren't paying attention at all!" The harshness of his words quieted every whisper in the room.

"No, Mr. Butler, I was paying attention," Nathan pleaded and then paused thoughtfully. "*...Just not to you.*" The class burst into such hysterical laughter that Mr. Butler was unable to silence it before the bell rang and we all began to file out the door into the hall. We left Mr. Butler, belly to the corner, snatching at a piece of dust, having assigned us no homework at all.

7

A Move Up for Me

I navigated my way down the crowded halls, bumping and pushing my way to my next class. People were laughing and talking about what Nathan had said to Mr. Butler. Of course, I was the only one who really understood the honesty of the situation. Nathan was never a smart-aleck, although the truth comes out that way sometimes. I remember really enjoying Nathan's few hours of fame, but I was also worried about Mr. Butler's inevitable retaliation. He wasn't the kind of man who would laugh things off. But by the time Nathan fumbled his way past Halley Cat's empty desk into Ms. Baird's class, the incident with Mr. Butler was old news, and Nathan was right back to attracting the wrong kind of attention.

The halls were just as crammed as always with students headed down to P.E., but at least we were all headed in the same direction. As we bumped and pushed down the hall, I slid my way over to make a quick pit stop in the restroom before heading on down to the locker room.

As usual there was a line, so I dropped my books next to the wall and waited for my turn.

You never saw any *Specials* in the boys' room at this time of day when any shenanigans would be masked by the noise of the mass exodus down the hallway outside. Being victimized in the general population of school made *Specials* very aware of their surroundings, and even though they could never go totally unscathed, they certainly knew how to avoid trouble.

There was a lot of loud talk and laughing all through the restroom as my turn finally arrived and I stepped up to the urinal. I needed to go so badly that I didn't even notice who was in the room with me as I started to unzip my pants. I fidgeted a little, getting ready to relieve myself, not realizing what was happening, when I felt the hands on my shoulders. I was oblivious to the silence that had fallen over the restroom, but I was keenly aware that someone had grabbed me, although it hadn't registered why.

Without turning around, I instinctively shirked my shoulder and rolled my elbow back to shake myself free. Surprisingly, when I threw my elbow back it popped something hard. A resounding "Ohhhhhhhh!" echoed through the restroom.

"Wow, look at that," I heard someone say right before the chant "fight, fight, fight" started to bounce off the tile walls.

As I turned, trying to make sense of what was happening, my eyes fell on a kid named Stan Lynch, one of Jimmy's friends, lying on the floor up against the wall. Some other boys were shouting, "Get up, get up, Stan!" Stan lay there, holding both hands over his face as the blood leaked through his fingers and all over his shirt. I heard, "Get him, Chris, kick his butt, bust him again!" amid the urges for Stan to rise and fight.

It was all an accident. Stan had mistimed shaking me, and as I threw my elbow back to knock his hands off, I caught him squarely in the nose, sending him bleeding to the floor. Thank goodness that he was hurt bad enough to keep him from getting up and continuing the supposed fight. Although it was only an accident, history records it as one of the only fights I ever won. Stan and I were escorted to the nurse and then to the office where the principal allowed me to finally relieve myself in his personal bathroom. After that, I didn't care what punishment he gave me.

I guess I knew from the beginning that it was the blood on my hands that started my brief and unfortunate association with Jimmy Malone. I overheard him talking about my fight with near admiration, and even though I had always hated Jimmy from afar, oddly enough, I welcomed his newfound acceptance. It was a move up for me.

Jimmy was a tall, lanky kid who had been held back in school twice, giving him a decided physical advantage over the rest of the boys in my grade. He was loud and mouthy as he roamed the halls stepping on people's heels, slamming locker doors, and flipping books, all to the delight of his crew of laughing hyenas. It was customary for Jimmy to extort ice cream and lunches from his favorite victims, having them pay for it all on their school account. Behind his back, we all called Jimmy an "old nothing," referring to his failure of two grades, but to his face we were silent, or we laughed when he flipped spit on someone else.

Jimmy was a bully, extorting our approval the same way he extorted ice cream; always with a crowd that was always on his side. In a way, I guess, we encouraged the behavior that we both dreaded and despised. But even with all of that, I was more than satisfied that my fight with Stan had attracted Jimmy's favorable attention. It felt good to be noticed.

A few days later, Brett caught my attention between classes. "Hey, hey, Chrissy, come on in here, we have something to show you," he called over the crowded hall, motioning me into the restroom. I could feel the hair on the back of my neck stand on end. I knew this couldn't be good. I thought about ignoring him and saying that I didn't hear him calling me over all the noise, but I had already looked over and he knew that I had seen him.

"Hurry up," he said with a smile as he waved me over to the entrance of the boys' room.

"What do you want, Brett?" I asked as the students changing classes bumped around me.

"I just want to show you something funny." He grinned big as he put his arm around my shoulder and walked me into the restroom.

When I turned the corner, Brett's arm still around me, I felt my heart drop to my stomach, and I knew something was terribly wrong. *Why had I come in here?* Jimmy was leaning against the wall, talking quietly with a couple of his henchmen who seemed to be waiting in the urinal line.

He looked over as I walked in, put his finger to his nose and whispered "Shhhh," as if he didn't want me to spoil a big surprise. Then he raised his eyes and nodded so that I would notice Stan waiting in line to take a pee.

I shook my head at Jimmy and made a move to walk back out, but Brett's arm tightened around my shoulder. I'm sure that I could have broken away, but not without making a scene, and I certainly didn't want the focus of what was coming to shift from Stan to me. Jimmy looked at me with a smile while silently nodding "yes," reassuring me that I was not his prey.

As Stan finally stepped up to relieve himself, Jimmy moved off the wall as his other two jackals tightened in to flank the unwary Stan. Brett and I moved in together as well. I was nervous. There were five of us closing in with a grinning Jimmy, and there was Stan, still feeling safe facing the wall in his sacred moment.

Then Jimmy made a long, loud exaggerated snort noise, the kind you make when you suck back through your nose into your mouth producing that nasty mixture of snot and spit. We all followed with a chorus of our own snorts…*we waited…and then…*we all let them fly. By the time Stan realized that he was in any trouble, he was covered in loogies dripping from his hair into his collar, all over the back of his shirt, and on the side of his face. I fled the bathroom laughing with the rest of Jimmy's followers, believing that Stan had gotten what he deserved for trying to "shake" me that day.

With the exception of a few stragglers, the halls were mostly empty as the five of us trotted on to class. I was bringing up the rear, running past the closed doors signaling that anyone coming in now would be counted as late. By the time we rounded the corner to our hall, there was only one other student left walking by himself along the lockers on his way to class. Jimmy, Brett, and the others ran safely past the boy, but on a whim I swung over, came up behind the lone student, and tipped his books, sending them all over the hallway as I ran past. I felt strong.

Jimmy and Brett looked back, smiled, and gave me a "thumbs up" as they entered their classroom. Opening the door late to science, I stopped to give one quick look back down the hall at Nathan, down on his knees, trying to collect all of his books and papers that lay scattered all over the floor.

8

Eighteen

It was kind of weird. Halley Cat was rarely at school anymore, but the day I tipped Nathan's books there she was, sure enough, on the bus ride home. I watched them talk and laugh and whisper things to one another freely as the noise of the bus droned over their conversation. Nathan even reached up and patted her on the head as if she really were a cat, and then he laughed his geeky laugh that sounded more like a goose honking than anything else.

I just stared out the window, watching as everybody else got off the bus. What an inconvenience—the one day I might want to explain something to Nathan, the one day that I might actually have something to talk about, the one day that I'm feeling a little sorry…she shows back up on the bus. As I watched Nathan not needing me, my shame turned to anger, and I started thinking that Nathan had gotten what he deserved, just like Stan did.

The next few weeks were hard, and ordinarily I don't like to think about them. I spent a lot of time in the principal's office for various offenses that I committed against my classmates to the amusement of Jimmy and Brett. I'm sure most of the boys I shook in the bathroom or stole ice cream from could have easily whipped my tail, but with school rules against fighting on my side and being under the tacit protection of Jimmy Malone, I operated without any fear of physical retaliation from my victims. I know that makes me a coward. As my shenanigans continued, my stature in Jimmy's gang grew, but I could never shake the feeling that I always had something more to prove.

Nathan stopped coming back to sit with me on the afternoon bus ride home, contenting himself to stay up front listening to the radio with Bill after everyone else had been dropped off. Even at home, I didn't see much of Nathan for the next little while, and since Flat Rock didn't want me without him, Cherry Field began to feel more like a prison than ever.

I moped around the house nearly bored to death for a couple of weeks before I finally got the idea to ask Mom and Dad if I could have some friends sleep over on a Friday night. I made sure that I asked for a Friday night because Saturday night leads to Sunday morning, and I knew that my dad would insist that we all go to church. I was pretty sure how the friends I wanted to invite would feel about Sunday school, so I decided to stick with the Friday to Saturday scenario instead.

Since I rarely invited anyone out to Cherry Field, my parents were more than delighted to allow me to have both Jimmy and Brett come out Friday after school to spend the night. Throughout the week's interrogations over what kind of pizza and snacks my guests preferred, I was very careful not to reveal too much information about my friends or what they liked to do. I was so clever in keeping my parents from the truth that, in the end, even I didn't really know what I was bringing home to Cherry Field.

Dad picked us up late from school that Friday because both Jimmy and Brett had detention, but I told my parents that they were meeting with the science club. The ride home was painful, with my dad asking a bunch of goofy questions and my friends mostly responding with one-word answers and rolling eyes. Some hoodlums at least put on a little pretense for parents, but Jimmy and Brett were way beyond that concern. We hadn't been in the car for ten minutes and I was already uneasy and embarrassed by their behavior in front of my father. I was hoping that it was only the distance to the house and the close confines of the car that made everything seem worse, and that my friends' demeanor would improve at home around my mother.

I was worried about what my father might do if Brett or Jimmy even hinted at disrespect for Mom, so I knew that it would be better if I kept everybody separated once we got out to Cherry Field. The sun was already sinking below the trees when my dad got tired of trying to start a conversation with my guests, so he reached over and flipped on the radio, making no attempt to hide his disgust.

As the rest of us sat silently now in the car, something on the radio caught my dad's attention and he reached over again to turn up the volume. It was the news, of course. The announcer was saying something about two more bodies found over in Dunn and that the police were calling them copycat murders. Dad leaned over to turn on the headlights and pushed his fingers back through his hair the way he does when he's upset, as the news continued. The lawyers for the man arrested for killing all those kids were demanding that he be released immediately, saying that the authorities had made too many mistakes and they had just been looking for a scapegoat. They were saying that the new murders proved he was innocent. Then something was said about carpet fibers and that the police weren't about to let the guy go, and my dad changed the station to music.

By the time we got home, it was totally dark, and my mom had pizza kept warm in the oven. She made some remark about it being a late day and a hard week at school as we walked in and I made the introductions. Even with my mom's continuing prompts for Brett and Jimmy to tell her about themselves, we mostly ate our pizza without conversation. I was relieved, because I knew my parents wouldn't like what we usually talked about. I was initially excited about my new friends spending the night, but now with Jimmy and Brett in my home, I felt nothing but tension and even a little shame. For even though it was my mom fussing about pizza and snacks, and my dad offering up his lame old jokes, they were not the ones who were embarrassing me.

After we ate, I ushered my guests up to my room, which wasn't even close to meeting their approval. It was too babyish, I had no contraband of any sort stashed in a secret hiding place, and gravest sin of all, I didn't have my own television. Of course, they did find my little safe bank, threatened the combination out of me, and then divided up the money my parents insisted I put in the offertory at church. Since I wasn't allowed to spend the money, I acted like I didn't care, but

I did. Sitting up in my room, I realized that I had dug myself into a hole that there was no good way out of. I felt small and intimidated, offering only a weak resistance to anything Brett and Jimmy wanted to do or wanted me to do. Whether willingly or against my better judgment, I always yielded to them, even in my own room. I guess if you are going to play with a wolf, you better not bring him home.

Jimmy and Brett were town kids, so the only thing that I really had to offer them way out in Cherry Field was the woods. I told them about Boulder Creek and Flat Rock and that we would have to climb down a cliff to get where we were going in the morning. They seemed intrigued, and I played it up as much as I could, exaggerating a little here and there, making everything seem more dangerous than it actually was. I didn't bother to tell them about arrowheads and triangle rocks, but I did say that some guys long ago found some gold in the creek and had used the money to open a theme park down in Florida.

Brett and Jimmy got so excited about that stupid story that they wanted to sneak out of the house and head out to the creek right away. But I pressed my advantage with the town kids and told them that even though it wasn't widely known, Cherry Field was infested with bears and coyotes. I told them that although the predators mostly stayed in the woods during the day, at night they roamed through our yards stalking any pets that may not have been let in before dark. I even went so far as to tell them one of our neighbors was pulled from his porch swing a couple of years ago by a huge bear that was silent as a snake and faster than a horse. My guests listened intently as I spun my yarns, and even though it felt good to have their attention, it felt better letting them know that

I had to contend with things much greater than the two boys sitting on my bed. I liked making them feel small.

"How in the world do you live here, man?" Brett shuddered.

I stared at him hard, pausing for effect before I answered. He seemed more vulnerable somehow. "Very carefully," I drew out in the most ominous tone I could muster.

He took a deep breath looking up to the ceiling.

"Ah bull!" Jimmy snapped the moment. "You are so full of it, Chris. There is no way people would live out here with all of that." Jimmy slid off the bed and strode to my window looking out into the night.

"Why do you think it's so cheap to live here, Jimmy?" I offered back, still using my ominous tone. Jimmy didn't answer right away; he just put his hands on my window sill and leaned closer to the glass contemplating the darkness outside.

"I like it," he finally muttered to himself, "I like it." But even so, having grown up in the suburbs with the street lights to take the edge off the darkness, Jimmy wasn't prepared for the pitch black of a Cherry Field night. And though I had only told my tales to keep Jimmy and Brett from sneaking out of the house on my parents, I enjoyed seeing both of them unsure of themselves for the first time.

9

Stomping Ground

Mom made pancakes for us the next morning, and I was the only one to say "thanks" before we finished up and headed out the door. Jimmy and Brett made light conversation about some girls at school as they followed me around Ms. Hall's garden.

"What do you think about that Halley Kate chick?" They were talking to each other, but Halley Kate's name caught my ear.

"Yeah, man, I think she's pretty fine with that raspy voice and red stripe."

"Yeah, yeah, you know what that red stripe means, don't you?"

But before Jimmy could answer his own question about Halley Cat's red stripe, we stepped out of Ms. Hall's yard into the woods, cutting the conversation short. I guess the primeval woods of Cherry Field demand their moment of reverence from even the likes of Jimmy Malone and Brett Cower. The majesty of the forest certainly didn't impress them for long, as they quickly started to chuckle and chat again in raised voices about teachers and girls at school as we walked along. They rustled loudly through the leaves behind me, and they moved clumsily in the underbrush that I intentionally led them through.

I pushed through some low-hanging branches, holding them back for Jimmy, but as he passed he let them whip back, catching Brett right across the face. Jimmy laughed, but Brett complained bitterly as a large welt sprang up quickly on his left cheek. We climbed over a fallen tree, down into a small ravine, and up the far side. I pulled myself up using a low-hanging dogwood, failing to mention the more convenient grip was a "Devil's Walking Stick," with its long needle spikes well camouflaged against its bark. Jimmy sounded like a scalded dog when he grabbed the thorn tree to follow me up the bank. He slid back and fell right on his butt, holding his wrist and looking at his bleeding hand. This time Brett laughed as Jimmy picked the thorns out of his palm, and I acted surprised that Jimmy didn't know to avoid the "Devil's Walking Stick" on the bank.

I added about thirty minutes to the usual walk to the creek, leading my guests through all manner of minor perils, failing to warn them until after the fact, and then pretending to be surprised at their lack of experience. Too bad Fair Play Middle School doesn't hold its classes out in the woods. Too bad the Postcard Church doesn't hold Sunday school classes out here either.

By the time we got to the bluff where we have to climb down to Flat Rock, Jimmy and Brett had stopped talking altogether. They were tired and a little beaten up, and they were both paying much closer attention to how I picked my way through the woods, trying to copy every step.

"Hey, Chris, who's that down there?" Brett asked, pointing out a lone figure on the far bank as we finally approached the edge of the bluff.

I held my hand up to my forehead, shielding my eyes from the sun, and peered down just in time to see Nathan disappear behind a veil of kudzu on the forbidden side of Boulder Creek. "Uhhh, I don't know, guys, maybe we shouldn't go down there."

I was petrified of what would happen if my two friends came upon Nathan in the middle of the woods. I was afraid of Brett and Jimmy, but I had chosen to be with them, and I wasn't ready to find out what that might really mean. It was one thing to tip someone's books or slam their locker with teachers around to make sure nothing could get out of hand, but it's another thing altogether to start something out here, far away from all protection, where nobody would know to look. These two didn't concern themselves with boundaries, and out here, there were none to be imposed.

"No, no, no," I stammered, "I don't know who that is. We need to head on home. My parents wouldn't want..."

"Forget it, man, no way, we're going down there, Chris," snarled Jimmy. "Now you show us how."

"My parents don't allow me to go over there, Jimmy. That's where the coyotes like to nest, in all the kudzu."

"Bull!" shouted Jimmy. "Now you get us down to the water or else the ugly one here is going to throw you off this cliff." He motioned to Brett as the ugly one. Brett stepped up and began socking his palm and rubbing his fist like a well-trained goon.

The advantage of being in the woods was gone, and I had no choice but to show them down to Flat Rock. The water seething and hissing around the rocks held no allure for my two friends, who were now obsessed with getting to the far bank to find out who the trees and vines were hiding. If we had been a few minutes later, we would never have seen Nathan, and if we had been a few minutes earlier, he would have spotted us first and known to go back home. Our timing could not have been more perfectly horrible.

As soon as we reached the bottom, Jimmy and Brett charged right off Flat Rock, barreling recklessly through the water, driven like two wild beasts bent on getting to the other side. The creek retaliated, sweeping both of them off their feet and sending the two on a quick, bumpy ride downstream. But the water wasn't high enough today to do much more than give them both a good soaking and sore butts before they emerged safely on the other side. I tried to follow, picking my way over the usual route across the creek, falling once in my haste, and wading up out of the water to the stony beach that had been my previous boundary.

Brett and Jimmy were running up and down the far bank before finally spotting a narrow hidden path through the wall of leafy vines. I saw Jimmy point it out to Brett, and then without hesitation, they both went crashing in and were swallowed from my eyes by the forest's curtain. Their search for the secret path had delayed them, allowing me to nearly catch up, so I ran down the beach and dove in right behind them.

There was nothing like this on our side of the creek. The path was more like a hallway built of vines and underbrush, hidden by a low canopy of privet and dormant honeysuckle that were so tightly woven, they must have grown that way on purpose. This would be an easy place for anyone to stay hidden, and I prayed as I ran that my two guests wouldn't be able to find Nathan at all. I moved as quickly as I could, ducking and running sideways for part of the way, not even aware anymore of the danger I was chasing or what I would do if I caught it. I could hear Brett and Jimmy up ahead of me and suddenly, as if I had just run through a spider web, I was wrapped in the overwhelming feeling that we shouldn't be here.

The tangled passage seemed to be thinning as I finally caught up with Jimmy and Brett, who were now flat on their bellies, lying down behind a patch of thick privet.

"Shhhh," Jimmy whispered, motioning me to join him in his hiding place almost as if we were on the same team again. He seemed to have forgotten all about threatening to throw me off the cliff or about luring me into the forbidden woods on the far bank. I wanted to forget about all that too, and now everything seemed to be okay again, so I crouched down and moved up silently next to where the two boys were taking cover in the underbrush.

"Look," Jimmy pointed through the bushes, "what's that?"

"Wow," I exhaled under my breath keeping my astonishment a secret. "I don't know, Jimmy; I'm not allowed to come over here." But even though I said I didn't know, it was easy to see that it was an old rotting cabin, barely visible and overrun with the woods. It looked as if the forest had reached up with its viney hands and pulled the structure right off its stone column foundation on one side, making it look a little like a lopsided fun house. Although you could still see some handrails, most of the porch was gone or rotted away, and the remnants of its steps lay in dust out front.

If the cabin had been in better shape, it would have been a boy's dream, but as it was, with no floor and full of starving mosquitoes, it turned out to be nothing more than a cool landmark and a fertile stomping ground for my imagination. Although I had been mesmerized by the discovery of the old cabin, the spell was quickly lost on the boys lying next to me in the bushes.

"What is that kid doing?" Jimmy whispered so Brett and I could just hear. His eyes were trained on Nathan who was sitting on a fallen limb at the edge of a small clearing in front of the cabin. The brush was so twisted and thick here that the little cabin yard looked kind of like an oval-shaped animal pen, with the only easy escape being down the path we had just come. Nathan was bent over with his head in his hands and his elbows on his knees, and looked like he may have been crying or sleeping. *How did Nathan know about this place?*

"Hey, I know that kid. He's one of those geeky *specials* from school," Brett announced, still keeping it low so as not to reveal our hiding place.

"Does he live out here or something, Chris?" Jimmy sneered, still not taking his eyes off of Nathan.

With Jimmy's question I became suddenly aware of every breath I was taking. It seemed so loud I was certain that Nathan would hear. My heart began to pound so hard I had to push myself up off my belly to give it some more room. I couldn't breathe deeply enough anymore, and my chest started to ache as my heart continued its tirade. I had attacks before, but this was different as I could feel anxiety pulling itself around me in a full embrace. There was a low drum in my ears like the sound of rain falling steadily through the canopy, and the trees swayed above whispering secrets about the intruders lying in the underbrush.

Jimmy and Brett hadn't noticed a thing, remaining solely focused on the *special* sitting on the limb. Something big, something big, something big, we shouldn't be here, we shouldn't be here! I felt the panic taking hold as the woods around us magically fluttered to life.

I had never seen so many! They were moving in from all directions, easily navigating the thick brush and circling in down from the trees. They paid little attention to us as they moved in from behind and fluttered gracefully by on their way to the clearing. There were black ones and red ones and yellow ones and orange ones, so thick that it was getting hard to see Nathan, who was now standing and smiling like some sort of hero in a ticker-tape parade of butterflies.

Nathan held up his arms and beamed as the colorful little creatures lighted gently on his shoulders and his head, as if they had come out of the woods just to visit him. The whole thing was so calm and peaceful; it reminded me of a silent snow falling into its own blanket. This was something amazing and beautiful. I was so taken by the moment that I stood up from my hiding place and raised my arms as the flutter-bys flew past. I wanted them to touch me too, but none did. And although I hung back with Brett and Jimmy, every fiber of my body screamed to be part of this wonder like Nathan was.

"On guard!" Brett yelled as he and Jimmy broke from their hiding place, running into the clearing with privet switches in hand.

"Ha, ha, ooooh! Weeeee!" they yelled as they began whipping the branches around and around slicing through butterfly after butterfly in midair. They were swinging and stomping and congratulating each other over all the clean kills, as the bodies of the colorful, innocent creatures began to pile at their feet. I watched dumbly as the two that I had invited laughed and hopped around wreaking havoc through the most beautiful thing I had ever witnessed. The whole terrible scene had become mind numbing and repugnant.

"Stop! Stop! Please stop!" I heard Nathan screaming as he moved in to disarm Jimmy. Much to Jimmy's amusement, Nathan, red-faced and crying, was doing his best to snatch the switch from Jimmy's hand. Jimmy laughed, easily keeping his weapon away from Nathan. He called Nathan a stupid "*special*," and when he tired of the game, he did what he really came for and sent Nathan to the ground with a solid punch to the stomach. Nathan lay on the ground doubled up and gasping for breath amid the other dead butterflies.

Jimmy, with Brett by his side, stood over Nathan taunting him to stand up. He called him all sorts of foul names, and when it was finally evident that Nathan wouldn't be getting up, Jimmy looked down with disgust and said, "Brett, I guess I'm just going to have to stomp this punk where he lies."

Then slowly he raised his foot over Nathan's head, smiled over at Brett, and was just about to pull the trigger on smashing Nathan's head when I surprised him with a hard right to the face. I felt the crack of bone on bone as I hit him with all my pent-up rage, knocking him back over a log and into a sticker bush that was able to hold him long enough for me to wheel back around on Brett. I wasn't done.

Brett still had his eyes on his friend in the briars when I caught him square in the mouth hard enough to cut my knuckles on his teeth. His lip exploded and blood shot up his face, but I didn't knock him down. He tackled me and sat on my chest cussing as Jimmy dug himself out of the thorns. Brett held my arms and Jimmy went to work on my stomach and midsection until he was too tired to beat me anymore. The butterflies had all disappeared by the time Brett let me go and I crumpled to the ground beside Nathan.

"Hey, you know what we oughta do, Jimmy," the fat-lipped Brett suggested, "let's go get some of those vines over there and tie these two pukes up and leave them here for the bears and coyotes."

Jimmy thought that was a great idea, but the vines they wanted proved tougher than the two worn-out bullies. They waded deep into the underbrush, and although they tugged and pulled with all of their might, the leafy vines would not give up the hold they had on the surrounding trees. Brett and Jimmy decided that tying us up was too much trouble, and when they discovered that the foliage was strong enough to support their weight, they climbed in deeper and nestled themselves into a couple of natural hammocks while they waited on me to recover enough to show them the way home.

Nathan and I lay on the ground listening to the two thugs talk politely with one another about teachers and girls and how great it was to beat us up. They even talked about how cool all those butterflies were and how they couldn't wait to get out of this Godforsaken place and go home. I couldn't wait for them to go home either, but still I stayed on the ground listening to Brett and Jimmy just a little longer than I needed to. My two guests seemed to be really enjoying the moment, relaxing in their leafy hammocks after a hard day of killing butterflies and beating me and Nathan. I wanted to be a good host, and I knew they were going to need plenty of rest for the long walk home, so I wasn't in a real big hurry to tear them away from all that poison ivy they were lounging in.

Brett and Jimmy didn't make it to school all the next week. Dad dropped them off early enough on Saturday for the neighborhood kids to get a real good look at Jimmy's black eye and Brett's split lip, and by Sunday evening, the poison ivy had both boys in the hospital. On Monday my teachers and classmates were all amazed that I had been in a fight with both Jimmy and Brett, handing both of them visible battle scars, yet they had left me without a mark. Bruised ribs don't show like black eyes or fat lips, but I didn't mention any of that. All anybody really knew for sure was I had tangled with the two meanest kids in school, and now they were both in the hospital. That alone was enough to keep me from being picked on for the rest of my time at Fair Play Middle.

10

Flitty Art Teacher

I never understood why we all seemed to think that it was such a big deal at school when we received our schedule changes for the quarter. We still had the same exact academic classes with the same exact teachers. The only thing that really ever changed were the mandatory electives that we were all forced to take at the end of the day. But generally, they did do a better job of mixing the students in elective classes from quarter to quarter, so as luck would have it, I wound up taking art with Nathan and Halley Kate.

Nathan was delighted that we were all assigned the same table of four with some kid named Robert, and to tell the truth, I didn't mind our seating arrangement as much as I minded having to take art. I can't remember our teacher's name, but I do remember that she loved art, feeling that it was the only real way for students to be free to express themselves and their connection to the world around them. She believed we experience art, we live art, we are all artists, and what we choose to create can never be wrong or less than anyone else's.

Our heads were spinning as she moved gracefully among the tables on that first day with big arm motions and gentle smiles, making each of us believe that this class would be a delight, where we would go un-judged as long as we tried. Then she danced to the front of the room and announced that we would have one clay project, one still life drawing, one collage, and one paper-mache sculpture for the quarter, each with its own rubric, and that the best ones would be selected and displayed in the glass case outside the front office.

The class, entranced by the near free spirit of our teacher, nodded as she covered the syllabus, but her spell was lost on me as soon as she said the word "rubric." She wanted all of us to feel free to create, but in the end we weren't free at all; we would be ordered, compared, and graded just like any other class. At least in math I knew that my effort would be fairly judged, but in art, I never had that confidence or even understood how it was possible. I guess that may have been why Nathan never revealed his true artistic ability for a middle school art teacher to fawn over.

"Hey, Chris," Halley Kate said with a big grin as she sat down and shoulder bumped a smiling Nathan.

"Hey," I offered back, trying to sound friendly and surprising myself with an unusually pleasant response.

Halley Kate put her arm over Nathan's shoulders and reached over the table to put her other hand on top of mine. "I am so glad that the *bus buddies* are in this class together." She paused, smiled, and then continued in her raspy voice, "and *all* at the same table too. How fun is that?"

I was a little surprised, because I hadn't realized that the Halley Cat considered us "*bus buddies.*" I mean she and Nathan were always the ones talking, and I mostly ignored both of them until after she got off the bus. Still, her hand was warm and her laugh was honest, and I couldn't help feeling, somehow, that she was stronger, no, better than me...*in a good way.* It was in a way that made me want to be more like her...free and kind. I felt comfortable.

I'd like to say that I had a little more confidence because of the whole Brett and Jimmy thing, but in all honesty, I never would have sat next to either of my table mates had it not been assigned. At least this way I had a legitimate reason for sitting with the geek of the school and the red-striped delinquent who didn't seem to care what anybody else thought.

As it turns out, one of the most important things that any teacher ever did was to assign my seat next to Nathan and Halley Kate. I wish I had known that at the time.

We were introduced to the clay bin and to the supply closet as Ms. Flitty Art Teacher danced between our tables handing out big sheets of paper with only instructions to express ourselves. Robert raised his hand announcing to Ms. Art Teacher that he had failed to bring a pencil to class, for which she scolded him openly. She said something about being in middle school now, and would he forget to take a pencil to math, and why would he think that art would be any different. I guess of all the things free spirits can tolerate, forgetting to bring a pencil to class is not one of them.

I pulled my piece of paper in front of me and began to sketch my customary hockey goalie. Even though it was a little odd for a kid like me to be sketching a hockey goalie, I could actually make a decent picture without having to draw a face or hands or feet or even legs. Nathan had shown me how the mask, the skates, and the big gloves would allow me to reasonably avoid drawing any detail while still producing a good sketch.

Really, the goalie and an airplane coming in off the horizon were the only drawings that I could make look right, so those quickly became the staples of my artistic career. The good thing about art is that we were allowed to talk with the people at our own tables as we worked. So we mostly chatted quietly about nothing while Robert worked on his scuba diver, Halley Kate on her landscape, me on my hockey goalie, and Nathan, tongue sticking out, scratched away at whatever he was drawing.

“Wow!” Robert gasped under his breath after a while, causing both Halley Kate and me to look up at what Nathan had been doing.

“Oh my gosh,” breathed Halley Kate, looking over at Nathan’s sketch. She put her hand on the top edge of the paper and gently slid it away from Nathan so she could get a better look. With her mouth hanging open, she looked down at the drawing and then back up at him. “Nathan, this is beautiful,” she whispered. “Is this real? Where is this place?”

I saw the boulders, the seething water, and the woods on the far bank pressing in. I saw the opening in the thicket that leads back to the cabin and a pair of faint butterflies fluttering down by the water’s edge. It was nearly magical, and for a brief instant I thought I heard the trees rustling through the rush and gurgle of water. I’d been there, but never like this.

"It's Flat Rock," I answered softly.

Robert, Halley Kate, and I sat in awe, lost in Nathan's picture, wondering about the woods, listening to the water, and watching the trees gently sway as Ms. Art Teacher busied herself at another table.

"Is it really real?" Robert whispered.

I nodded, "Yes."

Watching my response, Halley Kate looked back down at Flat Rock. "Why haven't you told me, Nathan?" Her voice cracked just enough to force a slight pause. "I want to go. Nathan, I want to be there." With the whir of art class all around us, she was now staring hard at Nathan, fighting to hold back the tears.

"Sure," he whispered, sliding the picture back over to himself. He picked up his pencil, and we all watched as he stuck out his tongue and scratched away. It was like magic. He handled the pencil with such great agility that every time his hand passed over the drawing, some new detail was revealed. In less than two minutes, he put his pencil down and slid the sketch back over to Halley Kate. She took a deep, shaky breath and a single tear welled up in her eye, dropping into the creek below.

There she was with her pants rolled up wading in the water near the far bank. Her head was tilted down, and she was brushing her hair back over her ear as she searched over the creek bottom, and even though everything was in black and white, you could see her red stripe clearly from Flat Rock. The sun was glinting up off the water, making it look like she was kicking up sparkles with every step. There was something so natural about it all, almost as if she belonged there. She was the most beautiful thing I had ever seen. Sitting at that table, seeing her that way, that's when I fell in love with Halley Kate. I think Robert did too.

Halley Kate was still choked up just a little when she finally managed to ask, "What am I looking for?"

I looked over at Nathan and smiled. "Arrowheads," I answered.

"At least that's what I look for when I go," Nathan followed in a hushed voice. Then he slid the picture back and looked it over. "Do you want this, Halley Kate?"

"Please," she whispered.

Nathan quickly folded up the masterpiece and shoved it into Halley Kate's book bag. Then he reached for another piece of blank paper, pulling it over to start another sketch.

"Well, let's see what you four have been doing over here," Ms. Art Teacher announced as she floated over to our table. "We have a hockey man, a very nice landscape, a very interesting scuba guy, and what about you, young man?" Her eyes fell on Nathan and the blank sheet of white paper lying in front of him. "What's this?" she loudly inquired, holding up Nathan's paper to get the attention of the whole class. "Must be a polar bear in a snowstorm!"

Nobody got her joke so she continued, "Nothing but white!" Then she put her palms on the table and leaned way down so that only we could hear, "If this seating arrangement is going to be a problem, I can certainly separate you."

We all assured her that sitting together wouldn't be a problem. "Yes, well, today is just a participation day. So you three start off this quarter with one hundreds, whereas you, young man," she glared down at Nathan, "are starting off with a big fat zero."

11

Love Letter

Even though something still wanted to hold me back, as soon as everybody else had gotten off the bus, I slid up to the seat behind Nathan and Halley Kate. This was a first for me. It seemed a little odd, and I didn't want to intrude, but what Nathan had done in art class made me want to be closer to the red-stripe girl. So as the bus bumped along, I somehow overcame my embarrassment and plopped down behind my two "bus buddies," just in time to hear Halley Kate ask, "Why didn't you show her your picture, Nathan?"

Trying to avoid the question, Nathan looked stupidly back to me as I sat down. "Hey, Chris, what's going on?" I smiled and nodded, hoping that Halley Kate might get the answer that I never could.

Halley Kate gave me a welcoming look, but she wasn't ready to let up on Nathan. "Why didn't you tell me that you could draw like that? And why in the world would you take a zero in art when you're probably the best artist in the whole school?" She was staring at him hard and kept saying that she didn't understand and asking him "how" and "why," but Nathan said nothing, keeping his eyes in his lap as her flood of questions washed around him. She seemed angry and frustrated.

When Halley Kate paused, I added, "Why don't you just tell her, Nathan?" as if I had some deep, secret knowledge of why Nathan kept his talent to himself. I think that I may have fooled Halley Kate, but Nathan rolled his eyes at my pretense of insight.

We all bounced and jostled as the bus rumbled closer to Halley Kate's stop. "Nathan," she said much softer now, "I'm not sure if I'll be at school tomorrow, so before I have to get off, will you please, please tell me why you didn't show her your picture?" She put her hand on his shoulder. "Please," she begged again.

As the bus rolled along Nathan never looked up at Halley Kate, keeping his head hung and his eyes down, simply trying to weather the storm of her pleading.

Pshhhhhhh, the school bus hissed to a stop and the doors squealed open. "Time to go, young lady," Bill called out, "let's rock-n-roll…it's a long way to Cherry Field…gotta go, gotta go!"

Halley Kate stood up, grabbing her book bag off the floor.

"It wasn't mine," Nathan muttered.

"What? We saw you draw it, Nathan. Of course it was yours," Halley Kate stated flatly, standing over Nathan as Bill tapped his fingers on the dash.

"Yes, I did," Nathan agreed, lifting his eyes just a little, "but it wasn't mine…*to show.* I mean, I gave it to you, Halley Kate." Nathan paused. "It's yours, why didn't you show it to the teacher?"

I could see in her face that she had no answer for his question, but I knew that she would no sooner have shown that picture to the art teacher than she would have given up a love letter.

Bill was getting edgy. "Will you take me there? Nathan, Chris, will you guys take me there sometime soon?" Her last request trailed as she looked back from the doorway and finally stepped off the bus. I wanted to say "Yes," but I guess I wasn't ready, and neither was Nathan.

"When the bus stops, the conversation stops. You boys can't be keeping the young ladies hanging out. You'll have plenty of time for that later. You guys got me?" Nathan and I both nodded that we did as Bill chastised us through the rearview mirror and wheeled the bus out on the road to Cherry Field.

Some days it's hard to break free from the rhythm of a bus traveling through a remote area uninterrupted by stops. So it seemed like a long time before Nathan and I spoke again.

"So," I piped up, "do you think that we should invite Halley Kate out to Flat Rock sometime? I mean, it sounds like she really wants to go." Nathan, with his head against the window, made no response at all, and I almost thought he had fallen asleep. "Hey," I poked him, "did you hear what I said?"

"Yeah, yeah," Nathan muttered, turning around, "I heard. I was just trying to decide if it would be a good idea. I mean, she's a girl."

"Yeah, I know," I agreed. "I just kinda think that she would like it. She liked being in the picture, that's for sure."

Nathan offered nothing more on the subject, so I decided to let the topic drop. As I remember, the whole bus ride seemed a little weird that day. Usually it was Nathan doing all the talking, but today it was me who wasn't ready to end the conversation. Even though I had a lot of questions, my shame had kept me from mentioning the "butterfly day" with Jimmy and Brett. So I was pretty sure that my next cast would bait Nathan right back in to talking with me. "So, Nathan, have you been back to the cabin?" I asked.

Nathan's eyes began to well a little at the question and an unusual sadness seemed to creep over his face. I hadn't made any amends over the butterflies, and his reaction stirred the guilt that I still harbored. He nodded slightly, leaned over and whispered just loud enough for me to hear over the noise of the bouncing bus, "I've gone back a couple of times, Chris, but not since I found it."

"Found what? What are you talking about?" I asked a little louder than I had intended.

"It is something you need to see, Chris, something important." Nathan, stone faced and distant now as if he had drifted a million miles away, was responding to me the way people do right before falling asleep.

"Well, what is it? What did you find?" If Nathan was trying to be mysterious, he had me. "Just tell me. What is it?"

Nathan smiled slightly and then paused to truly consider my question. "It's what I have been dreaming about, Chris. It's what I've always dreamed about," he said, and then he turned his head and leaned it against the bus window for the rest of the ride home.

12

Something...at the Cabin

Well, Halley Kate was right, she wasn't there the next day, leaving me, Robert, and Nathan to survive "clay day" with Ms. Flitty Art Teacher all by ourselves.

"Well now, class, today is the day you start expressing yourselves through clay!" She seemed delighted that she had made a rhyme. "Our very first graded project this quarter will be whistles. Your clay piece will have to be hollow and roundish with at least two holes, so that when you blow in one, you get a nice loud whistle out of the other. Some of my former students actually put key holes on top so that they could play separate notes, but that is certainly not a requirement for our project. Now, I want you to be creative with your whistles. You can make them look like animals or cars or fruit or anything else you can think of. I have had some wonderfully unique designs from my students over the years, and I am really looking forward to seeing what you young artists are able to produce."

Truthfully, I was a little excited about the idea of working with clay. I thought it was kind of neat, and it seemed like it was going to be a lot easier than drawing. On rare occasions we had worked with clay in elementary school, and I remembered being pretty good at making worms, so I was fairly confident that I would do well on this project.

"We will have three days to sculpt our clay pieces; then we will let them harden, glaze, and fire them. After we have our final products, the very best pieces will be displayed in the big case by the front office. It will be an honor for the artists whose pieces are chosen. Now, before I allow you to go to the clay bin, I need to show you one very important thing."

Ms. Flitty Art Teacher held up a lump of clay in her hand, laid it on the table in front of her, and began squishing and rolling it and squishing it and rolling it. "Before you begin your projects, you must always knead your clay very carefully like I'm doing here. If not, you may get small pockets of air in your clay piece, and when they are put in the kiln to be fired, the air trapped inside will expand causing a very small explosion that could damage your clay project and possibly the clay projects of your classmates. So please, please, please, make sure that you knead well. Now as I come around and touch your table, you may go get some clay out of the bin."

When our turn came, Nathan, Robert, and I all retrieved a nice big wad of clay from a plastic bag hidden away in a rustic-looking plywood box that was called "*the bin.*" I'm not sure, but I bet the Indians never made their pots and whistles from clay out of a plastic bag like that. The stuff smelled like rubber dirt, and I started to get the feeling that making clay whistles wasn't going to be as much fun as I had hoped.

Robert sat down and started massaging, squeezing, and rolling his clay all around just like Ms. Flitty Art Teacher had demonstrated. If there was going to be a kiln mishap, it certainly wouldn't be because Robert left air pockets in his project. Nathan had a different approach; he started socking his clay flat, all the time muttering something about beating those air bubbles right on out of there. He'd wad it right back up and beat it flat again. I mostly just squeezed mine through my fingers a couple of times and then started right to work forming my future whistle into the shape of a submarine.

I had a vision, I knew exactly how a submarine was supposed to look, and I knew that if my hands could simply manufacture what I could see so plainly in my mind, my sub whistle was a shoo-in for the glass case by the front office. I was focused and I was diligent. I was delighted with how my masterpiece was taking shape. I didn't even bother looking around at my classmates' work, and I kept my arm wrapped around my own to prevent anyone else from getting a clear look and copying my brilliant idea. I couldn't believe how well it was going! I was amazed that I would easily finish my sculpture three full days ahead of our deadline!

I had my head down, scratching and shaping, scratching and shaping, becoming more and more pleased with how my submarine was taking such beautiful shape. The sweat was beading up on my forehead when I finally looked up; I leaned back, stretching my arms over my head, and I was sure my work would be the first that Ms. Flitty Art Teacher would gush over. As I sat there gloating and waiting for my classmates to begin noticing the incomparable piece of fine art sitting before me, I heard the first one. A low, hollow whistle, followed by a whole chorus of low, hollow whistles beginning to fill the art room. Ms. Flitty Art Teacher began hopping up and down, clapping frantic little claps as if she had just won a free dinner at bingo night.

"Yippee! Yippee!" she bubbled. "You guys have your pieces all hollowed out and whistling nicely, so tomorrow you need to think about how you want to design the outside and what you want your end product to look like. Just like I said at the beginning, first make it hollow, then get it whistling, and then let your creativity take you and your project anywhere you want to go. Yippee!"

I sure didn't remember her saying any of that stuff about making it hollow or getting it to whistle first, and I felt my heart start to sink a little as I stared down at my solid little submarine with no prayer of ever making a toot. I took my fist, and I squashed it flat. The only sculpture worse than mine was Nathan's fried egg. Ms. Flitty Art Teacher took one look at it and rolled her eyes with a huff, but she let Nathan wrap it in wet paper towels and put it on the counter with the rest of the projects anyway. I, on the other hand, would have to start again tomorrow.

For the first time ever, I sort of missed Halley Kate on the bus that day. After our first day in art class together, Halley Kate seemed to get a little prettier every time I saw her. She had a funny way of including me, almost as if Nathan and I were a package deal, and I found myself looking forward to our afternoon chats on the days she was on the bus ride home. Even though I knew that Nathan was missing Halley Kate too, he seemed to be in pretty good spirits that afternoon.

“Hey, Chris, did you get a good look at what I made in art today? .... A big ol’ fried egg, sunny side up, just the way Grandmom likes ’em. I’m planning on painting it white and yellow and serving it to her in bed on her birthday.” He snickered a little waiting for my response.

“I saw it,” I muttered, thinking about the destruction of the little clay sub that couldn’t.

“I sure don’t think that the art teacher cared much for it, though. Maybe she thought that it was too easy to make or something, but it’s so perfect for Grandmom that I really don’t mind if Ms. Art Teacher likes it or not. Besides, it’s only art class and some things are meant to be easy. Don’t you think so, Chris?”

I just stared at him and shook my head. “You know, Nathan, you were supposed to make a whistle.”

“What,” he frowned, “who said that we had to make a whistle?”

“That’s the project. Ms. Art Teacher said that we all had to make clay whistles.”

“But don’t you think that’s a little stupid, Chris? Fried eggs don’t whistle. They’re not even the right shape for that. They may pop and crack, but I’ve never heard a fried egg whistle before. I don’t even know if Grandmom likes whistles much. I’ve never seen her blow one. Are you sure about this, Chris?”

I was both astounded and amused at Nathan’s response to the whistling requirement that had been imposed on our clay projects. I nodded to indicate I was pretty sure about the instructions.

Nathan tilted his head a little to one side, mulling over the option of compliance. Then he looked back at me and said, "Well, I'm pretty sure clay fried eggs don't whistle." He paused. "But I sure know Grandmom will be whistling mad if I actually fail art." He chuckled a little bit at his last comment, as if he didn't really care whether or not his project would ever make any noise at all. I didn't share his freedom though, and as the bus bumped along, the awful thought of not getting an "A" in art class began to prey on my mind.

"Hey, Chris, I have something I need to show you, you know." Nathan was staring at me, but I hadn't noticed. I was still lost in the consideration of my fate in art. "Something on the other side," he continued in the background of my thoughts. I guess he wasn't satisfied with my lack of response, so he turned fully around in the bus seat, got up on his knees, leaned over the back, and knocked on my head with his knuckles. "Earth to Chris, Earth to Chris; come in, Chris. Where are you, Chris?"

"Hey, hey, cut it out, Nathan! That hurts!" I rubbed my head where he had knocked on me. "I'm trying to think! That hurts! I have things to think about! I have worries, you know!"

Nathan was still leaning over the back of the seat listening to my whiny protest at his attempt to get my attention, and when I finally finished, he leaned in even closer, right up to my face, and whispered, "Oh, I know you have worries, Chris, art class and all, but I have something very important to show you, something...*at the cabin.*" The rumbling bus bounced hard in protest to what Nathan was about to say, nearly throwing him back over the seat into my lap.

"Get back in your seat, boy!" Bill growled through the rearview mirror. The big bump had caught Bill by surprise too, making his chastisement for not following bus rules seem more harsh than usual. "We hit a bump like that again, and you boys aren't seated like you're supposed to be, I could bounce you clean through the roof of this bus. Sit like you know how! You got me?"

We both nodded to Bill through the mirror, and Nathan slid back down into his seat with his back to the side so that he could keep talking to me. When Bill finally broke his glare, Nathan turned back to me, smiling. "Wow, that was great! Next time I'm going to push off a little and see if I can touch the ceiling with my feet!"

Nathan had made an extra effort to get my attention, but after the "big bounce," he seemed to forget all about what he wanted to tell me. He just sat there smiling and talking and reliving how he was nearly tossed to the back of the bus. He beamed like a kid at a carnival telling his friends about the "Rocket Spinner" ride as the bus rolled on closer and closer to Cherry Field.

"Nathan. Nathan. Nathan!" I interrupted. "You knocked on my head to tell me something about the cabin. So what was it?" I acted a little frustrated, but the truth was, I had been dying with curiosity ever since Nathan mentioned finding something out there.

"Yes," he said, dropping his eyes as the excitement from the "big bounce" fell from his face. "We can never take Halley Kate to the cabin, never, ever, ever. She can't even know about it. Do you understand, Chris? Boulder Creek is as far as she can go. We can take her there, but never into the woods on the far side and never, ever to the cabin. Do you promise, Chris? Do you promise to never take anyone else to the cabin ever again? Now that I have found it, that place is only for you and me. Don't even talk about it with anyone else, not even your parents. Do you promise, Chris? Do you?"

He was so emphatic that small tears began to bubble in his eyes, but still his words were as hard as I have ever heard, with no sign of weakness or compromise. Whatever he had found at the cabin was his secret, not to be shared with anyone else, including Halley Kate, and if I wanted to know, I had to pledge to keep it my secret as well. A large part of me thought that this was all stupid. Nathan probably found some old dishes or something and was convinced they came from a caveman family that used to live out by Boulder Creek. I hate to promise over silly things.

Still, I had this strange sense that without my pledge things would never be the same, and I would be giving up my Cherry Field companion, Boulder Creek, and whatever lay beyond the far bank forever. For our adventure to move forward, Nathan required only a promise, and without it, I was sure I would lose everything that made Cherry Field tolerable. After all, the woods, the creek, and certainly the cabin wouldn't have me without him. So I guess it was out of self-interest that I gave my word to keep his secret, but as with most things I do, it was a promise that I would eventually betray.

"Yes, Nathan, I promise."

"Really, Chris?"

"Really, Nathan, I promise."

He watched my eyes as I gave my word twice, and then his voice went smooth and low as if someone had ironed the shakes out of it. "I know why they were there, Chris. I know why they built the cabin."

"Who, Nathan, who are you talking about?"

"The people who were there before us, the ones who lived down by the creek, they were miners, Chris, they were miners." He paused a long moment. "I followed some butterflies down the path to the cabin one day; they like it when I come...have you ever seen anything so amazing before?"

I lowered my head in shame and shook it to let Nathan know that I hadn't. He continued, "I don't see them so much anymore; maybe they're out of season or something. Anyway, I was walking around the little clearing out in front of the cabin…by the way, that would be a great place to go camping sometime, don't you think?"

I nodded that it would.

"All of a sudden, I almost fell right into it. I slipped down on my butt and had to scramble to keep from sliding straight in."

"What was it?" I hadn't been in the woods or out to Flat Rock for a little while, and I guess I was more intrigued than I had anticipated. "Come on, Nathan, what was it?"

"It's a mine, Chris." He paused and then whispered right through the bus noise, "And I'm pretty sure that it's a gold mine."

Great, I thought to myself, *he had me believing that he found something for real, but this is nothing more than Nathan's lame imagination.* But as he kept talking in that low, smooth voice, I was more and more convinced that he might really have something worth keeping secret.

He told me that we could only go to the mine together so in case something happened we would always be there to help each other get out. He almost fell in once and that's why he wouldn't go back without me. He said he didn't know how deep it was and that we might have to do some digging, but we should always hide the dirt so no one else would know about our gold. We would need some spades, some rope, and some other supplies, and he was sure there was still some gold in that old mine or maybe it would be silver, but either way, we were going to be rich. He was straight-faced and confident as he told me all about it that day on the way home. I was so excited that it was hard not to believe that every bit of what he had said would be true. We were really going to be rich!

The loud crunch of gravel followed by the squeal of the bus's brakes signaled that we had arrived at the Cherry Field turnaround, and it was time for a snack and homework. The ride seemed a lot shorter today than usual, I thought, as the bus hissed and the doors squeaked open. I lifted my backpack to my shoulder and headed down the aisle thinking of gold and silver with Nathan just behind.

"Thanks for the ride," I blurted out to Bill as I turned the corner to find my mom standing in the doorway of the bus. After Nathan and I had bumped past her on the stairs, Mom called up to Bill, "Hey, don't worry about coming out tomorrow; my husband will be driving the boys to school in the morning."

"Thank you kindly, ma'am," Bill called back, "that means I get to sleep just a little longer, if I can, and maybe have a cup of coffee with my wife before I head out. Thank you and I'll see the boys the day after."

"Maybe," Mom answered. "I have your number and I'll call you if not."

Bill waved, and the three of us stepped back just a little to watch him make his turn out onto the highway, rumble down the road, and disappear.

It was unusual for Mom to be at the bus stop or for Dad to take us to school, but I gave very little thought to either of those things as we watched the bus sputter away. Nathan, on the other hand, had noticed both. As I turned to make the trek up the hill to the house, I saw Nathan standing back away from us, backpack on the ground, pale as a ghost and trembling. He looked as if he were waiting for some awful dread to be confirmed.

"Nathan, honey," Mom walked over, put her hands on his shoulders, and knelt down in the gravel, "it's your grandmother. She's at the hospital." Nathan welled up with tears as big as apples and fell into my mother's arms as if she were his very own.

13

Nineteen

When you get older like me, everything begins to condense in your memory and minor details seem to get squeezed out. I guess if this wasn't the case, it would take a lifetime to remember a lifetime's events instead of skipping right to the essence of what truly matters. Anyway, that's my excuse for failing to remember the season, but it seems to me that cold weather was just coming on at the time Nathan's grandmother took ill.

"Nathan, honey," Mom was saying, "we are going to go to the hospital, but first I need you and Chris to go pack up anything that you may need from your house, clothes, underwear, toothbrush, anything at all, and take it up to Chris's room. You're going to be staying with us until your grandmother comes home, okay, sweetie?"

Nathan nodded, still in her embrace, and then he stepped away and tried to clear his face with a long swipe from his shirt sleeve. "Yes, ma'am," he choked, "thank you."

We packed up a lot of Nathan's stuff, including his sketch pad and some pencils, and moved it all up to my room while Mom changed out the linens on my twin beds. We just kind of dumped everything at the foot of my guest bed into a sloppy little pile the way boys usually do. Mom started to clean out a couple of my drawers, but then noticing Nathan sitting on the bed watching her through small tears, she stopped and told us both to go hop in the car.

I rested my head against the car window on the way to the hospital, watching the trees and vines go speeding past to Nathan's intermittent sniffles and muted sobs. Even though Mom had given us no information on Nathan's grandmother, she was old and she was at the hospital and I started to get a bad feeling about what could happen. Without his grandmother, I wasn't sure what Nathan would do. He didn't have anyone else in the whole world. Of course there was always his mother, if she could be found—if anyone would really want to find her. But Nathan leaving Cherry Field to go live with his real mom, that's the stuff that honest to goodness tragedies are made of. That's the kind of story that people just make up for drama or to make their readers get all emotional. Nathan, I'm sure, was only thinking of his grandmother, but as he sat there in the car gently weeping for her, I worried more about what would become of him.

As it turns out, bad things happen to innocent people just the same as if they were guilty, and that's just not fair. I don't know why adults seem to accept this so easily.

"*This just in from WXI News.*" The music on the radio was interrupted by some late breaking news report: "*The body of thirteen-year-old Keith Jerome Laird has been found in a wooded area off State Highway 71 just outside of Piedmont. The boy, who went missing six days ago, has been positively identified. The Joint Federal Task Force has been called in to investigate. Officials are saying that characteristics of the crime are highly similar to the previous child murders, and a general advisory has been issued for all parents and children in the area to take extra precaution.*

In a related story, Robert Roberts, previously charged in the murdered children cases, has been exonerated and is due for limited release. Authorities have confirmed that Roberts was present and accounted for in a halfway house out of state during the time of at least four of the murders. As condition of his release, Roberts will be required to check in with authorities and his movements will be tracked by law enforcement. Roberts' lawyers say that justice has been served, and now the Task Force can get back to the business of solving these crimes and protecting our children..."

The radio announcement played faintly somewhere in the background of my thoughts. Suddenly my body strained against the seat belt and the tires squealed against the road as my mom drove into a curve a lot faster than she realized. We went clear into the other lane, and I felt the car fish tail a little as Mom regained control, bringing us safely back to our side of the road. She seemed very calm about Nathan's grandmother, so I figured that something else had caused her to neglect her speed.

"Are you boys okay?" she asked, a little shaken up.

"Gahlee, Mom! What's going on?" I'd never seen her drive like that before.

"Are you boys okay?" she asked again, but calmer and more assertive.

Nathan and I both nodded that we were fine.

"Sorry about that, boys. I guess my mind wandered a little. Let that be a lesson to both of you. When you start driving, always pay attention, and keep your mind on the road."

Again we nodded that we understood.

"And stay away from people you don't know," she added as an afterthought.

14

Uneasy Feeling

The hospital was just like every other hospital: a dirty kind of antiseptic with big doors and wide halls, making us wait for some very busy people whose schedules were well protected by people who didn't seem very busy at all. Mom asked at the desk, and we were ushered back to a small waiting room where Dad was sitting. Dad had discovered Nathan's grandmother collapsed on her front steps, and he and Mom had lifted her into his car so she wouldn't have to wait on an ambulance to find Cherry Field. It was a lot faster for Dad to take her, and I could see he was glad that part was over.

Nathan's grandmother was unconscious in intensive care, hooked up to about a million machines, and although Nathan was allowed to see her through the glass, the doctors would not allow him to go into her room. Nathan shifted between sitting in the small waiting room with Mom, Dad, and me and standing outside his grandmother's window down by the nurses' station. I went to keep him company outside her room a couple of times, but seeing his grandmother lie there with her thin gray hair all pushed back and all of the contraptions around her bed gave me a terribly uneasy feeling. Her deep-creviced skin was ghostly pale and her eyes were so deeply set and dark that it was hard for me to tell if they were open or closed.

The nurses all said that it was just like she was sleeping, but there were times I was sure she was watching me outside her room, judging my secrets and the way I treated her grandson. When I looked at her, I saw Death in the room, but I dared not mention it for fear of attracting his attention. So I spent most of my time at the hospital in the little waiting room with my parents. Mom often walked down to keep Nathan company when he went to watch his grandmother through the glass, leaving me and Dad to sit and stare as the time crawled by.

The hour got later and later, so Dad finally took me home, leaving Nathan and Mom behind. After all, I did have school in the morning.

15

God's Hands

It seemed like I had barely closed my eyes before my dad was quietly shaking me awake in the predawn darkness. He signaled me that Nathan was in my guest bed and not to wake him up. Without turning on the light, I collected my clothes as best I could and then crept down the hall to the bathroom to get dressed. Mom was still in bed, and Dad didn't feel like rattling any pots and pans, so we decided to stop by the donut shop for breakfast on the way to school. I briefly wondered if Bill was still asleep or having a second cup of coffee with his wife. At least somebody was getting some rest.

The car seats were slick with the cold. "Dad," I finally broke the silence in the dark, chilly car, "is everything going to be okay...with Nathan's grandmother, I mean?"

"I don't know, son." His eyes were on the road and his voice was still gravelly with the morning. "The doctors say...well, they say that she's not doing that well, but they really won't know anything much until she wakes up."

I paused, listening to the road under our car in the darkness. "Dad, what's going to happen?" I wasn't looking for comfort as much as I was looking for assurance from the man I'd found it in so often before.

"I can't say, son. I just can't say. It will all have to be in God's hands now." He reached over and patted my leg. I leaned away, putting my head in its customary spot against the window, letting the vibrations from the road numb my cheek as we sped toward town. I had been worried before, but as soon as Dad said that part about *"God's hands,"* I felt the hope begin to drain down my legs and leak right out of my feet. *"God's hands"* is what people always say when something really bad is about to happen.

We ate our breakfast (if you can call donuts breakfast) quietly stitching our conversation out of direct statements and one-word answers, the way men always do early in the morning. Dad told me it was alright that I didn't have my homework and I should walk straight over to the hospital after school. I would have plenty of time to catch up on my school work there. He also told me not to tell anyone about Nathan's grandmother, which I thought was a little odd, but I agreed without questioning. Sometimes it's hard to tell if Dad is up to being questioned. The whole morning was somber and we both accepted that our conversation was naturally broken and labored. We were content not discussing our deeper thoughts, making our breakfast together comfortable and easy. I felt closer to my dad that morning and even a little relief from the terrible circumstances waiting to swallow us outside the donut shop. Somewhere I found solace in the imperfect man sitting across from me, far from invincible, but I always believed he would find a way to make things a little bit better.

16

Doesn't Make a Toot

I passed the day with my mind occupied by things other than school. I was dinged three times for not having my homework, and it seemed like my teachers were disappointed that I wasn't more appropriately apologetic for my failure. The day drifted, and I found myself in art class sitting at my table alone with Robert. No Halley Kate, and even though I missed her company, I was glad that I wouldn't have to keep Nathan's grandmother a secret from her.

Ms. Flitty Art Teacher was saying something about how excited she was and how well we were all doing and how hard it was going to be to choose a piece for the coveted glass case. She said that we should all get right to work, be creative, be free, and express ourselves fully. I just stared down at the blob of clay in front of me. Robert's project was whistling nicely. He had constructed two little spouts for blow holes to make its hollow sound more pronounced, and he was now busy sculpting the whole thing into a pretty recognizable stegosaurus. I looked around and saw teapots, cars, all manner of animals, a smiley face head, and even a submarine. All of my fellow artists were hard at work on their individual masterpieces, pausing every now and again to hold it to their lips and show the rest of us how loud they could whistle.

I felt the beads of sweat on my forehead as I started the belated work on my clay piece. I'm ashamed to say that the only thing I prayed that day was that Ms. Flitty Art Teacher wouldn't notice how far behind I was and point it out to the rest of the class. She danced between the tables singing out that we only had one more day as I worked feverishly to make my lump of clay finally whistle. But I couldn't. It was almost as if I had some kind of weird artistic handicap that genetically prevented me from coaxing the high-pitched hollow sound from clay. I would ball it up, hollow it out, cut a hole to blow in, cut another hole for the air to escape, make it look just like everyone else's, put my lips to it, and, and…*nothing*. I tried over and over again, bubbling with frustration and losing hope with every subsequent attempt. Ms. Art Teacher clearly said that if it doesn't whistle wet, it won't whistle dry.

"Time is certainly running out on you, Mr. Chris." Ms. Art Teacher had floated up behind me without my notice.

"Yes, ma'am," I stammered with shame. "I've been working and working, but I just can't seem to get it to whistle."

"Everyone else seems to have their pieces whistling, Chris," her words dripped from her mouth as she motioned over the rest of the class like she was the Good Witch of the North.

"Yes, ma'am, I know." I looked up at her with tired eyes. "Does it really have to whistle? I mean, this is art class, so shouldn't we be graded on our creativity and not our ability to hollow out clay?"

"Well, Chris, you're right. You do need to be creative, you do need to express yourself, you do need to put your feelings into your clay, but most of all, you do need that tooter to toot." She giggled at the word "tooter."

"Yes, ma'am." I silently fumed. I couldn't bear to look at her anymore, so I dropped my head and asked, "What happens if it doesn't make a toot?" *I'm pretty sure she missed the pun.*

"Well, Chris," she put her hand on my shoulder, still sounding like Glenda, "you know as well as I what our rubric says. 'Any whistle that doesn't whistle starts out with a D.'" She quoted the rule as if she hadn't been the one to write it herself. Then she floated to the front of the room in her imaginary bubble, instructing us all to wrap our projects tightly in wet paper towels and place them in an orderly fashion over on the counter. I wrapped up my lump and set it right next to Nathan's forgotten fried egg that had been neatly concealed the day before in wet paper towels that were now bone dry. I sure was glad school was over.

My eyes were heavy and so were my books as I trudged across the school yard of Fair Play Middle. I made it out to the main street, down four blocks past the stores and shops that crowded the sidewalk, and finally through the vast hospital parking lot sparsely dotted with vacant cars. The premium visiting hours always came after work later in the day. I felt a little put out, but truthfully the walk was less than a mile, so I didn't let my agitation show when I finally sank into the waiting room chair next to my mother.

"Hey, Mom."

"Hey, Chris, how was your day?" She put her book in her lap, reached over and stroked the back of my head.

"It was tiring," I sighed. "Where's Nathan?" Nathan wasn't with my mom in the room.

"He's walking around the hospital, I guess. The waiting is pretty hard, so he's been passing the time wandering around the halls. He might be up looking at the new babies, if you want to go find him."

"No thanks, I'm just too tired," I sighed again.

"Well, sweetie, your dad will be here to take you home after a little while, but 'til then, why don't you walk down to the cafeteria, get a Coke, and then come on back here and get some homework done?"

Mom and Dad both did that, phrased statements as questions trying to make their parental commands seem a little more palatable. I think it was more for their own benefit than it was for mine. Whenever Mom started with "*Why don't you,*" it wasn't because she was about to ask you a question, it was just the way she began telling you what to do. I guess she thought it made everything a little more compassionate, and it did—unless you made the mistake of thinking that her orders were actually requests instead. I was tired and didn't want to think about it. So I took the money she offered me and skulked down the wide hallway toward the cafeteria to get myself a Coke.

By the time I bought a pack of crackers, taken a few sips of my Coke, refilled it again, and watched my feet all the way back to our waiting room, Dad had arrived and was talking in the hallway with Mom and Reverend Lane. As it turns out, one of our esteemed church council members was having some bunions removed from his feet, and while the reverend was here visiting anyway, he thought that he would pop down and check on Nathan's grandmother. At the time, I held no expectations of the clergy, so I didn't realize how disgusted I should have been. To avoid having to speak, I sipped on my drink as I slid past the three standing in the hall and stepped back into our empty little waiting room. I slunk down into a chair as the adults talked outside in what should have been hushed voices.

"So what are they saying now?" I heard Reverend Lane ask my dad.

"Well, they don't know what caused her collapse, but they're saying it could be anything from a stroke to some sort of severe reaction to who knows what. The bottom line seems to be that the doctors don't know and can't tell. They have told us that the longer she stays out, the less likely she'll be to regain consciousness. I don't know what's considered a long time, but she's been out almost two days now, and I think the machines are all that are keeping her going at this point." My dad paused. "To tell you the truth, it doesn't look real good."

"What about the boy? What's his name?"

"Nathan," whispered my mom.

"Yes, Nathan, what about him?" Reverend Lane's voice was deeper and much clearer than either of my parents'.

"We're taking care of him for now," Mom answered, "but after his grandmother, that boy doesn't have anyone else in the whole world." Mom knew better than that, so I guess it was an issue of trust that forced her into an honest lie.

"It sounds like a very sad situation. I'll have MaeBelle put it on the prayer list in the church bulletin this week."

"I've already called MaeBelle and Ms. Lamb's Sunday school class, but thank you anyway, Reverend," I heard Mom say.

"Alright then, folks." Reverend Lane paused and, while still addressing my parents, leaned back into the doorway just enough to see me in my seat. We made eye contact, but still, it was like he was staring into an empty chair. "It's all in God's hands now," was all he had to offer in that deep, affected voice.

He turned back to my parents as my mom invited him to please come back tomorrow to speak with Nathan. The reverend looked at his watch, said something about checking with MaeBelle and that he would try.

I busied myself with homework while Mom read her book and Dad went down the hall to make phone calls or something. I didn't see Nathan at all, and I was more than relieved when Dad appeared in the doorway to announce that it was time to take me home. He gave Mom a kiss on the cheek and a little whispered conversation while I collected my books and papers.

Dad and I stopped by the Fair Play Diner for an early dinner on the way home. I fingered through my onion rings as Dad stared out the plate glass window into the street, occasionally running his fingers back through his hair. Even though I was worried, I didn't ask what was on his mind. He tells me things when he thinks I'm ready or he has no choice, and since I dreaded what he might have to say, I contented myself to sit in silence and stare down at my food. I wondered why Mom had lied to the preacher about Nathan not having any other family.

The second Coke at dinner made sleep evasive that night as I lay in the bed trying to will myself into slumber. I pretended I was on a cloud, I pretended I was on a boat, I concentrated on letting sleep overcome me from the toes up, but no matter what strategy I employed, the events of the week reeled in my mind, keeping me from drifting peacefully away. I tossed and turned in bed for what seemed hours before I realized that I was standing on Flat Rock with Nathan. He beckoned me to come along as he hopped nimbly off the rock and sprinted quickly over the dry creek bed to the far bank. He stopped and called to me before turning to disappear down the path on his way to the cabin.

Not to be left behind, I jumped down off Flat Rock to follow. This was so cool! The creek was like a turtle on its back, lying there dry with all of its secrets exposed. I could see large chunks of gold up under the big boulders, and it seemed that with every step I took on the naked creek bed, I kicked up another arrowhead. This was wonderful! I called out to Nathan to come back and help me collect them, but he didn't answer. The woods on the far side had already swallowed him up, keeping him at the cabin and well out of earshot. I could see him standing in front of the cabin waiting on me as butterflies danced in the clearing, but I was too busy looting the creek's private things to follow.

This was so great! Everywhere I looked I found something more precious than the last. I made a pouch with my shirt and was filling it with arrowheads, jewels, and gold. Where was Nathan? Surely he should be on his way back to look for me by now. Then he could help me collect everything that Boulder Creek had ever kept hidden from us. This was amazing!

My shirt was nearly full when I stooped down to collect another treasure, reached out, and took a snake firmly in my grasp by mistake. My heart leapt and I stumbled backwards, nearly putting my hand on another snake as I reached out to break my fall. I needed to get out of the creek bed, but snakes that had been invisibly sunning themselves began dropping down off the rocks, and everywhere I thought to move revealed another waking viper of some sort! Serpents of all kinds and sizes were writhing and twisting all along the dry creek banks! I hadn't seen them before. I was afraid to stay and I was afraid to climb out. My voice was paralyzed and mute when I tried to call for anyone's help, as if it were even possible to save me.

I looked down. *Why are my tennis shoes wet?* was the last thought that crossed my mind as a wall of water came crashing down, knocking all of the wind out of my body. The creek was furious with my treachery. It slammed me to its depths and held me there as a soup of snakes rushed by. The angry water swirled and tossed me about, and just as I was about to reach the surface for air, it sucked me back to the depths to take its due for my betrayal. The water was black and cold. My waterlogged clothes bound me like ropes, and no matter how hard I struggled, the powerful creek easily pinned me to its bottom, threatening to hold me there beyond my last breath. I felt the rocks against my head and the sand in my underwear as I writhed on the creek bottom before finally realizing the futility of the battle and succumbing to the water.

Then as if to say "Don't ever mess with me again," Boulder Creek puked me out onto the shore of the far bank, leaving me lying there naked and exhausted. I looked up and saw Nathan watching me from the trees, and I was embarrassed.

"Chris! Chris!" I heard Nathan's voice calling softly somewhere in the distance. Then I sat straight up in bed with a giant gasp. "Gahlee," Nathan whispered, "what did you do, eat onion rings for dinner or something?"

I looked around, thankful to be in my dark bedroom. "I had a bad dream," I breathed and started to untwist the covers from my sweaty legs.

"Yeah, I figured that." Nathan moved quietly to get back into his bed. "With all the thrashing and flailing and gulping air, I thought it would be best to go on and wake you up."

"Yeah, yeah, thanks," I panted, still sitting up in bed. "I'm sorry I woke you up, Nathan." I looked, but I couldn't see Nathan at all. Cherry Field nights are black, and we never sleep with any lights on in the house.

"Nah, you didn't wake me. I was having a bad dream too." Nathan paused to yawn. "I dreamed that you were drowning in the creek, and I was trying to help, but it was real weird because no matter how hard I tried to run to you, I could never get any closer. You were only lying in enough water to cover your face, and I knew that you could hear me, but I just couldn't get you to stand up. I kept yelling, 'Stand up, Chris, just stand up,' but you wouldn't do it. It scared the crap out of me." Nathan paused. I could hear him yawn again in the dark. "What about your dream, Chris? They say if you tell them, they go away and you don't have to dream them again in the same night."

It was a bad dream, no, a nightmare that I remember vividly even to this day, but the fact of the matter is, I think that Nathan's dream scared me more.

"I barely remember it," I lied, "something about my teeth falling out."

"They say that's caused by worry, Chris." His voice was starting to fade out. "You don't have anything to worry about, Chris. You shouldn't worry." Then he added, "Wake me in the morning; I'm thinking about going to school." His voice trailed off into sleep, leaving me there alone in the Cherry Field darkness.

17

Nathan's Chris

I was too afraid to fall back into the same dream, so I spent the rest of the night staring into the darkness and listening to Nathan sleep. Time dragged painfully by, and I was glad when Dad finally cracked the door and whispered that it was time to get up. I shook Nathan as he had asked, and we both dressed for school in my room.

"Are you sure that you want to go to school today, buddy?" my dad asked Nathan.

"Yes, sir," Nathan answered in his squeaky voice, "Grandmom will be okay for a little bit without me, and I'd kinda like to see Halley Kate."

Mom got up with the rest of us to make breakfast, but Dad said not to worry, that we'd stop by the donut shop and get something. Nathan slipped on his "still too big" black leather jacket that his mom had supposedly sent him a couple of years before, making him look like a geeky road warrior wanna be. It was heavy with a big buckle at the waist, and the sleeves reached down halfway across his palms. The black jacket was cool enough, but when you put that together with his high water pants and tennis shoes with knotted laces, Nathan almost looked like he belonged in some sort of institution. I had no idea why he chose today of all days to wear that thing to school, but I was too tired to protest or try to talk him out of it.

Mr. Butler was talking about figures of speech that morning while Nathan stared out the window, and I sat there wondering if Mr. Butler ever had nightmares. Maybe it was because I was tired, but the whole day seemed strange. I saw Mr. Butler up in the front of the room lecturing while the rest of the class talked freely, but all of this only served as background noise while my thoughts wandered lethargically.

"Nathan!" The sound of Mr. Butler's voice singling out Nathan broke the trance I had fallen under. "Give the class an example of a cliché," he continued after he had secured Nathan's attention.

I guess Mr. Butler had been talking about clichés, but Nathan obviously thought he was referring to material that had been covered in class during Nathan's recent absences. Nathan fidgeted a little, looking around the room for any clue that might help him answer the question, and when he found none, he finally offered up an honest excuse instead. "My grandmother's been sick," he responded and then put his face down into his hand like the words had caused his head to hurt.

"Very, very good Nathan!" Mr. Butler boomed with delight. "Usually you hear it as *'my grandmother died,'* or *'my dog ate my homework,'* or something like that, but that was a very good answer, Nathan. Good job! And, by the way, I really like your jacket."

As Mr. Butler continued on with his lecture, Nathan slumped down further into his desk while I pondered the merits of sarcasm against ignorant praise.

Mr. Butler was still talking when the bell rang, and we all got up to file out into the hall. Using both arms, Nathan clutched his books to his chest and walked with such small steps that it looked like he was tiptoeing out behind us. The sight of him holding his books like a girl and his itty bitty prancing steps was so comical in contrast to his tough-looking black jacket that it was impossible not to notice. Although my scrape with Jimmy and Brett had more or less insulated me from a great deal of teasing that went on at school, Nathan was not nearly that fortunate.

I bumped and shouldered my way as usual down the crowded hall, stopping at my locker to deposit some books and retrieve others before my next class. Nathan and his black jacket had been swept along in the river of bodies down to his locker where he would stop and do the same. I shuffled through my notebooks thinking of Nathan's grandmother and how terrifying she looked in her hospital bed. Nathan was so close to the edge of such vast uncertainty that I wondered why he even bothered to come to school today. I wished he hadn't.

Nobody around here knew anything about what was really going on, and it made me terribly uncomfortable. If I could have just told about his grandmother, the passive sympathy of our schoolmates would have provided some shelter from the abuse his oddities always seemed to invite. It would have been easier for me to help if everyone else knew the story. I guess I have always been better at doing what's right when there's a cause than I have ever been at just doing what's right.

"Ha! Ha! Ha! Look at you, belt-buckle boy. You sure are bad!" I heard the loud, jeering voices down the hall rise above the rest of the usual student shuffle. Students were stopping to watch, causing a long jam-up back down the hallway. I did my best to push through the crowd, squeezing through and stepping on the feet of protesting students I passed by.

"Hey, hey, black jacket man, you sure look tough in that black jacket. Are you a tough guy, belt-buckle boy?" There was some laughing, but most of the kids standing around seemed disgusted at the spectacle, and yet they continued to just stand and watch.

"Look how big that jacket is." I heard a girl's voice join in. "What in the world is that big giant buckle for? What does your mom do, buckle you to the *special* tree with it?" Then she laughed through her nose like a wounded hyena. I kept pushing through until, even though I was still hidden in the crowd, I had a full view of the scene. I was never clear on what Nathan did to set this off, but he was now backed against the wall by two boys and a girl who were spewing loud, venomous insults at Nathan, to each other's delight.

"I said I was sorry," Nathan whined. "I said I was sorry, why can't we just leave it at that and leave me alone?"

"I said I was sorry. I said I was sorry. Leave me alone!" the girl mimicked. "Why don't you just go home and cry to your mama? No, she probably doesn't even like you. You should go cry to your grandmamma instead. Just make sure you don't rust this big jacket buckle with all your tears." She reached over and flipped the big buckle hanging low on his black jacket. Nathan tried to knock her hand away, but he was too slow, and it made the boys laugh even harder.

Then, when it seemed that the bullies were just about to lose interest, Nathan wiped his nose and, with big tears beginning to swell up in his eyes, smiled at the boys and said, "You just wait until my friend Chris gets here! You are both going to be so sorry. You know what he did to Jimmy and Brett, so he won't even break a sweat with you. You just better look out!" Then he pointed at the girl. "You're just lucky Chris would never beat up a girl."

I cringed at his words. I knew I should help, but instead I tried to sink deeper back into the crowd. Backing up, though, proved to be much more difficult than moving forward had been. Nathan hadn't scared anybody but me with his threat, and the taunting just intensified after that, as the boys were more than willing to wait for me to show up. I stood in the crowd wanting to simply fade away before somebody recognized me as Nathan's Chris.

I don't think I was too scared to fight; fights get broken up pretty quickly at school, but I was petrified to stand up for him in front of all of these people, to always and forever be associated with the most uncool *special* at Fair Play Middle. It was something I just couldn't do. I felt sick to my stomach knowing that Nathan's faith in me was so terribly unmerited. I remained frozen in the crowd.

"So where's your friend?" I heard one boy jeer.

"Yeah, so where's your friend, geek?" the girl echoed as she poked Nathan in his shoulder with her finger.

Somebody bumped me from behind as if to push me out of anonymity and into the limelight with the others, so I pushed back, not to be budged from where I was safely planted. When I realized that it was someone simply trying to get around me for a better look, I felt a small wave of relief roll over me. *This can't take too much longer and then we'll all be in class where I can pretend that I didn't see anything.*

"You're pulling my leg, Black Jacket. 'Cause you know and I know that *specials* are too dumb to have any friends. Nobody wants to be friends with you." The girl who poked Nathan was not letting up. "I'm going to ask you one more time…and real slow so you can understand. Where – is – your – friend?"

Even though I knew she couldn't see me from where she was standing, it seemed that this girl was no longer talking to Nathan, but only using him to humiliate me into action. She gave me every chance.

I got shoved from behind again, but this time whoever had been trapped in the jam-up sailed right past me, out of the crowd and on to center stage with Nathan and his tormentors.

"HERE – I – AM! Did I say it slow enough for you, you stupid cow!" Halley Kate exploded onto the scene with such force the shock waves nearly knocked the girl to the floor. Halley Kate dropped her books and turned on the boys. "Isn't it funny how you two are so, so interested in another guy's clothes? What is your problem, did your mommy dress you this morning? I mean look at your hair, what are you, a couple of girls?"

The boys stepped back, unable to respond to Halley Kate's tirade. The crowd began to laugh at Halley Kate's quips and taunted the bullies to respond to her insulting questions.

"Yeah, what is your problem? Did your mommy dress you? Hah, hah, you're getting your butt kicked by a girl!" yelled the formerly uninvolved bystanders.

With fiery finger points, head bobs, and a stream of witty insults, Halley Kate had both boys backed against the wall unable to speak and looking for any chance to escape her wrath. Her eyes cut right through the two cowards, and she snarled low, just loud enough for the rest of us to hear, "You guys are so lucky Chris isn't here."

"Hey, what is your problem, girly? Is this geeky *special* with the Fonzie jacket your boyfriend or something?" The girl bully forced a laugh as she recovered from Halley Kate's initial onslaught and had regained enough confidence for a counterattack.

You could almost feel the rush of wind as Halley Kate wheeled back around to meet her. As soon as she turned away from them, the boys she had pinned against the wall slid away and scurried into the nearest classroom like a couple of little white mice.

"Yeah, that's right, Laura," Halley Kate growled as she advanced toward the other girl, "he *is* my friend. That's something you don't have, little *Miss I Think I'm So Popular.* You're nothing but a sad sack with too much makeup and last year's clothes. You're the only friend you have, and that's not saying much."

Halley Kate's words were cold steel, and she didn't let up until all of them were laid out for Fair Play Middle School to see. Laura made some feeble remark about her red stripe, leaving Halley Kate unscathed and unstoppable. Mostly Laura stood against the lockers getting a harsh dose of what so many people wished they had said themselves.

When she was done, Halley Kate picked up her books, and she and Nathan walked together to class. Everybody in the whole hallway clapped and cheered for the red-stripe hero. The sound of applause brought Ms. Waits out of her room to investigate the commotion and to tell us all to hurry up and get to class.

Later, in art, Halley Kate's heroics were all that Nathan wanted to talk about. "You should have been there, Chris. Laura and her friends were giving me a pretty bad time about Mom's jacket, and I just didn't know what I was going to do. I didn't want to be late for class, but they just wouldn't let me go. Everybody, I mean everybody, just sat there in the hall watching me get so embarrassed. I can't believe a girl could be so mean and nasty, but that girl really is. Anyway, just when I thought I was never going to get out of there, Halley Kate comes flying in and gives all three of them a lot more than they ever wanted to have. She made the boys run away and she made that horrible Laura cry right in front of everybody in the whole school. It was great! You should have been there, Chris. And then, when it was all over, everybody clapped and cheered for Halley Kate just like she was Bat Girl or something."

He sat at the table with an untouched ball of clay sitting in front of him, jabbering incessantly and heaping shovelfuls to the weight of my guilt. Robert had only heard about the episode secondhand, and since his stegosaurus whistle was all but finished, he continued to ask Nathan about every detail, until finally Halley Kate spoke up.

"Hey, Nathan, that lump of clay lying there in front of you isn't going to magically make itself into a whistle. Today is the last day to work on this, you know." In almost no time at all, her fingers had nimbly crafted a clay tulip bud with two little butterfly wind spouts. She hadn't been at school all week, and in less than half a class period, she had sculpted the most wonderful whistle our table had ever seen. It made Robert's stegosaurus look silly. She held it up to her lips to blow, making one long, pure, beautiful note.

"Yeah, I know," Nathan answered. "I think I'm just going to turn in my fried egg. It's around here somewhere, and I don't think she'll mind too much if it doesn't whistle so well. What about you, Chris, what have you got going there?"

I looked down at the perfect baseball-sized sphere sitting in front of me. As I had been watching Halley Kate craft her whistle and listening to Nathan go on, I guess that I had been rolling my clay around and around until it was a smooth, solid ball. I liked the way it looked. With only fifteen minutes left to work on this project, I had no chance of ever making it whistle, let alone making it all creative like the rest of Ms. Flitty Art Teacher's students. I had resigned myself to a zero on this project when inspiration finally took hold. Something that Ms. Flitty Art teacher had said swirled in my head, mixing with images from some old Saturday morning cartoons, and I knew that I was indeed capable of the greatest creation that no one would ever know about.

I took my thumb and jammed it deep into the solid sphere I had rolled so neatly. Then I wiggled my thumb just a little to make sure I had a nice hollow spot dead in the middle, surrounded by thick walls of clay. Without anyone else noticing, I sealed the hole up, covering all evidence from the outside that my project was now a solid ball of clay with a marble-sized air pocket right in the very center. I pinched up a couple of fake air holes, giving my creation the appearance of a true whistle, and then I reached over and snatched a piece of Nathan's unused clay and rolled it out on the table to form a long, thin fuse. I wrapped the fuse on top of my clay ball, finishing off my sculpture by scratching the letters "TNT" on the side.

Wow, I couldn't believe how cool it turned out. It looked just like one of those round black bombs that you always see in the old cartoons…the ones they always hide in birthday cakes and stuff. I looked around the room, and my cartoon bomb whistle looked as good as anyone else's except for Halley Kate's. As we all got up to put our final work on the counter to dry, hers truly stood out against the rest. Mine, however, didn't, as it easily hid among the cars, animals, and submarines waiting to be glazed and fired.

18

In the Garden

Nathan seemed a little melancholy as we walked together across the grass in front of the school on our way to the hospital. I got the feeling it was more about missing the bus ride with Halley Kate than it was his grandmother's condition or the uncertainty of what may happen if she worsened. He wanted to stop by B & B Hardware on the way over, to see if Mr. Brant might have a reasonably priced pulley in stock. That's exactly how Nathan put it, *"reasonably priced."* I didn't bother to ask him why he was suddenly interested in a pulley, but I was plenty willing to make the stop, knowing full well that any delay would cut down on the time I would have to spend waiting around at the hospital. A front bell chimed as we pushed the door open and stepped off the street into the crowded little shop.

The sign outside clearly stated that this was a hardware store, but the whole front half of the shop was filled with interesting little knickknacks, porcelain bowls, figurines, glass balls, wooden angels, brass cooking utensils, all kinds of eye catching bric-a-brac and wicker. The aisles were tight and the shelves were packed with all manner of expensive breakables. One wrong turn and a boy could find himself working here every weekend for a year to pay for the damage.

Moving toward the back of the store, everything took on more of the traditional hardware feel. There were chains on spools, drawers with every screw imaginable, barrels of nails with scales hanging above, some fishing gear and other dust-covered inventory ordered but never sold. It was a great store, assuming a split personality reflecting the different dreams and desires of its two owners. Ms. Brant, a loud and forceful woman, had always wanted a gift shop filled with beautiful pieces of overpriced impracticality. Her husband, Mr. Brant, on the other hand, wanted an old-fashioned hardware store where he could spend the day talking with his customers and coaching them on the fine art of home repair.

They fought over floor space all the time. If you were there late in the day, after Ms. Brant had tallied the receipts, it was not uncommon to hear her yelling at her husband through the store, just to gloat over how much better her gifts had sold than his hardware. But in the end, I think it was the strange chemistry of things that don't seem to belong with one another that kept this little shop afloat for so many years.

Nathan walked back to the hardware section and was talking with Mr. Brant while Ms. Brant glared at me fidgeting among her things. I decided to go back and look at the pocket knives that were on display in a dusty little case well out of her sight at the far back corner of the store. Nathan and Mr. Brant disappeared into a back room, and when Nathan finally emerged, he was carrying about forty feet of rope and an old pulley that was painted flat black. "Hey, Jan," Mr. Brant called to his wife from the back of the store, "put the pulley and the rope on *my* account."

Ms. Brant watched us closely as we made our way back through her things up to the front counter. "Yeah, fine," she yelled back to her husband, "but when I tally at the end of business, I'm not including this stuff with your receipts."

Mr. Brant muttered something about his wife and then disappeared again through the doorway to the back room. Nathan, with the rope neatly wound and hoisted over his shoulder, handed me the pulley to carry as we nodded good-bye to Ms. Brant and stepped back out to the street. I don't think we had even walked three steps because as soon as the door swung closed to B & B Hardware, Nathan turned to be captured in a full embrace around his legs. Nathan twisted a little bit to avoid falling over. I had never seen him look so coordinated as he regained his balance to keep from toppling over the little boy who was now hugging him affectionately. Nathan looked like first prize at the fair. He didn't try to break away; instead he put his hand down on the boy's head and craned around to look for the child's mother.

"Mommy, Mommy, look, look, look, it's him!" the boy began to shout excitedly as a woman pushing a sleeping baby in a stroller hustled up.

"Peter," she scolded, "don't you ever run away like that again! We're out here on the street and you could have gotten hurt! You always have to hold on to Mommy's hand. Do you understand me?"

But little Peter was far too excited to pay much attention to his mother's chastisement, and he began to bounce up and down joyfully while still holding on to Nathan. "Look, Mommy, look who it is!" he chirped repeatedly as Nathan stood there calmly waiting for the boy's mother to assert control.

"I'm so sorry," Peter's mommy explained as she tried to pry her son off of Nathan's legs. "I don't know what's gotten into him. He's usually leery of strangers, and I'm really not sure how he thinks he knows you."

Even with his mother tugging at him, Peter was determined to hold on to Nathan, but when all three of them nearly fell over with the force of her pulling, she finally gave up and swatted Peter's fanny with her hand. The little boy started to wail as his mother finally freed Nathan from his grasp.

"It's okay, ma'am. It's okay, ma'am. He's a nice little boy. I don't mind at all. It's okay." Nathan tried to comfort the woman while she wrangled with her son and continued to apologize.

"Mommy, Mommy, it's him, it's him!" Peter was now pointing up at Nathan as tears streamed down his little face.

"I don't think so, honey." The woman apologized once again to Nathan. Then she took her son by the hand and, pushing her stroller, headed off down the sidewalk. Peter turned to watch us as he followed his mother with tiny steps and great big tears. He seemed to be crying more over the injustice done for seeing what his mother could not than from the pain of the spanking he received. From her window, Ms. Brant had quietly watched all that had happened.

"That was weird," Nathan huffed as we started back on our way to the hospital.

But the day had already been way too much for me, so to keep the conversation to a minimum, I just nodded in agreement. I didn't even bother to ask about the rope or the pulley.

By the time we got to our waiting room, Dad was already there. He and Mom had their reading books and looked like they were prepared to stay way beyond my hopes. They asked us about our day, but neither one of us mentioned what had happened in the hall at school, indicating instead that the day had been uneventful. They told us Nathan's grandmother was still "sleeping" and that Reverend Lane would be by later to talk with Nathan.

I knew that Nathan wasn't a fan, but he didn't protest and thanked both my parents for everything. He said he was headed for the hospital chapel, hesitated as if he had something more to say, and then disappeared through the doorway. Oddly enough, my parents never asked about the things we brought from the hardware store, so I set them, unexplained, on the seat next to me and started on my homework. But my mind wasn't on it.

"Mom," I broke the silence, "what's going to happen if Nathan's grandmother doesn't wake up?"

Mom and Dad both laid their books in their laps in perfect unison, almost as if they had practiced. "Well, honey," Mom started, "I don't know. We haven't really thought that far ahead."

"What about his real mother?" I asked.

Mom looked to Dad for him to answer. "Well, buddy, we're not sure. It's just a real bad situation, and it keeps looking worse every day. I asked you to keep Nathan's grandmother to yourself because your mother and I needed some time to see what we thought about everything. You know, son, the right thing isn't always the easy thing."

I hate it when my parents talk around in circles. Adults always seem to think that if they ease in to telling you something it somehow makes the news easier to swallow, but really the suspense of not having a clue what they are getting at just makes it all worse. When adults tell you stuff, you get to dread what they are about to say first without making it any better in the end. Whatever Dad was getting to wasn't going to be good.

"Your mom and I talked about several options in the event Nathan's grandmother doesn't wake up. We don't have a lot, but we're pretty comfortable, so we talked about letting him stay with us. We wanted to see what you thought about it, but we figured the same school and the same friends would be a much better situation than his real mom might be able to provide. There is a very good reason that Nathan lives with his grandmother, and we thought staying with us might be a better option than leaving Cherry Field."

I sat there staring blankly at my dad, listening to what he was saying and not knowing how to feel about any of this.

"But," he ran his hand back through his hair as he went on, "Reverend Lane seems to feel that we should do our best to reach Nathan's real mother, and if that doesn't work out, he feels strongly that Nathan should move up to the Saddle Ridge Christian Home for Boys. He says his good friend from seminary school runs it, and they will be much better equipped to support Nathan

than we are. He thinks it would be best for both Nathan and our family. He says he is trained in these matters, and as the servant leader of the church, a prominent citizen of Fair Play who knows all of the personalities involved, moving Nathan to the home will be his written recommendation to Child Protective Services, when it comes to that."

Mom was in tears, and Dad knew that in his anger he had told me too much. "But of course," he continued calmly, "this will only happen if his grandmother doesn't wake up."

By the time Dad had finished, I was hunched forward in my chair with my elbows on my knees and my head down in my hands. My books and papers lay on the floor where they slid off my lap as Dad had been talking. I didn't bother to pick them up. I could hear Mom sniffling, but I still didn't know what I was feeling. I didn't know what to make of any of this. Nathan at my house or Nathan gone from Cherry Field forever... *what would it all mean?*

"Will she wake up?" I had an unanticipated crack in my voice as my question came from underneath my hands.

Mom moved over and put her arms around me. "The doctors say 'no'. They say that they don't have any idea what happened, and in cases like this, three days is probably too long."

I was still trying to digest what my parents were telling me when, "Hi ho, gang!" a cheerful Reverend Lane stepped into the waiting room before putting on his sad but hopeful face. Gauging the mood of the room quickly, the reverend's next words were more somber and worry-filled, "How's she doing?"

Mom hugged me tight and then shook her head, letting Reverend Lane know that there was no change. He saw something in my mother and me that prompted him to cross the little waiting room and put his hands on our shoulders. “I know this is a tough time for us all, but we have to have faith in the Good Lord’s plan. We don’t live in a perfect world, but He will always see us through even the most difficult times.” His words were perfect and smooth, just as if he had rehearsed them a thousand times before. He bowed his head over us and prayed, “Your will Lord, Your will. Everything is in Your hands,” and then he moved back to step out of the room.

But before he could make his full escape, my dad lifted his head and asked, “Don’t you want to see Nathan before you go, Reverend?”

“I thought this *was*...” Reverend Lane looked to me and caught himself in mid-sentence, “...of course I do,” he continued.

“He’s in the chapel...Chris, how about showing Reverend Lane where that is?” Then my dad leaned back in his chair, running his hand through his hair, perhaps not noticing the irony of his request.

I could hear the strides of the big man on the tile following close behind me. It seemed that he took one step for every two of mine, so I quickened my gait just enough to prevent him from overtaking me. I could hear him sniff and clear his throat, but I kept my pace so this part would be over as quickly as possible. I had no interest in any uncomfortable conversation with this man. When we reached the elevator, I finally turned and spoke, “Reverend, would you like to take the stairs or the elevator?”

"Well, young man," he answered in his smooth baritone voice, smiling and patting his midsection, "I should probably take the stairs, but let's make it easy on ourselves today." He reached past me and pressed the button for the elevator. We rode one floor up in silence.

The elevator slid open directly across from the open double doors of the chapel. Realizing that we had reached our destination, the reverend announced, "Well, here we are," and strode with long, heavy steps straight into the room like it belonged to him. Not knowing what else to do, I followed him in.

The empty little chapel was overstuffed with four rows of big pews facing a tiny altar with some artificial flowers and a gold cross. Though they were obviously phony, tapestries and drapes hung on the walls to give the appearance of windows in the room. The floor was carpeted and the lights were dimmed, making everything appear more religious than it really was. Nathan was sitting in the center of the first pew with his head down, not bothering to turn around as the preacher stepped boldly into the chapel and cleared his throat.

Reverend Lane waited for a moment, but Nathan, head still bowed, offered no invitation. So the reverend let out a sigh and squeezed his way along the wall to where Nathan was sitting. I sat down watching from the last row. From the back, the big man looked massive, and I could hear the pew groan a little with his weight as he slid up next to Nathan and patted him on the leg.

"How are you doing, young man?" the reverend asked in his deep, soothing voice.

Nathan looked up with wet eyes. "It's been three days now, sir. Why are you asking me how I'm doing now?

How do you think I'm doing?" Nathan's voice was a little jerky from the tears, but I could tell that he was feeling wronged by the preacher's belated visit. Nathan dropped his eyes meekly. "They won't let me go to her. They won't let me see her. They won't let me talk to her. Will you talk to the doctors, Reverend? Will you get them to let me see her? *Please?*" Nathan tuned up and whimpered as he begged.

"I don't think that I can do that, young man." Reverend Lane crossed his legs and leaned in toward Nathan. "The doctors know what's best. They are well trained and they know what to do in these situations."

"But they don't know anything!" Nathan protested tearfully. "Please, please will you just ask for me, *please?*" Nathan pleaded while Reverend Lane simply shook his head.

"God has a plan for you, Nathan."

"I know," Nathan sniffled in agreement.

"Whatever He has in store," the preacher smiled down at Nathan, "it will all be for your own good. It is all in God's hands. One thing that you can always count on is that in all things God works for the good of those who love Him…"

"…who have been called according to his purpose," Nathan concluded without looking up.

"Very good, young man," beamed Reverend Lane, "you know your Bible verses."

"I know that one," Nathan responded dryly.

The preacher patted Nathan on the leg again and offered his hand. "Why don't you take my hand, young man, and we'll pray together."

Nathan stared down at Reverend Lane's open palm and shook his head. "I don't think I want to do that, sir."

"You don't want to pray for your grandmother, young man?"

"No, I just don't want to pray with *you*, sir." The reverend's smile fled from his face and his ears began to redden. "I have heard you pray for sick people before, Reverend, and you start all of your prayers by saying, 'God, if it be your will, please heal…' but that's not what I want to say to God right now."

"You don't want God's will to be done, young man?" Reverend Lane raised a stern voice.

"If God wants my grandmom to never wake up again, then no, I don't want it. I want Him to change His mind. I've been here begging Him to change His mind, but all you want to say is that everything is in God's hands." Tears started to stream down Nathan's cheeks as he was getting upset again. He started to raise his voice to the preacher. "You think that God does everything and that He doesn't listen and He'll never do anything differently no matter what we say. What good are those prayers, Mr. Lane? How are your prayers going to help Grandmom if you won't even ask God to do something about it, if you are only going to chalk it up to '*His will*,' no matter what happens?"

Nathan looked to the preacher through sobbing, expectant eyes. "You're afraid He won't answer you, so you make all of the excuses up front so you won't have anything to explain or be embarrassed about. I don't want to pray those prayers. Those prayers aren't any good, and they won't help anything at all."

Reverend Lane wasn't used to being challenged, especially by a child. His face was red and angry. Using his pulpit voice, the preacher chastised Nathan, "NOT OUR WILL, BUT HIS WILL...Who do you think you are, boy, to question God? The world does what the world does, and God helps us get through it all. Right now, the doctors say your grandmother probably won't be waking up, so you need to take my hand and pray for what to do next." *He didn't need to pray for guidance. My dad already told me what Reverend Lane planned to do next.*

The big man grabbed for Nathan's hand, but Nathan slipped through his grasp and stood up out of the preacher's reach. "You better sit back down right now, boy, so that we can pray; so that I can ask God what to do with you!" Reverend Lane was losing his temper, and his words seemed more like threats. *Did he forget that I was still sitting back here?*

Nathan backed farther away from the preacher and then suddenly fled sobbing out the chapel doors, calling my name to follow. Reverend Lane glared back at me from his seat. I somehow felt the need to apologize, but I was too afraid. I slid off my pew and ran out behind Nathan. I was sure that my parents would never believe what had happened, so I kept it to myself until just now.

I chased Nathan past the elevator down the stairwell, and even though I took the stairs two at a time, he was too far ahead of me to catch. I heard him crying and the echoes of his feet as he busted through the doorway at the bottom of the first flight. He had a good head start, but I was sure I could catch him and calm him down before he got back to my parents in the waiting room. I sprinted past a gurney waiting for a patient in the hall and dodged around a cleaning cart, ignoring all the adults cautioning me to slow down as I ran by. I was moving pretty quickly, closing the gap on the much slower Nathan.

He was just up at the nurse's station now, and I knew that I would easily catch him before he ran, crying, to my parents. I wasn't sure why, but I needed to talk to him first. Suddenly, instead of continuing on down the hall, Nathan took an unexpected turn and bolted straight through the big swinging door into his grandmother's room. *He's not supposed to be in there!*

"Hey! Hey! He went in, he went in!" I heard someone yell as the staff mobilized like hornets swarming out from behind their big counter. I was on my stride and sailed through the door behind Nathan just ahead of the flood of nurses. I fully expected to see Nathan wailing and crying at his grandmother's bedside, but he was much calmer than I anticipated as he stood beside the dying woman.

"Hey, you have to leave! You can't be in here!" Someone in white grabbed my arm, but I jerked it away. "Orderly! Orderly! We need some help in here right now!" someone else was yelling as hospital personnel began to fill the room.

"Grandmom. Grandmom." Nathan was at his grandmother's bedside, gently shaking her arm as if he were trying to wake her up from a nap. "Grandmom, wake up. It's time to go home now. We need to go home." He was weeping softly and gently begging her to open her eyes. As the pitiful sight played out before us, the commotion in the room began to subside when the guardians of intensive care saw that we were doing no harm.

A young nurse was at the bedside checking the old woman's vitals, and when she was satisfied, she put her arm around Nathan and said, "It won't happen that way, honey; she'll have to wake up all on her own time." The young nurse waved the others out so that only the three of us were left alone with Nathan's sleeping grandmother and all of her blinking machines. "If you want to hold her hand for a minute, you can," the young nurse graciously offered, "but we can't stay long."

I didn't want to get too close, but Nathan reached down and took his grandmother's hand and kissed her gently on the forehead. "Please wake up, Grandmom. I need you. I need you here with me," he whispered.

"Okay, time to go." The young nurse touched Nathan's shoulder to guide him out. "Say good-bye now, but if the doctor says it's okay, maybe you can come back later."

Nathan nodded and turned away, disappointed and grieving. I felt like we were leaving a funeral as we shuffled our way out. But just when we were pushing back out through the door: "Hi, boys, how was school today?" Nathan's grandmother spoke up as clear as day.

The young nurse pushed the emergency call button and leapt across the room to attend Nathan's grandmother.

"I was in the garden, boys, when I heard you calling. Sorry I wasn't here when you got home. I came as quickly as I could. I sure hope that I didn't worry anybody."

The room flooded again with people in white dresses and blue scrubs as Nathan hugged his grandmother, and we were politely shoved out into the hallway.

The doctors let us all talk to Nathan's grandmother one more time before sending us home to get some rest. We stopped by the Fair Play Diner for supper, and Dad bought us all "Peanut Buster Parfaits" for dessert to celebrate. As usual we blessed our meal, but tonight Mom insisted that we bless our parfaits as well. We all obliged, holding hands, making an awkward ring in the booth, as our waitress paused and waited for us to finish before pouring my parents more coffee.

19

Unfinished Egg

Nathan's grandmother got better, and she was released from the hospital in about the time it took our clay projects to fully harden. Ms. Flitty Art Teacher danced around the room to a chorus of hollow whistles as we slapped the colored glaze on our creations, preparing them for the kiln. Nathan tried to blow into my TNT whistle, and when he couldn't get any sound, he told me not to worry, that his fried egg didn't toot either.

"It might whistle after it gets fired," I stated firmly to Nathan.

"Don't count on it," answered Robert. "If it doesn't whistle wet, it won't whistle dry. Too bad for you, Chris, I never heard of anybody failing art class before." Then Robert snickered from behind his stupid stegosaurus.

Halley Kate silently brushed the color on her tulips with the skill of a true sculptor, while Nathan's egg was just a mess of white and yellow glaze. My bomb was basic black with a white fuse, and I was just finishing up the red lettering when Ms. Flitty Art Teacher popped by.

"Well, Chris, I'm glad to see that you were finally able to make something work. Halley Kate, that looks wonderful! Robert, you've certainly been creative…I don't think I have ever seen a green dog before." She was almost singing her commentary as she glanced over our table. "Mr. Nathan," her voice dropped in exaggerated disappointment. "It looks like you didn't bother to even try the project. If you didn't take the time to do what I asked you to do, I'm not sure I should bother taking the time to put that *thing* in the kiln. What's it supposed to be anyway?"

"It's a fried egg," I spoke up.

"Well, yes. I can see it's the right colors. Nathan, I know that you were out a few days, but you did have plenty of time to work on this. It's like you just ignored the whole concept and decided to do something easy. Did you even try to make a whistle?"

"I forgot," Nathan muttered without bothering to look up.

"Well," she raised her head a little and looked down her nose, "I think I might just forget to put your little egg in the kiln with the other pieces, and I might just forget to put in a grade, so that next time, you might not forget to do as you're told."

As I sat there listening to Ms. Flitty Art Teacher scold Nathan with her usual lilt, I smiled to myself at the thought of his egg being banned from the kiln where my massive air pocket disguised as a whistle would soon be fired.

The next day, Ms. Flitty Art Teacher stood in front of the class with a tear in her eye and some very bad news. "I have some very bad news for you, class." She was so dramatic that it seemed whatever tragedy had befallen was nearly too much for her to bear. "Class," she sputtered, "I won't be able to grade your clay projects after all. It seems that someone's piece had an air pocket." She hung her head like she might be unable to go on. Then she summoned up all of her courage and continued, "I've seen expanding air pockets damage one or two pieces in a kiln before, but yesterday, class," she choked a little, "well, this one... this was a big one. This one not only destroyed every whistle in this class, but all the whistles from my other class as well. They were all being fired together, and there was nothing left but dust and broken rubble." She choked and sniffled at the thought. "I'm so very sorry about all of your hard work, but I certainly won't be able to count this project as a grade." Then she sat down heavily at her desk, being thoroughly exhausted from the whole horrible ordeal.

As it turned out, the school parent night was a couple of days later, and after the blast, Ms. Flitty Art Teacher had very little artwork to display in the coveted front case. She had intended to display the very finest of our clay whistles, advertising her talent and skills as a teacher for all of our parents to see. After the explosion, however, she scrambled, building her display with leftover drawings and old water colors, all centering around a single clay sculpture entitled *Unfinished Egg* that she had unwittingly saved from destruction.

Nathan eventually gave the egg to my mom for Mother's Day or something, but now it is sitting here at the corner of my desk on top of the water bill and some property settlement papers. I've grown very fond of it over the years. Maybe because it reminds me of Mom, maybe because it reminds me of my time with Nathan, or maybe because it survived my crime when nothing else did.

20

Full of Deals

We could still see our breath as we went crunching through the woods. Except for a few pine trees and some scraggly mistletoe, everything else was in deep slumber, making it feel like we were sneaking through someone's bedroom or across their grave. I could hear Nathan panting behind me as he followed, shuffling through the dead leaves. The cold air amplified every sound, and walking along, I got the feeling that we should try to be a little quieter out of reverence for the sleeping. The big pines that disappeared in the canopy on warmer days now stood like giant guardians, reminding us that we were still accountable even as the rest of the forest hibernated. *I wonder what trees dream about.*

Nathan had his pulley, his rope, and a big pail that he found under his grandmother's porch. I was carrying my dad's camping spade and a shovel with a broken-off handle that had been standing in the corner of our garage for as long as I could remember. I didn't ask permission, but I didn't think that my parents would miss either of the tools. The bluff was hard and slick with the cold, and with all our equipment, the thirty-foot descent to Flat Rock could have been disastrous if not fatal. So after several minutes of deliberation, Nathan and I decided not to throw our stuff over the edge and climb down after it, but elected instead to walk the long way around.

This was the safe, slow way that my father had mapped out for us when we were younger and he used to take us out here to play in the water. Dad hadn't been out here with us in years now, yet his rules about walking around the bluff had never changed. By now, however, Nathan and I had been scaling the drop-off with great regularity and expertise. Climbing the bluff was just part of the path to Flat Rock and became such a normal course for us that Nathan and I never considered it might still be forbidden by my father. Even so, we never mentioned it to my parents either way.

The creek bed was gentler down below Flat Rock, and the water passed around the bend with more of a gurgle than a roar. I guess it was resting up after the sprint through the boulders, licking its wounds and making ready to go crashing through different rocks somewhere else downstream. There weren't enough tall rocks, so it was impossible to cross the creek here without getting wet all the way up to your knees. Nathan and I trudged through the cold water, dumped our gear on the bank and, using some roots, pulled ourselves up to shore. It was a long walk up to the cabin from here, but neither one of us was in the mood to delay. We hoisted our gear and squished up the far bank with wet socks and lakes in our shoes. Nathan moved ahead of me as we picked our way down the secret path and finally emerged from the underbrush in the presence of the crumbling cabin.

This was the first time I had been back since Brett and Jimmy, and I was amazed how well hidden the cabin remained, even without the full, leafy canopy of warmer months. Looking around from the little clearing, it almost seemed like the woods had taken special care to keep this place a secret. Perhaps it had simply been waiting to share its treasure with two worthy boys.

Nathan, out of breath, dropped his gear and plopped down on an old log. My wet shoe had started rubbing a blister on my heel, so I was ready to sit down as well. I stuck my shovels in the ground and eased down next to Nathan. I was tired, but I was excited. The thought of finding gold out here in this secret place had been keeping me up nights, dreaming about all the things I wouldn't have to do anymore.

"Well, buddy, here we are," I said, leaning over and whispering for no apparent reason.

"Yeah, here we are," Nathan repeated coolly.

"We spent most of the day getting all of the stuff down here, so if we're going to have any time to dig for gold, I guess we'd better get to it." I was anxious and looking around, but I still hadn't spotted Nathan's mine.

"Yeah, you're right about that, Chris. I guess we'd better get to it." He parroted me again but still didn't move off the log, even after I stood up.

"So where's the mine, Nathan?"

"Remember what I said, Chris? This has to be a secret. You can't tell anybody about this place or our mine… *ever*." He was looking up at me, and he seemed a little edgy, reminding me of my former pledge.

"Yeah, yeah, I know. We talked about this already, and I'm not telling anyone about this place." I was looking around and getting a little impatient.

"That means no Halley Kate, no parents, no Grandmom, no friends, no teachers, no preachers, no firemen, no police, no FBI, not the mayor, not the governor, not the president..." Nathan would have kept on going all afternoon, but I held up my hand to stop him.

"I have already promised, Nathan. How many more times do you want me to say it? Gahlee, are you really that paranoid that your *grandmother* is going to come down here and take our treasure out of some hole in the ground?"

He looked up at me for a long time as if he were seriously considering my question.

"Okay then," Nathan finally agreed as he stood up, "whatever we dig up, we split fifty-fifty. Deal?"

"Deal," I nodded.

"But if one of us quits," he continued, "then there is no splitting."

"What do you mean?" This last caveat to our partnership had me a little confused.

"I mean," Nathan bent over to pick up the pulley as he explained, "if one of us quits or stops coming to dig, then the other gets to keep everything and there's no more fifty-fifty." Nathan sounded more like a businessman or a lawyer than a boy in the woods. Then he spit in his palm and offered me a handshake. "Deal?" he asked.

He was looking me straight in the eye with his hand held out. I spit in my hand and shook his. "Deal," I confirmed.

Nathan smiled and picked up the rope and the bucket. "Come over here and take a look at this," he said, nodding his head forward as he walked past me. I turned to follow him to the edge of the clearing right up to where the underbrush, knotted with vines, formed a tight wall of dormant vegetation. Nathan stopped, staring down at something at his feet, but the shadows dancing through dappled sunlight on the ground made it impossible for me to see what exactly he was looking at. I moved to walk past him for a better look, but Nathan threw his arm up hard across my chest stopping me in my tracks. "Be careful," he said, "I don't have any idea how deep it is."

Even with his warning, my eyes still had to adjust to the speckles of sunlight and shade playing over the bed of dry leaves on the ground before I realized that what I thought was just another shadow was a silent, yawning pit. *I would have stepped right into it.* Exposed privet roots grew like teeth along the top edge of the dark hole making it look like a mouth in the forest floor, waiting to be fed. I was terrified and fascinated all at the same time.

"Are you sure it's a mine, Nathan?" I finally asked.

"What else could it possibly be?" he answered without taking his eyes off of the pit.

"It looks more like a well to me. I mean it's mostly round, and it seems to be the right width, and it's pretty close to the cabin. Don't you think that these people would have been more likely to dig a well than a goldmine?"

I was trying to be reasonable, but I wasn't sure if what I was saying made any sense at all.

Nathan broke his gaze on the hole and sighed as if I didn't understand anything that was going on. "Chris," he asked, "why would anybody dig a well this close to the creek?" He didn't wait for my answer. "No, it has to be gold, or maybe silver."

Nathan seemed to have a good point at the time, so I let it go without further argument and really hoped he was right. "How far down do you think it goes?" I asked after pausing to consider what to do next.

"I don't know, but I guess we'll find out in a few minutes." Nathan pulled a small plastic flashlight from his pocket, but the light was dim, so he had to shake it to get the last little bit of life from the batteries. We cleared away some of the leaves around the mouth of the hole to keep from accidently sliding in and then we got down on our bellies and snaked our way up to the edge. We hung our heads over; Nathan shook the dying flashlight back to life and directed its beam deep into the abyss.

"Oh no," I heard Nathan gasp as my eyes were still adjusting to the dim light. I craned just a little more to get a better look, but I felt myself begin to slide, so I reached around and grabbed Nathan by the coat sleeve. My heart was racing as I steadied myself, slid back from the edge, and stood up.

"What's wrong, Nathan? What did you see down there?"

Nathan was just working his way back up to his knees. "Come here, Chris, I'll show you." Nathan was now kneeling next to the pit seeming confident and unafraid, but I was still quivering a little from my near fall. "Come on, Chris," Nathan waved me over, "come take a look."

I crawled over on my hands and knees as carefully as I could to where Nathan was kneeling. "Watch," he said as he shook the flashlight back to life one more time and then tossed it into the hole.

As I peered over, I anticipated seeing the dim little light falling out the other side of the earth, but instead, it thudded, rested on the bottom, sputtered, and finally went out about six feet down. I dropped my head to my hands in utter disappointment as my goldmine was quickly reduced to nothing more than a shallow hole in the ground. This was just somebody's old abandoned well, and I was ready to grab my tools and head back home. But Nathan didn't see it the same way.

"You know what this means, don't you, Chris?"

"What?" I answered gruffly, brushing the dirt off my coat and pants.

"There's a lot more gold down there than we thought."

"You're crazy! What makes you think that?" I was starting to get a little angry.

"Because the first thing that anybody does when they have too much gold to carry is to bury it, right? These guys have a goldmine in their front yard, but they have to leave, so before they go, they fill it in. That way nobody would steal it while they're gone. Don't you see, Chris, this proves that there's treasure, and all we have to do is dig for it! We're going to be rich!"

Nathan was so excited about realizing what happened to the gold that he started skipping and dancing all around the little cabin yard like he had just scored a touchdown. Somewhere in the back of my head I knew that this was all idiotic, but Nathan was so sure of himself that it was hard not to believe in the possibilities. Besides, what else was I going to do to kill time all the way out here in Cherry Field?

"We may not see it now, Chris, but something tells me that all we need to do is dig, and there will be treasure in that mine soon enough! Are you in or out, Chris? Remember the deal! Are you in or out?"

"I guess I'm still in," I sighed. "But you'd better quit jumping around like a spastic ballerina, or I'm going to shove you in that hole and cover you up for good!"

He stopped dancing around almost as soon as the words left my mouth. "Okay, okay," he capitulated while retrieving the rope and pulley, "but it's getting late, so let's test these out now, and then come back tomorrow and get digging."

The pulley was a weird-looking thing with two discs that you had to thread the rope through. Mr. Brant had shown Nathan how. I think the two discs were supposed to make everything much lighter. There was a handle on the top with a strap and a buckle so that the contraption could be anchored around a beam or limb from below. There was this cool little lever on the side that, when it was on, would allow you to pull stuff up, but if you let go of the rope it would just hang there and wouldn't fall.

Nathan and I called it putting it on "one way," and we used it whenever we had to pull anything heavy up out of the mine. We buckled the pulley around a tree limb that hung out over the hole and we used it for hauling out buckets of dirt, all of our tools and each other as well. We just stepped in a loop below the bucket and held on to the rope as the other one hauled us up. It worked great.

Nathan wanted to test all of his equipment on that first day, so even though I could easily jump to the bottom of the hole and then climb out unassisted, Nathan insisted that we set up the pulley to see if we could pull each other out. I felt kind of silly being lowered into a hole that was barely over my head, but I played along figuring at least Nathan couldn't drop me too far. Surprisingly enough, however, Nathan was able to manage my weight easily, and I reached the bottom quickly and gently as he let the rope slide through his fingers. The pulley bound to the limb held strong.

"How does the bottom feel?" Nathan asked standing over me.

"Like dirt," I answered.

"Can you reach down and get the flashlight, Chris?"

"Uhhh, I don't really want to. It's pretty dark and I can't see a thing."

"Come on, don't be a chicken. Just bend down and feel around for it," Nathan instructed from above.

He called me a "chicken." I should have been a "chicken." I could have reached down into a nest of snakes or grabbed hold of some other kind of animal waiting to maul any idiot stupid enough to jump down in this hole. But boys in the woods don't usually think about things like that, and neither did I. I wanted to be able to stand up quickly, so instead of getting on my knees, I just squatted and kind of duck-walked around the bottom. There was a lot more room down here than I thought. The whole thing was probably about four feet around with thick clay walls, and even though all I had to do was stand up to be back in the light, I felt a world away. The rich smell of heavy earth was all around and I started feeling comfortable, almost snug, as I fished around in the dark for Nathan's broken flashlight. I liked being down there, hidden from the rest of the world, in the hiding spot of a secret place.

"Hey, Chris, have you found it yet?" His question came right as my hand brushed over his flashlight.

"I have it!" I called up from the mine as I stood up and handed it to Nathan.

"Here, let me give you a hand up." Nathan offered me his hand to hoist me up, but the clay walls were too slick for traction and the goldmine was unwilling to let me go that easily. So Nathan had to toss me the rope, put the pulley on "one way," and haul me out like a Carolina coal miner.

Nathan wanted to climb into the mine, but it was getting late, so I convinced him to wait until tomorrow and he could be the first to dig. We took down our pulley and hid it with all of our tools in the thicket on the other side of the clearing. Nathan was still worried about someone finding the mine, so we pulled a big board off the cabin and put it over the hole. Nathan insisted that we cover the wooden top with leaves, so we did.

We took the short way home up the bluff and walked without talking the rest of the way through the woods. Right as we were about to step out into Ms. Hall's yard,

Nathan caught me by the shoulder and broke the silence. “Whenever we leave the mine, we must always take care to cover our tracks. We can’t leave our tools out, we can’t leave the mine uncovered, and we have to scatter our dirt. We don’t want anyone else to find our gold. Okay, Chris?”

I guess it was important for him to address this one last thing with me before we left the woods, so I nodded okay, not really knowing what it would mean.

He spit in his hand and offered it to me. “Deal?” he asked, smiling.

This day had been full of deals. “Deal,” I confirmed, spit in my own hand, and shook his.

21
Skunk Salad

We dug as much as we could over the cold months, but the days were short and progress was slow. My parents wouldn't allow me in the woods on particularly gray days and demanded that Nathan and I be home well before dark on others. Between school and church, Saturdays were the only days we could dig, and those were often canceled either by weather or parental decree. Nathan always seemed anxious about digging, and when we were able to go to the mine, he stayed down in the hole, working far longer than I ever did.

The walls of the pit swallowed any noise trying to escape from the bottom, so I would sit up top all alone, waiting for Nathan to shake the rope as a signal for me to haul up the bucket full of dirt. As per Nathan's instructions, I would always sling the contents of the bucket deep into the thicket, making sure to hide our work on the mine. It was cold and the dirt was hard, but the secret work seemed to insulate us somehow from the troubles of the world. What we were doing together seemed very important to our survival out in Cherry Field, something that I would never expect anyone else to ever understand.

Nathan was a little funny about the whole thing. He always insisted that we keep our deal, hiding the tools and covering the hole before we left the mine. He was paranoid that someone might horn in on our gold. I tried to tell him that it didn't matter because nobody else could ever find this place, but a deal was a deal, and he wanted to be sure. So even though it was a big pain to put everything away at first, it wasn't worth an argument, and hiding all the equipment became just another unconscious ritual. Nathan was doing most of the digging, so eventually, taking down the pulley, hiding the tools in the thicket, and covering the mine became solely my responsibility. It wasn't a big deal, and I did it as automatically as I cleared my own plate from the dinner table at home: pull Nathan up, unstrap the pulley, wind pulley with the rope and put it in the bucket, hide the bucket and the spade in the underbrush, pull the board over the hole, cover it with leaves, brush off my hands, and it's time to go. I could do it in less than five minutes.

We were only able to deepen the well about two feet that winter, and it was more about having something to do than the thought of finding gold that kept me going back with Nathan. I did think about finding gold, though, and I spent it a thousand times over in my mind while lying in bed waiting to drift off to sleep at night. I thought I might buy a pool and a really cool car, and later on I'd build a big mansion with a bowling alley and an arcade. Only people I invited could come over to play, but I would be the best at all the games.

"Hey, Nathan," I asked, traipsing home through the woods one day, "what are you going to buy with your half of the gold?"

He stopped dead in his tracks so that he could answer me without having to compete with the noise of crunching leaves. I stopped, silencing the leaves at my feet as well. I wanted to know what he dreamed of.

"Well," he started, "I'm thinking about buying a beach house...for my mom." He paused and looked away, somewhere else through the cold, sleeping trees. "That way...I could go visit her sometime." His thoughts drifted far away, but only for an instant. "We'd better hurry up and get home, Chris, before your folks get mad," he said, and then walked right past me leading the rest of the way through the woods. I never asked him what he would do with his money ever again.

As the weather warmed, the work on the mine started going a little faster. Nathan marked the rope with painted stripes, one every foot, so that we could measure the depth of our hole. All he wanted to do was dig. It used to be me seeking his company to alleviate the boredom of Cherry Field; now it seemed that at every opportunity he was on my front porch reminding me of our deal and dragging me out to the cabin. My parents still wanted us home long before dark, but their restrictions about being in the woods relaxed with the longer, brighter days, and for a while, Nathan and I were digging almost every day. We were down a full ten feet now with no treasure, and I was becoming uneasy about being lowered to the bottom when it came my turn to dig.

The bottom was earthy and pitch-black except for the faint glow of the flashlight. The walls were shear and heavy with slick clay, making everything else seem a thousand miles away with only the sound of my breath to keep me company. I felt a little like a circus performer with his head in a lion's mouth wondering if this might be the time that the beast wouldn't let go. Still, I dug for the treasure, although not half as well as Nathan.

He always left the mine shaped and smooth with a flat floor. Not only did he deepen the well at a faster pace than I did, he was also very careful to keep the walls rounded almost like a narrow, inverted silo. The symmetry of the mine seemed as important to him as its depth, and it was his weird obsessive digging that made the mine sometimes feel more like a chamber than a hole in the ground. I would usually chop out a few buckets of dirt and then shake the rope to be lifted out, but Nathan would stay down there for hours.

On Saturdays, we took our lunches so that we could stay and work in the mine all day long, mostly with Nathan down below and me sitting up top like the guy in charge of the air hose for a deep sea diver. I sat quietly at the foot of the cabin waiting for Nathan to shake the rope as a signal to haul up the bucket and scatter the dirt. At the end of the day I always did the same thing: pull Nathan up, un-strap the pulley, wind pulley with the rope and put it in the bucket, hide the bucket and the spade, pull the board over the hole and cover it with leaves. I was getting sick of it. I'd almost rather be bored to death than to have to come back here, even if it meant giving up my half of the gold.

"Find anything?" I sneered at Nathan as I was winding up the pulley one day. Nathan was exhausted and sitting on the log as I went through my routine of hiding the tools.

"Just more dirt," he answered, "but I have a good feeling if we dig just a little more, we'll find something."

"We're already twelve feet down, Nathan! How much further do you want to go? I mean we haven't even hit a rock much less any gold. All we're digging is hard, nasty clay." I kept talking as I hid the bucket and the spade. "You know what I think? I think that we were wrong. I think this hole is nothing more than an old, dry well, and I'm sick of going down there and I'm sick of waiting up here for you!" I stepped past Nathan and started off in a huff down the thick little path away from the cabin.

"Wait, Chris!" I turned to see Nathan following me with welling eyes. "Please don't quit. I can't do this without you. Can we just dig two more feet? Fourteen is my lucky number, and I have a good feeling that we'll find something if we go just two more feet. Please, Chris. I'll do all the digging. You won't have to go down into the mine at all. *Please.*"

He was exhausted and pleading so hard with red eyes that I just didn't have the heart to refuse. "Okay, but only two more feet, and then we're done digging for gold." And with Nathan at my heels, I stomped off, forgetting to cover the mine.

Not covering the mine was my mistake, but of course I made Nathan take part of the blame. By the time we got back to dig those last two feet, a skunk had fallen in the hole and died. You couldn't really smell it unless you stood right at the edge of the mine, but when you did, the stink was bad enough to blow your hair straight back. I tried to tell Nathan that the skunk would eventually rot and the smell would go away, but he was convinced that he had to remove the body if we were ever going to be able to work down there again.

I have no idea why I agreed. I guess I thought it was a little funny, but I set everything up and lowered Nathan into that giant hole of massive stink. Hearing him hooting and hollering about the smell from way down in the mine made me laugh until my stomach hurt. The stink was bad enough up here, so I could only imagine how horrible it must have been down where it was thick and settled.

Nathan yanked on the rope for me to bring him up. I stood way back, as far as I could, as he emerged with a dead skunk by the tail.

"Gahlee, Nathan! Are you crazy? What are you doing?" Nathan was holding the dead animal in one hand with his face turned away to protect his nose.

"Here you go, Chris," he laughed, "catch this." He swung the skunk up by the tail like he was going to toss the thing over to me. He was only pretending, but it was startling enough to make me step back and trip in the bushes.

"Will you get rid of that thing?" I yelled up at him, but he was already on his way. With his head turned and his arm extended to keep the dead animal as far away as possible, he walked back down to the creek and threw it in. The body with most of the stink washed away downstream and out of sight. I made sure to cover up the mine this time after I packed up and hid all our gear.

The smell was so bad that we wouldn't be able to dig for a couple of months, but that certainly wasn't the worst of it. I didn't come out smelling like a bunch of flowers, but Nathan stank so bad that I made him walk twenty yards behind me on the way home. We told my parents that Nathan had accidently surprised a mama skunk in the woods and that she had sprayed him pretty good. My parents both vacillated between gagging at the smell and laughing out loud at our misfortune.

Dad drove to town for all the vinegar the grocery store would sell him and delivered half his purchase to Nathan's grandmother. Mom finally let me in the house after she had filled the tub with vinegar, and even then I had to leave my clothes on the porch and run straight to the bathroom. She threatened to shave my head if I didn't dunk it all the way under and wash my hair thoroughly in the vinegar. I protested at first, but then grudgingly complied. Mom made me stay in the tub for over an hour, but after that and a very long, soapy shower, I finally shed all the evidence of skunk.

Nathan, unfortunately, didn't clean up so well. He had been fully exposed to all the dead skunk had to offer, and even though the vinegar was supposed to neutralize the odor, all it did in Nathan's case was to add a tang to the stink. I don't know if his grandmother just wanted him out of the house or she figured if I was going to school Nathan could too, but the next morning she sent him along with me to catch the bus. He wanted to talk to me about our adventure with the dead skunk, but I made him stand as far away from me as possible. Although his air didn't seem to bother him too much, I just couldn't take it.

"Oh my goodness!" Bill exclaimed when he opened the bus doors to receive us. "Boy, you smell like a skunk salad! If you're riding to school with me, you have to sit in the very, very back of this bus!" Nathan skulked to the back of the bus, away from his usual safe seat behind the driver. "…And open a few windows back there too!" Bill called as Nathan slid pouting into his seat.

The morning ride was rowdy with disgust, and everyone that could, crammed all the way to the front of the bus. Nathan stunk so bad that the principal pulled him out of class and made him sit in the clinic for the next three days. Poor nurse. She probably had to shove cotton balls in her nose the whole time he was there.

22

Twenty

Although it didn't seem to have much to do with us, the state police found another kid's body over in Sand Town about twenty-five miles away.

"Dear Heavenly Father, please comfort all of the families who have lost their children to this poor soul," Reverend Lane prayed from the pulpit. "You teach us that we are *all* sinners and yet You still love us all, and we know that everyone has value in Your eyes, even the one responsible for these horrible crimes. Let us all keep this in mind as we pray that law enforcement is able to capture the individual responsible for harming Your beloved children and that Your justice, not ours, be accomplished. We pray for both the trespasser and the trespassed against, as Your will, not ours, is done."

I felt my dad squirming in the pew as the reverend continued. "What a load of bull," I heard Dad whisper to Mom louder than he intended. "The one responsible is a monster, the devil himself, and needs no prayers or sympathy from us. We need to pray that he's stopped and that's all." Dad had grown critical of Reverend Lane ever since their conversation at the hospital. Mom raised her finger to her nose and shushed Dad. He scowled privately, sat back and ran his fingers through his hair.

When the choir stood up to sing, I noticed that with all of the finery and religious glamour the Postcard Church had to offer, one of the older ladies had kicked off her shoes and was wriggling her toes to the notes as she sang. At that moment she obviously didn't care if anyone else saw her naked feet, and I couldn't help thinking that's probably the way the angels did it: open and unashamed. Barefoot in the choir seems like an honest way to sing.

Nathan hadn't been to church or Sunday school ever since his grandmother had gotten sick. Most Sundays we would give him a ride into town, but instead of walking across the square with us, he would head out to the main road and walk down to the hospital. He was always back, though, sitting on the bench by the oak, waiting for us to finish and emerge with everyone else through the front doors of the church. I found his promptness remarkable for a guy I wasn't sure could tell time. My dad always offered to drop him off or pick him up from the hospital, but Nathan said that he liked the walk.

"Nathan, honey," my mom turned to ask from the front seat of the car, "wouldn't you like to come to church with us today?"

"Thank you very much, ma'am, but I kind of like going to the hospital chapel."

"What about all of your friends?" Mom asked.

"Oh, I have friends at the hospital," Nathan answered politely.

"Well, okay, but if you change your mind, just come on over."

Mom and Nathan had the same exchange on every Sunday drive since Nathan stopped going to our church. I thought that he was like my dad and had a change of heart about Reverend Lane, but the truth is, Nathan never really liked the pastor anyway.

The mine was still skunked, so after church and lunch I walked over to sit on Nathan's front porch steps. Neither one of us felt like going to Flat Rock, so I just sat there pouting as he sketched in his pad.

"I have bad news," I finally huffed. "My mother saw in the bulletin today that the youth are putting on a play at church."

"So?" Nathan asked.

"So, she's making me be in it. Can you believe that? My dad didn't even tell her 'no'!"

Nathan put down his pad and walked down the steps to sit next to me. "It's fine, Chris. I'm sure you're going to be great singing and dancing up there in front of everybody. Maybe you can play a woodland sprite or something else in a leotard." He was enjoying my misery.

I was incensed sitting there with my elbows on my knees and my face in my hands. "What do you care?" I asked through my fingers. "Ever since the preacher scared you off, you don't even go to our church anymore. I wish I didn't have to go either."

Nathan was quiet. So quiet that I finally looked up from my hands to see what he was doing.

"I'm not scared of Reverend Lame," Nathan said flatly as I looked up.

"Oh, you're full of it!" I argued. "Why else would you go to that stupid hospital chapel all by yourself every Sunday?"

Nathan smiled and puffed through his nose, "Because that's where God hears me best." Then he stood and walked back up the steps to his sketch pad, leaving me to stew about the stupid church play.

23

Secret Gallery

"Alright, class, everyone get settled." We were finally starting spring quarter, and Ms. Baird was saying something about expecting better grades and a fresh start. Nathan was in his usual spot over by the door, and Ms. Addler was already tapping on his desk to get him to pay attention.

"This quarter we're going to be doing something a little different, and those of you who don't like tests will really love it, because we're not going to take very many at all." There was a small sigh throughout the class, but we all remained attentive waiting for Ms. Baird to reveal the cost for relaxing the usual expectation. "This quarter we will be studying Africa, and each of you will be doing a comprehensive research project on an African country. The sheet that Ms. Addler is now handing to you outlines the milestones and requirements of the project. This will probably be the biggest, most challenging, and most comprehensive research project that any of you has ever done in your career as a student, and it's going to be worth seventy percent of your final grade.

"You will conclude all of your work with a first person narrative as if you are actually a middle school-age student living in your assigned country. You will describe your daily life, your family, your religion, and where you live. You will tell us everything about yourself as if you actually live in your country. Then you will stand up and give the class an oral presentation on all of your research to conclude the project. Are there any questions?" She surveyed the room. "Good. Now turn your paper over, and let's go over all of the requirements and due dates."

Ms. Baird then began covering a litany of details, checking over her reading glasses every now and again for our understanding. Whenever she looked up, we all nodded dutifully. Something in her tone let us know that this one report on Africa might be the single most important thing that we would ever do! *I wanted to do it right.* No matter how obscure her demands, Ms. Baird always shined a relevant light, turning the whole class into true believers. She was a teacher worth pleasing, and all of her students wanted to do so...all except Nathan.

As Ms. Baird continued, I glanced over toward the door to see Nathan picking in his ear with his pencil and staring at the ceiling while Ms. Addler gently tapped on his desk. I shook my head with disgust as I scratched down a few notes on Ms. Baird's outline. Nathan was assigned the Congo and I got Liberia.

When the bell finally rang, Nathan waited for me by the door. "Hey, Chris, I invited Halley Kate out to Flat Rock. Her dad is driving her out Saturday."

I heard what he said, but I was annoyed he didn't bother to tell me that he was going to invite her. I walked on by like I didn't see him. I'd wanted to ask Halley Kate. I don't know why I let Nathan get to her first.

All that week I lay awake in bed at night dreaming how the day would go with Halley Kate out at Boulder Creek. Usually my scenario began with Nathan having to leave and ended with a gentle kiss and holding hands with her. Ever since Nathan had drawn that picture in art class, Halley Kate had stayed on my mind, but in all my awkwardness I never had the courage to let any of my feelings show. On the contrary, I was so afraid someone might guess how I felt that I tried to remain distant, only getting close enough to pick on her a little or tease her about something. I wonder now why she ever considered me a friend. I looked for her at school and I genuinely missed her on all the absent days.

I don't understand why there always seems to be so much time when we can't even see one minute into the future. In some things, faith works against you, I guess.

Saturday morning I looked out the window and saw Nathan sitting on his front steps a good hour before Halley Kate was supposed to arrive. I wanted to be coolly amused at his eagerness, but my own got the better of me, so I walked over to sit and wait with him. Technically Nathan had invited Halley Kate out to Cherry Field, but I knew that he considered her to be our guest.

"What do you think we should do today?" I asked Nathan after sitting for a few minutes.

"Well," Nathan answered, "all Halley Kate really wants to do is go out to Flat Rock. She's been bugging me about it ever since art class."

The morning was warmer than I thought, and with the mention of her name, I could feel myself start to sweat. I took a deep breath in an attempt to control my pores and wiped my forehead with my sleeve. "So do you think that she can climb the bluff or do you think that we should take her the long way?" Both paths seemed to be a win for me because either I'm considerate enough to take her the easy way or brave enough to take her the hard way.

"Knowing her, I'm pretty sure she will want to climb the bluff, so maybe we should take her there first and just see. I don't know, that's a pretty long drop," Nathan debated himself. "No, I think we should take her to see it and then let her choose which way to go. If she wants to climb, we climb. If she wants to walk around, we walk around. After all, she is the guest."

He paused as he contemplated, "You know, Chris, she's probably the first girl ever to go out to Flat Rock. You and me, we're the ones responsible for her. We need to keep her safe out there. Nobody knows those woods like you and me." I nodded my head in agreement as Nathan and I sat waiting on his front steps trying not to sweat.

With every passing car our anticipation built until, finally, a blue sedan slowed enough to turn off the highway and crunch up the gravel drive. We stood, waiting to greet our visitors. The door popped open as soon as the car rolled to a stop, and Halley Kate bounced out smiling wide. She hugged us like we were her only friends in the world, finally reunited after some catastrophic event. She was so free with delight, it was nearly impossible not to be swept up in her excitement.

She giggled and chirped and talked really fast as her dad strode around the car to meet us. "Good morning, boys, how are you? You guys certainly live a long way out." He offered his hand. Nathan shook it, and then I did too.

"I'm Chris," I said.

"I'm Nathan," Nathan said.

"Well, which one of you boys is the artist?"

Nathan dropped his head and smiled shyly at the ground. "That would be Nathan, sir," I answered for Nathan.

"Well, Nathan, let me tell you," Halley Kate's dad put his hand on Nathan's shoulder, "your picture is the most beautiful piece of art I have ever seen. I look at that picture, son, and it's almost magical. I don't know how else to describe it. Not much gets to me, but when I found that drawing in Halley Kate's backpack, I was overwhelmed. I had it framed, but I can't seem to figure out where to hang it. I've had it in the foyer and in the kitchen and in the den, really just about everywhere in the house including my bedroom. It's amazing. I want to share it with all of my guests and at the same time I want to keep it only for myself."

My parents had walked over and Nathan's grandmother had come out onto the porch, so Halley Kate's dad was now speaking as much to the grown-ups as he was to Nathan. "I have a friend who is an interior decorator, and she says that you have to hang a picture around a house to find where it fits, but your drawing of Halley Cater...well...fits *everywhere.* Whether I hang it over the mantle or over the toilet, that's where it seems to belong. Funny, I've had the drawing for several months now, but I still find myself visiting it no matter where it hangs in the house. I guess you never get used to something that beautiful."

We all stood back and proudly watched as Halley Kate's dad gushed over Nathan's artwork. He obviously loved the picture, but it was still a little strange for me to see an adult so grateful to a child. He offered to pay for the picture, but Nathan wouldn't accept anything.

"Do you think you might come by the house some day and at least sign it for us, Nathan?" Halley Kate's dad finally asked.

"No sir." Nathan, who had never looked up, politely answered. Embarrassed, he kicked at the ground a little with his toe. "I never sign any of my drawings. Otherwise you wouldn't need to remember me." Nathan turned one foot over on its side, taking note of his ankle, "Uh oh, look there. I forgot to put my socks on this morning. Come on, Halley Kate, Chris; let's go up to my room and then get going to the creek."

As we traipsed up the steps and shuffled back through the house, we could hear introductions being made between the adults and Nathan's grandmother inviting everyone for coffee.

The three of us filed into Nathan's room to fetch his socks before heading out to the woods. I was only interested in hurrying Nathan along, but Halley Kate was immediately mesmerized by all of the sketches hanging around the room. Nathan and I were still talking when we noticed Halley Kate with her mouth hanging wide, slowly moving among his pictures as if she were approaching a timid rabbit. She was hypnotized as she stared and then sighed or gasped at every new masterpiece that caught her eye. She saw the embattled

Corg and all manner of other fantastic heroes prevailing over formidable villainous adversaries.

I had seen most of Nathan's drawings before, so I was more interested in Halley Kate's reaction to discovering Nathan's secret gallery than I was seeing the pictures myself. A sketch of a secluded cabin surrounded by weeping butterflies did catch my eye, and there was another one of Corg wrestling with a horned demon at the edge of the cliff over Boulder Creek. Recognizing some of the scenery Nathan used as backdrops somehow connected me to his drawings, and although I tried to remain focused on Halley Kate, I could feel myself being swept into Nathan's pictures as well. I was distressed that Nathan hadn't drawn Corg as the clear victor, and it looked as if his vicious adversary would drag him down in a suicide plunge to the rocks below.

My eyes went back to the cabin, and I felt shame and sadness as I watched the butterflies weep. There was a sketch of two awesome-looking heroes being chased out of a cave by a skunk that made me chuckle. Halley Kate and I ended up shoulder to shoulder, flipping through a stack of sketches that Nathan had left on a table, each one capturing us both in its story.

Nathan, ready now with both socks and shoes, had been as polite as he could be and was growing a little thin on patience. "Okay, you two, are you just going to hang around and look at a bunch of stupid pictures or are we going to the creek or what? You know, we really don't have a whole lot of time."

I think that Halley Kate would have stayed all day just looking at Nathan's work, but we broke away to make ready for the trip out to Flat Rock. Nathan stood to the side so that Halley Kate and I could exit his room ahead of him. As she walked past, Halley Kate stopped to face Nathan and took his hand. "You are wonderful," she told him without any shame and right out in front of me. Then she walked out as Nathan and I followed.

Halley Kate's dad was still having coffee with my parents and Nathan's grandmother on the porch when we came out of the house. Mom had packed three lunches for us in case we wanted to stay at the creek a little longer. We were told to have fun but to be careful. I picked up my fishing rod out of the garage, and we headed off to make Halley Kate the first girl ever to set foot on Flat Rock.

24

Lullaby of Boulder Creek

As we rounded Ms. Hall's house, we found her in a floppy wide-brimmed hat bent down on her hands and knees, scratching at the bed of her rose garden. She was an old woman, but Nathan and I always had a sense that it was best to keep her favor, so we always obeyed her rules about walking through her yard. *(Keep to the stepping stones and then walk way around the flowers and the vegetable garden.)* When she noticed us on the perimeter, she rose up to wave, and we all waved back. She was well known as a deeply religious woman who considered the demon alcohol to be an assault against man's soul. Ms. Hall would work like twenty farm mules until the sun got hot, and then she would go into her house, pull the shades, and according to my father, pop the top on a single hot beer for medicinal purposes. My dad seemed to admire her, but I'm not sure if it was because, or in spite of, her obvious flaw.

Ms. Hall watched us carefully from her knees as we made the trek along the side of her yard. The three of us fell silent under her stare, doing our best not to glance her way as we walked along. We were sure that we were following the rules, but you never feel quite as relaxed when your every step is being judged. By the time we plodded around her yard, arriving at the entrance to the woods, the old woman had stopped paying us any attention at all and was back hard at work on her roses. We stepped out of her yard and into the cool shadows of friendly trees as the wild privet closed like curtains behind us.

The smell of honeysuckle perfumed the air, and though I was a little nervous, the whole forest seemed content with our company. A sudden rush of wind through the canopy above sounded like applause as the trees all rejoiced that Halley Kate was finally here. Dancing shadows and dappled sunlight whispered a muted siren's song, coaxing us along our path deeper into the woods to where the bluffs overhung Boulder Creek.

Nathan led the way, and I followed behind Halley Kate, just in case she needed help climbing over a log or a boost up a bank. Even though I'd been here a thousand times before, somehow everything was different today, and all my dreams of being alone with Halley Kate ran right off into the trees. I felt as if I were walking through one of Nathan's pictures, noticing every detail from the bumble bee on the wild daisy over there to the lady bug caught in the back of Halley Kate's hair. I could feel myself breathing, but I couldn't hear the usual crunch of leaves underfoot. We paused along the way to pick a few early blackberries and then laughed at the sight of each other with purple teeth. The wind rushed again and all the trees laughed along.

I felt truly free, and the stupid church play and my Liberia report consumed no part of me as I followed behind my goofy friend and the red-stripe girl. I could hear the roar of water as we came closer to our destination. Boulder Creek sounded full and powerful today. Halley Kate would soon be the first girl to set foot on Flat Rock, but first, she would have to choose her way.

"Be careful up here," Nathan called over his shoulder to Halley Kate. "It's really steep and a long drop down to some pretty big rocks." A couple of more steps and we all stood shoulder to shoulder, toeing the rim, catching our breath and peering over the side at the boulders and water colliding below. From up top, the bend in the stream looked like a big, wide, toothy smile as if Boulder Creek was delighted to see the three of us out here together.

"Wow," Halley Kate gasped and backed away, sitting down to catch her breath. "We're up here pretty high," she coughed.

"Are you okay?" Nathan asked, sitting down across from her.

"I'm fine. I just need a little breather." Looking up, she held her hand to her forehead to take the sun out of her eyes. "How are we supposed to get down there?" she asked me.

"Nathan and I always climb. It's pretty easy if you know how to do it. But if you're scared, we can walk the long way around instead. No problem."

I was trying to be considerate, but as soon as I used the word "scared," I wished I hadn't. Halley Kate popped to her feet glaring at me. "Show me how," she ordered.

"Alright, alright." I put my hand up in a calming fashion. "We'll go the regular way. Just follow right behind me, and I'll tell you where to put your feet and what to hold on to. It can be kind of slippery sometimes, so let's just be careful, okay?"

"Okay," she puffed and then gave a little cough into her hand.

I took my fishing rod and sack lunch in one hand, sat down, and slid over the edge. This climb was so natural for Nathan and me that we did it as carelessly as running for the bus, but today was different, and I wanted to make sure that Halley Kate was still having a good time.

"I'm going to go a little ahead of you, and you'll see it's not really too bad at all. Just listen to what I tell you and we'll be down on Flat Rock before you know it." She whimpered a couple of times following my descent, so I coached her as sweetly as I knew how without going far enough to agitate her.

As we neared the bottom, Halley Kate's speed picked up with her confidence, overtaking me enough to accidentally kick me in the face, only to apologize over and over for the rest of the way down. I hopped down the last couple of feet to the rock, put down my pole and lunch, and then turned to help Halley Kate. As natural as it was, it felt too personal to reach up and steady her with my hands on her waist, so I stood and waited awkwardly for her to make the final leap to Flat Rock.

As soon as she touched bottom, she whirled around to me and started hopping up and down like a little bunny rabbit, chirping a mile a minute. "Thank you, thank you, thank you, Chris. That was great! I was so scared and so happy all at the same time. Thank you, thank you, I'm so, so, so, so sorry for kicking you in the face. It was just an accident. Are you okay?" She bounced herself over and threw her arms around my neck and squeezed me tight. I reached up, putting my arms around her back, and returned her embrace. My heart was doing its best to jump right out into the creek. I certainly wasn't ready to let go when she did.

"I'm coming down!" Nathan called to us from the top, and we stood and watched him, to Halley Kate's amazement, descend the drop-off with speed and ease. "Here you go," he said, pulling Halley Kate's lunch out from under his shirt as he stepped down to the rock. "I hope I didn't squash it."

"It doesn't matter," she answered, taking the sack from Nathan. "Everything always tastes better that way," and then she laughed and tossed it to the ground next to mine. She cocked her head slightly as if listening to the whisper of her name, and then turned and walked out to the edge of Flat Rock. Even though her back was to me, I was overtaken at how natural she seemed standing there silently overlooking the water. The drapes of kudzu on the far bank were like a movie screen from which this starlet had just stepped down into real life. She seemed like an angel to me. The woods and the creek had received her well, and it was obvious that she belonged.

At that moment I wondered how we would ever be able tear her away from this place. "It feels so good here," she finally piped up while rubbing her arms up and down. "Are we going to look for arrowheads?"

"Sure," Nathan answered, walking past me. The two of them sat down on the edge of the rock, pulled off their shoes, rolled up their pants, and plunked down into the water. The water was deeper there than Halley

Kate expected, and she squealed, reaching out to steady herself on Nathan as the creek soaked her to the waist.

"You coming, Chris?" she called up to me joyfully.

"Nah, I'm going to stay right here and cast a few. You and Nathan go search for evidence of lost peoples. Be careful, the rapids are pretty strong and the rocks are slippery." I turned to fetch my pole and then stood atop my perch watching Nathan and Halley Kate hold on to one another as they waded through the swift water, making their way to the shallows. They might as well have been a million miles away, wrapped in the roar of the creek and lost in each other's company. I guess I should have been jealous, but instead I had an overwhelming sense of déjà vu seeing them walk along the shore through calmer waters, heads down, laughing and searching for treasures just below the surface. The sun glinted off the stream, surrounding the whole scene in white and golden sparkles that sometimes lingered and sometimes cracked and disappeared like static electricity.

I never made a cast. I just stood like some weirdo watching my two friends wading back and forth in the shallow waters of the far bank. I guess it was days like this that made our ancestors believe in magic and miracles. A nice breeze whistled by, the trees swayed, the creek gurgled and hummed, and I expect if magic were real, the cabin would have torn itself free from the vines and brought its ancient self down to the creek bank to be with us as well. But that secret belonged to Nathan and me, so although I could feel it peeking through the trees, the cabin was excluded from our day.

I was lost somewhere in my thoughts when Halley Kate let out a blood-curdling scream of delight. "Look, look, look! Is this one? It has to be one!" The excited pitch of her voice was enough to cut right through the noise of the water and shake me from my trance. She plunked through the water as fast as she could to where Nathan was standing, showed him something in the palm of her hand, and then threw her arms around him, bouncing up and down until they both toppled over into the creek. She screamed another laugh and began splashing Nathan, to his amusement. He splashed back defensively, but she definitely got the better of him in their brief battle. They hugged again and then waded back to where I was watching. I reached down to pull a beaming Halley Kate up out of the water and then gave Nathan a hand up as well.

"Did she show it to you, Chris? Did you see what Halley Kate found?" Nathan was excited and out of breath, so it took me a few seconds to understand and shake my head 'no.'

"It's what I've been looking for all my life, Chris, and she found it on her very first day! Can you believe that?" We both turned to Halley Kate standing silently with twinkling eyes and an ear-to-ear grin. "Show him, Halley Kate," Nathan said in a calmer voice.

Halley Kate was doing her very best to contain her excitement and add drama to the moment. She slowly lifted one tight-fisted arm, rolled her wrist over, and paused. Not until I sighed with anticipation did she let her fingers begin to peel off one at a time to reveal whatever she held so tightly in her hand. Thumb first... one finger...two fingers...I was fully caught in her game to build the moment…three fingers…four fingers… and…and…*nothing* but her empty palm.

I gasped. Her eyes glistened, and her smile would have grown wider if her ears would have allowed it. Nathan snorted a little, trying to contain his laughter.

"What," I sighed heavily, "are you doing to me?"

Halley Kate didn't answer, she just grinned and slowly raised her other arm. I wanted her to hurry, but she was having fun, so I played along, resisting my natural instinct to be a butt-head. She rolled her wrist over in slow motion, and when my full attention was on her fist, she began peeling her fingers back one at a time. Thumb first…one finger…two fingers…this time I could see that she was actually holding something…three fingers…four fingers… and…wow! She really did it! Halley Kate had found a real honest-to-goodness arrowhead! I knew it was a real one right off, because it looked exactly like the one Nathan kept in his room from the souvenir shop.

"Can you believe it? Can you believe it, Chris?" she bubbled. "Nathan told me that most arrowheads are found under flat black rocks. So that's where I started looking, and I found this right up there on the beach. Nathan walked right past it. He almost stepped on the stupid thing and didn't even notice." She smiled over at Nathan. "No wonder you guys have never been able to find one." She tried to give it to Nathan and then to me, but neither of us would accept it.

With Nathan and Halley Kate back on Flat Rock, I finally made my fishing pole ready to cast a few over in the deeper water. Halley Kate seemed interested, and I had every intention of teaching her all that I could about snagging fingerlings with a small spinner.

"Hey, what was that?" Nathan stood up and walked across the boulder, peering off into the woods on the far bank where the cabin lay hidden. "Did either of you hear that?" he asked over his shoulder. Halley Kate and I both shook our heads, for whatever had caught Nathan's ear hadn't caught ours. We strained to listen. Ordinarily I would have accused Nathan of being full of it, but today seemed so strange that I wasn't ready to immediately doubt anything. "There! There it is again! Now don't tell me that you guys didn't hear that!"

"What? What do you hear?" Halley Kate sounded a little worried.

"It sounds like…it sounds like," Nathan searched for the words, "it sounds like…*nature calling*." Then he pointed at us and laughed so hard that he nearly fell off the rock into the water.

"You!" Halley Kate groaned and picked up a small pebble and threw it at the giggling Nathan.

"Gahlee, Nathan," I was almost as surprised as I was embarrassed, "I can't believe you just said that!"

"Yeah, I guess I better answer." Nathan grinned and then hopped down to splash his way across the creek. I watched uneasily as he trudged up out of the water and disappeared behind the veil of kudzu down the path to the mine.

"Where's he going?" Halley Kate asked.

"Just a little way into the woods, so hopefully, he'll be out of our sight," I answered. But I knew where he was really going, and I also knew that he probably wouldn't be back for a while. So there I was, just as I had imagined, left alone with Halley Kate on Flat Rock.

I stood, tossing my spinner into the water while Halley Kate stretched out on her back and stared up into the sky. I was nervous knowing we were alone with absolutely nothing to talk about, so I invited her to try casting. I showed her how to swing the pole and release the line. I taught her to place the bait with her throw and then to reel it in nice and easy to make it more attractive for the fish.

At first she flung the spinner unpredictably in all directions and I had to unsnag it from just about every nearby rock and limb. She eventually got the hang of it, though, and actually turned out to be more capable than Nathan at controlling the line.

We were mostly talking about fishing when she got tired and we both sat down. The sound of the rushing water was hypnotic as our conversation began to run dry.

"So," I started looking for almost anything to say, "I guess you and Laura really got into it at school. I heard you really let her have it." It was old news, but it was all I had at the moment.

"I guess," Halley Kate answered, looking away, "she made me really mad and I just couldn't help it."

Halley Kate obviously didn't want to talk about it, but I had nothing else. "Well, you certainly gave her what she deserved," I continued. "She's the meanest girl I've ever seen."

Halley Kate, still avoiding eye contact, threw her head back and stared straight up into the sky. "Yeah, I guess. I just didn't have any choice." She shook her head slightly.

I was focused more on keeping the conversation in play than I was on what I was saying. "You didn't have to do it. Everybody has a choice; that is, unless you believe in fate. Do you believe in fate, Halley Kate?"

She waited for a moment and then answered, "I believe there's a plan."

"Yeah, me too," I admitted. "But if you believe in a plan, do you believe in fate?"

Still staring up into the sky with her eyes closed, she sighed deeply contemplating the question. "I guess I believe more in destiny."

"What's the difference?" I asked.

She dropped her head, turned to me, and smiled. "My mom used to tell me that the difference between fate and destiny is all in *how* you get there and I guess that's what I think too." She paused a long time and I could see her thoughts go somewhere sad. I didn't know how to ask about her mother, so I waited for her break the silence.

"So how long have you and Nathan been friends?" she finally asked.

"He moved to Cherry Field in the third grade, so ever since then."

"He sure is different, isn't he?"

"He sure is," I agreed.

"I told my dad," Halley Kate continued, "that Nathan isn't like other kids I know. I can't quite put my finger on it, but somehow, I just feel a little better when I'm around him. You know?"

At that moment I thought about how lonely Cherry Field would be without Nathan, but all I could muster was a nod to indicate that I agreed with her. I wish I had been as free with Nathan as Halley Kate was with him. How could someone that I relied on so heavily in Cherry Field cause me so much embarrassment at Fair Play Middle? I was ashamed of my hypocrisy and secretly vowed that everything would be different next year at school. I knew that Nathan would always give me another chance.

"Hey, you two, don't eat lunch without me!" Nathan hollered from across the creek and then proceeded to wade on over. I was never so glad to have a moment broken in all my life.

Halley Kate kept her seat, but I rose to give Nathan a hand up. "Everything's workable again," Nathan stated louder than he thought as I pulled him to the top. I knew he was talking about the mine, but I can only imagine what Halley Kate thought he meant. She turned her head in embarrassment, but Nathan didn't notice. "Hey, guys, I'm getting hungry. Anybody else ready for lunch?" he bubbled.

I wasn't really hungry, but we all sat to down to eat anyway. For each of us, Mom had packed some squashed bologna and cheese sandwiches, a baggie of pretzels, a warm pudding cup, and grape drink in a little plastic bottle with a foil top. I ate a couple of bites of my sandwich and then used the rest to feed the minnows.

That's the best thing to do with warm bologna and cheese, so Nathan and Halley Kate followed my lead. We sat there talking as we munched on pretzels and pudding and then lay back on the rock to continue our deep conversation, staring up into the clouds.

I wish I could remember all that was said because we talked about everything and at the same time we talked about nothing. All things were in perfect perspective from Flat Rock, and any worry that we brought along was quickly swept away by the swirling water. When our conversation had finally run its course, we were content to lie in silence, lost in the lullaby of Boulder Creek.

"Hey, Chris," Nathan piped up after a while, "so when does your play practice start?"

"What?" Halley Kate exclaimed, turning up to her side and resting her head in her hand. "Are you in some kind of performance, Chris?" If she hadn't been there I would have strangled Nathan on the spot!

"Not really, well, sort of, I don't know," I stammered. "My mom is making me be in a play at church, but I'm not sure when it's supposed to start." I sat up and glared at Nathan.

"What's the play about?" Halley Kate asked. She was genuinely interested.

"I don't know. Church stuff, I guess."

Nathan rolled to his side, propping his head in his hand. "Does it involve tutus, Chris?" Nathan smiled, thinking he was funny.

"No way," I protested. "They don't have tutus in church!"

"They might."

"They don't!"

Halley Kate, amused by my exchange with Nathan, smiled and rolled to her back and stretched. "I want to come see you, Chris."

"There won't be much to see," I answered. "I'm going to sign up as a stage hand or something."

"I'll come see you anyways," she sighed, and then we all lay back to talk about dreams and watch the clouds for a little longer.

If I could have frozen time, I would have stayed in that day forever. The creek is full of tricks, though, and I started to get the feeling it was much later than it seemed, and we still had to get Halley Kate back up the bluff.

"Well, I suppose we had better get going," I announced reluctantly. "I don't think we want to see sunset from Boulder Creek."

"I love the sunset," Nathan commented as he dragged himself to his feet. "It means that everything is finished."

"Me too," Halley Kate agreed as she stood up, "but I've always kind of liked the sunrise better."

"Why's that?" I asked, collecting my pole and lunch bag.

"I just like knowing I'll be alive one more day and all of the hope and promise that goes with it. Most people like the sunset because that's the one they see more often and there's no doubt that it's beautiful. But me, I guess I just take the sunrise...*personally*." She looked over at Nathan and smiled. “It means that everything is just beginning.” I nodded my head, only halfway understanding what she meant.

Nathan scaled the bluff from Flat Rock with grace and skill, and then I followed Halley Kate up at a much slower pace. When we got to the top, she needed to sit and catch her breath before we started the rest of the way home. As we made our way back through the woods, the fading song of Boulder Creek sounded more like a dirge than a lullaby, and a breeze seemed to catch every tree and shrub so they could wave good-bye as we passed. I spent plenty of time out in those woods with Nathan, but the three of us together was somehow special. And I was content that even though we had snubbed the cabin, we had shown Halley Kate the very best that Cherry Field had to offer. I would have gladly done it all over again, but as you find out when you get older, once in a lifetime only happens once in a lifetime.

As we neared the final curtain that would let us out into Ms. Hall’s yard, Halley Kate reached up and took Nathan and me both by the arms. We stopped and she hugged me hard. She turned and hugged Nathan with equal vigor. Her eyes began to tear. “Thank you both for a wonderful day in a wonderful place,” she whispered, and then one after the other, we stepped out of the woods and back into real life.

We trudged around Ms. Hall’s yard and back to my house. We found that Mom and Dad had invited Halley Kate’s dad over, and he had stayed the whole time we were gone. It was a long drive, and my parents convinced him it would be no trouble to stay and chat. I noticed that our parents’ conversation ended abruptly as soon as we walked in the door, but whatever had been said left my mother misty-eyed.

"Hey, there's my Halley Cater," Halley Kate's dad exclaimed as we came in. He lifted one arm, inviting her to a half-hug. She slid on to his lap and obliged. "How was it? Did you have fun?" he asked.

"It was so great, Dad," she answered, exhausted. "The woods and the creek out here are just beautiful, and I actually found an arrowhead." I noticed that she was too tired to fish it out of her pocket and show him.

"Sounds like a really good day sweetheart and thank you boys so much for looking after her."

"Well, young lady," Mom sniffled, turning her head up to wipe the bottom of one eye, "anytime you feel like it, you are more than welcome to come on out. I'll even pick you up if need be."

Halley Kate had melted down on to her father and had her head lying up on his shoulder. Her dad smiled and patted her on the leg. "Wow, you seem pretty beat, girl, I guess we had better get on home." Then he stood and shook my dad's hand and gave my mother a hug. I heard Mom whisper "anytime" before they broke apart.

Halley Kate put her arms around her father's waist to prop herself as they made their way awkwardly through the front door. They staggered to the bottom of the front steps before her dad whisked her up into his arms to carry his Halley Cater the rest of the way to the car. Nathan and I both watched from the porch as he slid her in the backseat and closed the door. He started the car and guided it down the drive, disappearing on the highway back to Fair Play.

25

Twenty-one

As it turns out, play practice started the very next week even though opening night wouldn't be for another month and a half. I begged and I pleaded, I whined and I sulked, but all my protests left my mother's mind unchanged. I even tried to use my social studies report on Liberia as an excuse, but she was determined that I needed to participate more, and this performance was the perfect way to get my feet wet. Apparently the *powers-that-be* felt that putting on a play would be an excellent way for the youth to give back to the church, not to mention it was also an excellent fundraising opportunity.

My mom agreed. Mom knew the whole schedule, telling me that practice would only be two nights a week for the first month and four nights a week for the last two leading up to the big night. I was to walk to church after school, where they would feed us pizza for dinner, and then Dad would pick me up after everything was done. The only good thing was that I wouldn't have to ride the bus home, and I was pretty sure that Nathan would want to hang around and catch a ride with Dad too. At least I'd have someone to walk to church with.

My mom suggested I talk Nathan into joining the play as well, but I knew he would never go for it, so I didn't even try. Besides, the whole thing was going to be bad enough without Nathan fumbling around on stage in front of everybody. Anyway, Nathan decided he would rather ride the bus home with Halley Kate than hang out at the church, so at least for the first couple of weeks I had to walk from school alone.

I dawdled along the way so that I wouldn't be the first one to arrive. When I finally turned the corner and climbed the steps up to the church, I was received by a lady who directed me to the fellowship hall where about thirty future play participants were already assembled. I slipped in uncomfortable but undetected and then moved to the serving table for a slice of cold pizza and an orange soda. By the time I wandered in, the pizza was fairly well picked over, leaving only the least desirable flavors abandoned in their boxes congealing in grease. I ate two pieces.

I was one of the youngest, and I really hated being there. I mostly milled between the individual groups of three or four that had naturally gravitated to one another and were all engaged in very important and exclusive conversations. When anybody noticed me just standing around, I would pretend I had just remembered something very important and rush away or out of the room. I made that move with such regularity that I must have appeared mildly schizophrenic.

"Okay, okay, everyone! Can I have everyone's attention," Ms. Strozier yodeled from the front of the room.

"Everybody, come on and gather up now," she called out, waving her arms to get our attention. Ms. Strozier was a choir lady, and she must have been very important to the church, because she always sang the solos on Sunday mornings even though she wasn't really that good. "Gather round, gather round," she called in a singsong voice as the parents who were assisting her stood idly by, smiling. At first no one paid any attention to Ms. Strozier, but eventually conversations began tapering off, and we all collected around to hear what she had to say.

"Welcome, welcome, everybody. I certainly know a lot of you here, and I am very glad to see such a good turnout for this wonderful opportunity. I know it is going to be a lot of fun, and I'm sure that we will be a much tighter group after we have experienced the joy of Christian theatre together. It will be a great time to showcase the talent God gave you." Her parent assistants smiled and nodded in agreement with all that Ms. Strozier said.

"The name of our play is *A Collage of the Bible* written by yours truly." Her parent assistants applauded and so did we. "There will be two acts. Act I with Old Testament stories and Act II will be the story of the Gospel." She paused, clasping her hands together under her chin as if she were choosing her next words very carefully. "Now, we only have six weeks to put on this production, which includes learning our lines, building all of our sets, and making our costumes. So in order to hurry things along, I have already talked to some of you about being cast in our speaking roles. If I have talked to you about tackling one of these roles, please come up and stand behind me now."

About ten kids pushed their way up to the front and stood proudly, like the chosen few, behind Ms. Strozier.

She called them out one at a time, telling the rest of us the characters that each one would be playing as the parent assistants coerced our applause.

Her daughter, Bebe, would be playing Esther in Act I and would take on the role of Jesus in Act II. She acknowledged that it was a little odd for a girl to play Christ, but under a robe with her light brown hair and blue eyes, Ms. Strozier felt that Bebe's resemblance to Jesus was too striking to be ignored. "Now," she announced after introducing her final actor, "I will take *this* group with me to start running lines, and the rest of you head to the back to get your assignments from our two volunteers, Ms. Smith and Ms. Jones." She nodded to her two assistants, and they herded us to the other side of the room out of Ms. Strozier's way.

I stood in line with the rest of the supporting cast to be assigned the part of an anteater in the *Noah* story, a jeering Philistine in *David and Goliath,* and a stagehand for all of Act II. I was then dismissed to the back parking lot to start helping some volunteer dads with construction of the set. I spent the rest of play practice holding nails for somebody else's father.

Time dragged by at a painful pace before everything finally started to wind down and our parents began to arrive. I was relieved to see Dad and slid into the car without saying any good-byes. I doubt anyone noticed.

"So how was it?" Dad asked in his customary manner as he steered the car out of the parking lot.

"It was fine," I answered in my customary manner as well.

Dad tried to make conversation by asking all sorts of questions about my day and my part in the play, but I was reluctant to reveal too much, so he finally stopped fishing and turned on the radio. The sun had been on its way down when Dad picked me up and was now fully set. We sped along, unable to see anything other than what our headlights revealed. I noticed the car slowing a little as Dad eased off the accelerator. You had to be very careful on the road to Cherry Field at night unless you wanted to wind up with a deer through your windshield.

I let my mind wander around Nathan and Halley Kate on the bus, and I let my mind worry about my Liberia project and the church play. I thought how unfair it had been for Ms. Strozier to preselect her favorites, leaving the rest of us to build props like a bunch of drone worker bees. Even if they were rigged, I was upset that she didn't feel the need to hold any auditions at all. I thought that the choir lady should have had at least enough respect for us to lie. My mind drifted over to opening night, and I wondered if I had enough courage to teach Ms. Strozier about the virtues of placating the insignificant boy manning the curtain in Act II. I smiled to myself in the darkness.

Woooo! Woooo! The scream of a siren followed by a heavy flood of flickering blue lights streamed into our car through the rear windshield! Startled, I sat straight up and turned around to be blinded by the whites and blues that seemed more like they belonged to an alien vehicle than anything man could have made.

Dad slowed way down, giving the blue lights ample opportunity to pass us by, but instead the state trooper closed in even tighter and didn't back off until Dad found a place on the shoulder to pull off the highway.

Dad ran his hand back through his hair, rolled down his window, and waited for the policeman to approach the car. There was a lot of loud radio talk and the sound of a door finally opening, as we seemed to wait forever. A shadow moved toward us out of the lights as the trooper edged up to my dad's side of the car.

"What seems to be the problem, Officer?" my dad asked.

"License and registration please," the trooper responded brusquely, ignoring my father's question.

"Was I going too fast?" was my dad's next question as he handed his papers out the window, but there was still no answer. The trooper examined Dad's license and car registration under a flashlight and then thrust them back through the window to my father.

"Where are you going tonight, sir?" the trooper asked curtly while surveying our backseat through the window with his flashlight.

"Home," my dad answered.

Then the trooper leaned down into the open window, shining his flashlight past my dad and directly into my face. "What's your name, young man?" he asked in a slightly softer voice than he had been using with my dad.

The light stung my eyes so I held my hand up to shield them. "Chris," I answered nervously.

"Chris," the trooper's voice resumed its old tone, "please take your hand down so that I can see your face." I did as he asked, but I had to squint as the trooper examined me from behind the bright light. "Sir," the trooper was back to my father, "would you mind opening your trunk?"

"Why?" I could hear the irritation beginning to surface in my dad's voice.

"Sir, please step out of the car." The trooper sounded irritated as well, and I started to feel very nervous for my father. Dad retrieved his keys from the ignition, opened the door, and got out. I couldn't hear what was being said, but there was an exchange of words, and then my dad walked around to open the trunk. The officer had my father shuffle a few things around inside as he looked on with his flashlight. I didn't move. I just kept staring out the back window as the shadows moved back and forth behind the opened hood. I was only mildly relieved when the trunk was closed and my dad was sitting back behind the wheel. I thought we were going to be allowed to leave, but the trooper leaned back into the window. He wasn't quite done.

"Have either of you seen this boy?" The trooper passed a photograph to my dad for us both to examine. He held his flashlight steady so we could get a good look. The boy was about my age and build, but I didn't have any idea who he was or even why the trooper was asking about him. Dad passed the picture back shaking his head.

"Sorry about the inconvenience," the trooper apologized without sincerity. "This young man went missing about fourteen miles from here over in Crabapple yesterday afternoon. We have roadblocks set up around the town, but we're also doing stop searches in the vicinity, particularly out here on the rural highways. We're just hoping to get lucky. Anyway, drive safely, sir."

The trooper returned to his car, allowing us to pull back onto the highway before turning off his blue lights. He followed us all the way back into Cherry Field, though. The trooper pulled over to the side of the road and watched as we parked the car and walked to the porch. Mom greeted us with excitement at the front door. She wanted to know all about play practice.

26

Anything but Safe

Dad was a little unnerved by the experience with the trooper, and over the next couple of days my parents had several intense conversations behind closed doors. After that, Dad started waiting with me and Nathan at the bus stop in the morning, and Mom always greeted us there when we were dropped off in the afternoon. I didn't mind too much because by the time we got all the way out to Cherry Field, there weren't any other kids on the bus to see my folks on babysitting duty. There were now a litany of rules governing my walk from school to church and Mom even asked Nathan, as a personal favor, to stay after school and walk with me on play practice days. I thought that was a little too much for Mom to ask of Nathan, but I was worn thin by all of the safety lectures, so I let it go without complaint.

Nathan happily agreed. He loved my mom and would have done anything she asked as a *personal favor.* With the abduction in Crabapple, Fair Play really started to tighten down. Ms. Strozier called roll every night and parents had to park their cars and come into the fellowship hall to pick up their kids when play practice was over. Funny, I never even knew to consider what all of this really meant. Fair Play was doing everything it could to hedge the bet in a lottery no one wanted to win, but to its adolescents, the new rules were just another engraved invitation to rebel. Of course none of this mattered out in Cherry Field, where my parents never believed us anything but safe.

The very next weekend, Nathan begged me to go to the mine. I wasn't really sure that I wanted to, but he assured me that he would do all of the digging, so I finally gave in. Around the garden, through the woods, over the creek, and to the mine; the hike went quickly and without conversation. Nathan had found an old spool of rope in his grandmother's garage, and even though it looked more like a piece of clothesline, he insisted on taking it out to the mine. He called it the "backup rope," and he didn't see any reason at all that we shouldn't have it in the event of some great catastrophe, especially if he was willing to carry it.

I rolled my eyes and huffed, but he brought the extra rope anyway. He had it looped over one shoulder and across his chest like a Swiss mountain climber, but one end of the "backup rope" kept falling to the ground and getting tangled around his feet as he tried to keep my pace. He tripped and fell twice. I don't know what I had against bringing more stuff out to the mine. I guess I was just looking for a reason to be bent out of shape, so I naturally took it out on my most convenient and usual scapegoat. I hurried along knowing that the more quickly I moved, the more burdensome Nathan's rope would be and the more likely he was to get tangled and fall. I was being a jerk, but we sure made great time getting out to the mine.

I didn't start feeling the usual relief the woods offered until we moved down the path and stood once again in the cabin yard. Nathan was panting like a worn-out dog, but we were here, our "backup rope" was here, and the church play, the social studies report, and my parents *were not.* This secret place, this wonderful secret place, was always more than happy to shield us from any worries for as long as we chose to remain. I felt better. I was somehow comforted. I guess I kind of missed watching Nathan dig for nonexistent gold, and I vowed to myself that next time, I would show this place to Halley Kate.

Nathan shed the rope and plopped to the ground, sitting and breathing heavy. "Wow, Chris, we sure made it out here fast today."

"I guess," I muttered as I went about retrieving all of our gear from the hiding place under the brush.

"You find everything? I mean nothing got stolen, did it?" Nathan asked.

"Of course nothing's stolen," I answered, "nobody but you, me, and the stupid skunk even know this place exists. I'm not even sure why we bother to hide this stuff." I strapped up the pulley and threaded the rope through as I talked. Even though we hadn't been back in a long time, I set up all our equipment as automatically as if I had just done it yesterday. Nathan was the digger, so he never helped with either the set up or breakdown of the equipment. He was, however, always quick to correct me if he felt that I hadn't done something just the right way, particularly when it came to hiding everything at the end of the day. It was always easier to do things his way the first time than to listen to a bunch of nitpicking that would last all the way home.

I brushed away the leaves and uncovered the mine. There was a faint smell of musty clay, but no evidence at all of dead skunk…*thank God.*

"All set," I announced, turning back to Nathan, who had been watching approvingly from his seat on the log.

Nathan walked over to the edge, pulled out his flashlight, shook it a few times, and turned the beam into the mine, barely illuminating the bottom. "No animals," he whispered to himself before looking up. He picked up the spade and dropped it casually into the hole. "You ready to man the rope?" he smiled. I nodded, so he stepped into the loop, and I lowered Nathan and his bucket to the bottom.

I guess Nathan must have hit a patch of soft dirt, because the buckets were coming up faster than ever. By the time I hauled up a load, dumped the dirt in the brush, and dropped the bucket back down, Nathan was already yanking on the rope for me to pull it back up again. Except when we ate lunch, I didn't even have a chance to sit down, and I was pooped when I pulled up the last bucket and it was time to go home.

The rope measured the well as just a little better than fifteen feet when I hollered down to Nathan that we had to leave.

"Already?" he whined from the bottom of the hole. The mine was very stingy with sound, so I had to lean way over the edge in order to hear Nathan grumble. I lowered the rope to pull Nathan up as my last load of the day.

"Hey, Chris," Nathan faintly called up to me.

“What now, Nathan?” I was in a hurry and not really in the mood to deviate from our usual routine.

“Toss me the other end of the rope.”

“What?” I wasn’t sure that I heard him right.

“Toss me the other end of the rope, so I can see if I can pull my own self out today.” We didn’t have a lot of time before we needed to be home, but I was interested to see if Nathan could actually pull himself out, so I did as he asked and tossed him the other end of the rope.

Now the pulley dangled over the mine with both life lines disappearing down into its dank, earthy throat. The whole contraption bobbed and turned oddly about, almost as if a fish were nibbling at the other end, as Nathan was getting set to hoist himself up.

Suddenly everything went taut with his weight and the “one way” on the pulley snapped on. All of this time, I had been reaching over to flip the “one way ”on manually so that I wouldn’t drop Nathan or a bucket on his head. I didn’t realize that the safety would automatically engage as soon as a load was being hoisted. That would certainly make hauling dirt up a little easier.

I watched the rope move slowly over the top of the pulley, one short stretch at a time as Nathan began to haul himself up out of the dark. One pull, rest, another pull, rest; I wondered if Nathan would really be strong enough to do this all by himself. Another pull, and one end of the rope dove deeper into the mine while the other slowly emerged. Another pull and then another, and I could finally see Nathan faintly as the darkness started to give way to the light from above. He was standing in the loop, swinging from side to side, doing his best to get his balance coordinated with his next tug. His tongue was sticking out of his mouth and almost up to his ear in deep concentration. He gave a big wide smile when he looked up and saw me standing over him.

Nathan was moaning and gritting his teeth, but I knew that he wouldn't accept any help, so I just stood back and let him have this victory. A few more tugs and he tossed the spade and flashlight up to the surface. A couple of more pulls, and his head finally popped up out of the hole.

I was really ready to go now, but he stopped where he was and started looking around as if he were searching for something that may have been left on the forest floor. "Ah shoot!" he exclaimed with disgust when he didn't see what he was looking for. He was still dangling over the hole with only his head above ground.

"What is it? What's wrong?" We didn't have time for him to go back down into that stupid pit if he had forgotten something.

"I can't believe this!" he shouted, looking around frantically before he rolled his eyes back and popped himself in the forehead with his free hand.

I was frustrated and starting to get a little worried about how he was acting. "What is it, Nathan? Just tell me!" I yelled.

"Well, Chris," he said much more calmly while still looking around, "it looks…well…it looks like six more weeks of winter."

I didn't think that was funny at all, but Nathan had a real big laugh anyway. I told him to get his butt up out of that hole before he fell back in and I left him there for the rest of the week. He pulled himself on up, still chuckling at his own joke. It was incredibly annoying.

Nathan was worn out from digging, so he just sat and watched as I fulfilled my mindless responsibilities of our gold mining partnership. I didn't mind; it was quick, easy, and automatic: unstrap the pulley, wind the pulley with the rope and put it in the bucket, hide the bucket and the spade in the underbrush, pull the board over the hole, cover it with leaves. I hid Nathan's stupid "backup rope" right along with the rest of our equipment.

27

Aru

The church play was drawing near and so was my report on Liberia. Nathan and I spent a lot of time in town after school at the Fair Play library researching our social studies projects on the days that I didn't have play practice. Ordinarily I would have procrastinated a little longer on my report, but practice was about to go to four nights a week, and my progress on Liberia seemed to be a constant concern of my parents. They'd ask me about it every night at dinner.

Of course I took those opportunities to complain about not having enough time for school work because of the play, but they didn't seem to care, telling me as I got older I'd have to learn to juggle more than one ball. So Nathan and I walked to the library after school to gather enough research to satisfactorily fulfill our obligation to our social studies teacher, Ms. Baird.

I have always liked the library with its rows of books and quiet ladies ready to help. The guardians of silence behind the desk or moving with their carts between the shelves demand a reverent hush so as not to wake the sleeping books before their time. With all the solemnity of a church funeral, the sanctuary of study commands its respect from even the most boisterous individual. And although it is a place of peace, the library is also a place of secrets, ready to whisper all to anyone willing to crack a book. I have always been intrigued…even when I wasn't too crazy about the labor reading requires.

Nathan and I spent three days after school taking notes for our project. I would collect my mountain of books and magazines and sit at a table while Nathan went off to work at a study carrel. He passed by often to fetch additional resources, appearing more intent on his report than I had ever seen before. He asked to borrow paper a few times as he filled his own with notes that only he could read. I guess he was really into the Congo. Other than that, I didn't pay much attention to Nathan, staying focused on my own Liberian task.

Ms. Baird's requirement of a narrative written as if we lived in the country we were researching seemed to make the work a little more interesting. Instead of just copying fact after fact into my notes, knowing that I would actually have to turn them into a story made me consider what living in Liberia might really be like. I imagined how the culture, the terrain, the economy, and education would all influence my life experience. I mulled over how living there might impact my view on the world and my hopes and dreams for the future. I could almost put myself into the Liberian countryside, and all of the mundane facts I dutifully copied into my notes began to transform into the causes and conflicts that would eventually be the basis of a pretty interesting story. I tossed it all around in my head a little bit, and before I had even finished my research, I had already developed characters and a plot that would easily weave around and illustrate everything I had learned about my country.

I guess this is when I discovered my love of writing, finding that it soothed me in nearly the same way as the walk to Flat Rock. Even though Nathan begged and pleaded, I didn't go to work in the mine for the next two weekends. Instead I stayed boarded up in my room crafting the story of Aru, the Liberian boy who found a massive jewel in the mountains and used it to immigrate his entire family to Fair Play. There were good guys, bad guys, and even some social commentary about our community. I wrote twice as much I needed to, but it was kind of fun, and I didn't think Ms. Baird would mind.

I finished my entire social studies project three weeks early, and I was more than satisfied with all that I had done. I even read Aru's adventure to my parents, who said they thought it was very good. I was generally skeptical of parents' praise, but this time seemed different; maybe because they offered no suggestions for the story's improvement.

28

A Full Twenty-one Feet

With my school work well in hand and no real lines to memorize for the upcoming church play, the ever looming Cherry Field boredom started to set in once again. Nathan was able to talk me into going out to the mine several more days to dump the buckets of dirt he sent to the surface and to handle all of the equipment. He dug like he was running out of time, and I guess he was, because I was getting sick of walking all the way out here to stand around and haul dirt. I had spread so much of the stuff in the underbrush that there was now a long, low mound just beyond the bush line. The forest had hidden most of our "pre-skunk" dirt under a bed of leaves and rogue weeds, but Nathan had been digging so fast lately that it was getting harder and harder to hide the dirt to his satisfaction.

Gold mining had been fun as long as there was hope of getting rich, but now it just seemed like yard work with my dad, and I was sick of it! The cabin watched me grumble as I halfheartedly hauled up the buckets and dumped them off to the side. I didn't spread a thing on the last day of our dig.

Nathan skipped lunch and stayed in the hole until the rope measured a full twenty-one feet to the bottom. Then he called for the other end of the rope and hauled himself up with relative ease. At the top, he stuck his head out and made the same stupid groundhog joke about six more weeks of winter and giggled as if it were still funny.

By this time, I was spoiling for a fight and in no mood for dumb jokes! Still, I didn't break routine, and as soon as Nathan pulled himself to his feet, I automatically started to take down and hide our gear like I had done so many times before. Nathan took his usual seat to watch me clean up before he noticed that I hadn't bothered to spread any dirt. He huffed back to his feet, picked up the spade, and without saying one word to me went to work on the pile that I had left sitting near the edge of the mine. He was exhausted as he labored to sling the dirt back into the underbrush, one slow spade full after another. I didn't care that he was tired as I finished up my chores, and it was his obvious disgust with me that prompted my assault.

"What are you doing?" It was a rhetorical question boiling in anger and frustration.

"Your job," Nathan answered flatly without looking up from his work.

"Is that right?" I fumed.

"That's right," Nathan continued in a flat tone, still without the courtesy of looking up.

I could feel the anger fill my face. "Is that so? Well then, I quit! I'm done! This whole thing is just stupid! There was never any gold. This isn't even a mine. It's just an old well, and no matter how far you dig, you're never going to find anything but a dead skunk that will send you to school stinking to high heaven! Nathan, you're just an idiot *special* who wants to hide tools and dirt in the middle of nowhere for no good reason!"

Nathan finally stopped spreading my dirt, watching me pull the board back over the mine and cover it with leaves during the course of my regrettable tirade. "I'm sick of this, and I'm never ever, ever coming out here again!"

"I don't even care anymore, Chris. That's just fine," Nathan snarled back. He walked over to where I was standing, spade still in hand, putting his face right up into mine. I didn't know what he was doing, but I wasn't going to back down. Nathan's eyes went narrow, and his lips were tight. "We can be done now," he growled, squeezing the spade handle tight, "but we can't leave all that dirt sitting out in front of the hole like that."

I had never seen Nathan this way before. He actually seemed a little menacing, and even though I thought about shoving him back away from me, the spade in his hand made me think better of it. I was the one to step back. "Great! Great! Hallelujah!" I threw up my hands in sarcasm. "We're done! We're done! We're done!" I continued to rant as Nathan stood his ground.

"Why can't we leave the dirt, Nathan? Why not? Are you afraid someone is going to come down here and steal it, or do you just have some weird *special* issue with dirt piles sitting in the middle of the woods? Well, I can tell you right now, I can leave that dirt right where it is, no problem. I'm gone! Do you hear me, *special*, I'm outa here now!"

Then I stomped off, leaving Nathan to finish my job all on his own. I didn't make it halfway home, walking through the woods alone, before my anger subsided and I was overtaken by so much guilt that I puked right there on the path. Still, I went home to sulk instead of going back to help Nathan fulfill my part of the bargain.

29

Missing

Even though I had broken our agreement, Nathan honored his with my mother and continued to walk me from school to church on play days. Practice had gone to four nights a week and Nathan escorted me over without complaint. As a matter of fact, he was eager to engage me in almost any conversation, but I was always intentionally gruff to cover the shame of what I said at the mine. I never understood how he could forgive so easily without even a hint of an apology from me.

So we never talked about the mine, and oddly enough, we never talked about Halley Kate either. Whenever her name was mentioned, Nathan would fall immediately silent or change the subject in his usual awkward fashion. I hadn't seen Halley Kate in a long time, and Nathan was unwilling to tell me how she was doing or even talk about her at all. I guess I should have sensed a secret. It became pretty clear which topics were taboo, and with very little practice, we managed to negotiate around them, making our trips to play practice as comfortable as possible.

Whenever the conversation turned to our social studies project, though, I was more than willing to go on and on about the adventures of Aru, while Nathan walked along listening. Every day was the same; we walked and talked, but when we arrived, Nathan always refused to go into the church. I invited him in for pizza, but he would decline, saying that he was looking forward to the play and didn't want to ruin it by accidently seeing any of the rehearsal. "That would just spoil it for me," he said every time he refused the invitation to a greasy cold dinner with orange soda. He said that he liked to sit outside in the square and watch the people go by, so I left him plopped on a bench to wait patiently for my dad to pick us up.

Mom never told Nathan explicitly to wait inside the church, so Ms. Strozier, who called roll religiously after the last disappearance, never knew to include his name on her roster. Mom never forgave herself for this uncharacteristic oversight, even after it no longer mattered.

"Alright, Nathan, it's the very last rehearsal," I said as I started up the church steps. "Why don't you just come on in and eat a piece of pizza?" I was pretty sure that he wouldn't come in, but the invitation was the only apology that I could muster.

Nathan huffed. We'd been over this every afternoon for weeks. "I told you and I told you, Chris, I don't want to spoil the play!" He seemed even more resistant about the whole thing than usual.

"Yeah, yeah, you're not going to see anything. We won't even start rehearsing until everybody eats. You can come on in, grab a bite, and then get back out here to do your *'people watching.'* There's orange *sooooda*." I said it like that to tempt him.

"The pizza and orange *sooooda* is for people in the play. That stuff isn't for the fans," objected Nathan.

"It doesn't matter. We're all so sick of it anyway; half of that nasty stuff gets thrown out. I mean how many nights in a row can kids eat pizza? No one's going to care." I don't know why on this night, of all nights, I was trying so much harder to convince Nathan to come inside.

"If I go in there, Chris, and Boss Strozier sees me, is she going to let me come back out to sit in the square?"

That's something that I hadn't really considered before, and I don't think I would have ever noticed unless Nathan had brought it to my attention. After we checked into practice, there was always an adult close by seeming very intent on keeping track of where we all were. Spend too much time in the restroom and someone would come looking; stray away from your work group and get called back immediately. We were always kept busy and in close proximity to an overseer of some sort. Once you were counted, you were then accounted for every single second of the evening until your parents picked you up; no strays and no lost lambs.

"No. You'll have to stay inside," I answered honestly.

"That's what I thought, Chris. So then I'll be stuck sitting there watching the entire play and ruining opening night. I'll see all the costumes, I'll hear all the lines, I'll know if someone messes up, and if it really stinks, I won't want to come back at all! If that happens, what in the world am I going to tell my date?"

"Yeah, right, like you really have a date," I smirked and moved up one on the church steps.

"Well, not really," Nathan admitted, "but I am sitting with Halley Kate and her dad, and I don't want to see your performance before they do."

"Halley Kate's coming?" I stepped back down closer to Nathan. I hadn't seen her in so long, and I had been so busy that I didn't realize how much I really missed her. Nathan wouldn't talk about her, but now to hear him say her name, I felt a big empty space sink into my stomach.

"Yeah, don't you remember? She said she was coming to see you even if you were just going to move props around, and you know how *she* is. I don't think that the president himself could talk her out of doing anything that she sets her mind to. You saw her climb the bluff."

"Where has she been, Nathan? Why hasn't she been in school?" I wanted him to tell me, but he had moved past the sidewalk and was already crossing the street into the square.

"I shouldn't have told you," Nathan called from the far curb, "but you know me, I'm a teller. That's just another reason it's not good for me to see anything ahead of time. I'll tell what happens! Go, do your practice. I'll meet you and your dad out back like usual." Then he walked out across the grass of the Fair Play town square to pick out a good bench, watch people, and wait for us to take him home.

Play practice was more miserable than usual. They finally handed out our costumes, issuing them to us one by one out of a trash bag, calling us up by our roles instead of our names. There weren't enough animals for the Noah story, so my costume had another anteater sewed right to the side to make it look like there were two of us. My unmanned mate hung limply at my side, looking like someone had just let out all of his air. Most of the animal costumes were pretty good, but mine looked like some sort of mutant Siamese elephant that Noah should have excluded from the boat ride.

It was hot, and the mask, or head piece as Ms. Strozier called it, was too big and trapped all of my pizza burps like an airtight space helmet. I sweltered on stage as patiently as possible, trying to see out of one of my eye holes as the smell of belched pepperoni fumed inside my mask. Hot sweat rolled off my nose, and I wondered if anyone had ever died like this. Finally the anteater head was more than I could bear, so while Ms. Strozier busied herself with positioning Noah on the other side of the stage (she wanted the audience to get the full effect of his soliloquy), I committed a heinous theatrical sin. I took off my mask during a dress rehearsal.

"No, no, no!" Ms. Strozier stomped across the stage wagging her finger at me. It took me a second to realize who she was talking to. "Anteater, anteater, put your head back on! You must never, never, ever de-costume on stage! I know it's hot, but it's hot for everybody! After all, the show must go on!" She snatched the mask out of my hand and shoved it back over my head. The pizza burps never got the chance to escape.

Later on I was dressed in a breast plate and a skirt, handed a rubber spear, and shoved out on stage to snarl like an irritated Philistine in the background of the David and Goliath story. There were about ten or twelve of us Philistines waving our swords and spears, sounding more like a bunch of pirates than ancient warriors. Ms. Strozier didn't seem to care as long as she could see her David and hear his lines clearly. Rehearsal started to move a little faster, and when Act I was finally over, I was relieved of all acting duties to man the curtain. I was a lot more comfortable watching from the wings in my regular clothes.

Ms. Strozier was particularly agitated, stomping to and fro across the stage, calling everyone but her daughter by their character names and constantly rearranging where we were supposed to stand. Her adult assistants, never daring to make a single suggestion, stood and watched her with the rest of us. She must have been under a lot of pressure having to fulfill God's plan with a bunch of amateur actors and well-meaning adults who thought that fun and fellowship were equally important to providing a crisp performance. Ms. Strozier looked exhausted when practice finally ended forty minutes late, apologizing to our parents who were now waiting for us in the back of the room.

Ms. Strozier called to our parents from her place on stage, "I'm sorry that we ran a little over, and I know it's a little late, Moms and Dads, but please make sure that your children sign out with Ms. Smith or Ms. Jones before they leave. We need to see that everybody has a ride home. And don't forget, we want all of our actors back here tomorrow by three thirty sharp. We need to get all our props set up and run through a few more things before the seven o'clock show. We will feed the kids pizza for dinner, and I hope that all of you will join us after the play for our cast party." Ms. Smith and Ms. Jones waited patiently for the conclusion of Ms. Strozier's announcements before they began checking us out to our parents.

My dad spotted me and raised his arm so I could see where he was standing in the crowd. I walked over, and we shuffled over to get in line to check out and finally go home. "Hey, buddy, how was it?" my dad asked, putting his arm on my shoulder.

"It was practice," was the only response I could manage. That kind of answer was good enough for Dad, although Mom always found it unacceptable. Dad was the better one to talk to when there was nothing to say.

Dad nodded as we moved up in line. "Why don't you go find Nathan so we can get out of here?" Just like Mom, Dad was in the habit of telling me what to do in the form of a question.

"Yes sir," I answered and then slipped through the crowd of adults and youth still waiting to be ticked off the clipboards held by Ms. Smith or Ms. Jones. I headed straight for the back door where Nathan usually met us. Typically Nathan would wait for me there and then sidle on up as Dad checked me out. I never thought too much about it, but I suppose that Dad always assumed that Nathan had been inside at play practice, while Ms. Smith or Ms. Jones had been under the impression that he had arrived with my father. He had managed to stay under the radar all this time, and no one, not even me, had ever realized it.

Through the windows I could see that rehearsal had run late enough for the sky to darken and the street lights to pop on. It was Friday, and I was ready to get home. I picked my way through the crowd to collect Nathan from our usual meeting place. I stepped through the back door to wave him on in so we could leave, but tonight, for the first time, Nathan wasn't there.

I held the door and leaned way outside to have a look around, but I didn't see him anywhere. "That's just great," I muttered to myself. I was tired, I was irritated, and I just wanted to cave into the car and go on home, but now I had to look around for Nathan. It was too early to be worried. I figured since everything had run late tonight, he probably came into church to use the toilet or find a comfortable place to sit, so I went to check the restroom and the sanctuary, but still no Nathan.

Dad is not going to be happy, I thought to myself. I went back to check our usual meeting place by the door one more time before reporting back to my father. I held the back door open as I stepped out. The night was warm and the crickets, held at bay by the streetlights, were beginning to surround the parking lot. I stood there surveying longer than I needed to, and for the first time I started to doubt that Nathan would be easily found.

Dad, who had let everyone else move ahead, was now standing behind the last few people at the very end of the line. He looked impatient as he watched me approach.

"So where's Nathan?" were his first words as I came close enough to hear.

"I don't know," I shrugged, "I can't find him anywhere."

"Did you look?"

"Yes sir. I looked in the restroom, in the sanctuary, and outside, but I didn't see him anywhere." My dad looked away, running his hand back through his hair. I could feel his frustration, and I was suddenly more tired than before. "Do you want me to go look again, Dad?" I asked.

"No, no, let's just ask this lady up here with the clipboard. She probably has him somewhere on her list." That's when I realized that Nathan's name wasn't going to be on that list; it had never been on that list, but I said nothing and waited for my father to discover Nathan's missing name for himself.

"Hi, Ms. Jones, how are you tonight?" Dad said to the lady with the clipboard as our turn finally came.

"No, no, I'm Ms. Smith. That's Ms. Jones over there checking out that line." She indicated the other adult assistant with her pencil. "But I'm doing pretty good; a little tired, but a good kind of tired. How about you?" Dad said that he was a little tired as well, and Ms. Smith then turned her attention to me. "And how about you, are you getting nervous about tomorrow night?"

"No, ma'am, I'm just an anteater," I answered as she smiled down at me.

Dad put his hands on my shoulders, "I've got Chris," he said as Ms. Smith dutifully found me on her list and scratched me off, "and I'm also supposed to pick up Nathan Lamb, but I don't see him around."

Ms. Smith's eyes shot back to her clipboard running her pencil down the side of the paper searching for a name that I knew she wouldn't find. "Nope, sorry, we don't have any Nathans at all," she announced, sounding like a grocer telling my dad that they were all out of grapes.

"He's been here every single night. He walks over from school with Chris," Dad explained.

"No, I'm so sorry. I don't think I've seen a Nathan Lamb once since the show began, and you know that we've been keeping very careful accounts on all the children." She looked down at me and leaned in toward my dad to complete her thought in a whisper, "Ever since that business over in Crabapple, you know."

My dad ran his hand back through his hair again. "Chris, Nathan has been walking you over after school, hasn't he?"

"Yes sir," I answered, "but he never comes in."

"What?" My dad's voice sound frustrated and harsh.

"He usually sits in the square and then walks around back when it's time to go home. I didn't know that was wrong, Dad. I'm sorry."

My dad sighed heavily and looked straight to Ms. Smith, who was just now catching up with Dad's concern. "Please get a few people to look through the building. Maybe he's in a bathroom or maybe he's just dozed off somewhere."

Ms. Smith nodded and made a bee-line for Ms. Strozier, who was still busy with something on stage. Almost everyone else had left, but Dad caught a couple other fathers as they were just getting ready to head out the door. "Hey, we have a boy missing. He's probably just hanging around the parking lot somewhere. Would you guys mind taking a look out back and around the church grounds? His name is Nathan." Dad's request sounded more like an order, and the others eagerly obeyed. Dad ran his hand back through his hair, "Stay here, Chris," he commanded and then bolted out the front of the church to search for Nathan in the street-lit square.

From her position on stage, Ms. Strozier organized a search of the building, but with the return of my father and the other men, it was quickly determined that Nathan was nowhere to be found. In the room, desperation was passing through panic and on its way to despair.

"Call the police," Dad ordered Ms. Strozier. She nodded her head and rushed off to the church office.

Fair Play is a small town, so the deputies were in the back parking lot even before Ms. Strozier returned from making her call. They questioned Dad and they asked me all about walking Nathan from school, about him sitting in the square, and about everything he said to me that afternoon. When they talked to Ms. Strozier, all she could say was that she had no idea, she didn't know about it, and that he had never signed in.

"Alright," the young deputy finally concluded, "we have called in an APB with the state police and we've already started setting up a perimeter around town. There is no way anyone is getting out of Fair Play without being seen. The state boys are stopping any vehicle they see on the outer highways. We're locked down tight, folks. Don't worry, we'll find him."

He paused to write something in his notebook. "Okay, here's what I need you to do. Take your kids, go home, and stay home. It's better if the streets stay clear. If you're out and about you'll probably be stopped, taking up time that would be better spent looking for the boy. Does everybody understand?"

All the adults nodded and started to filter out to their cars. Terrified and relieved all at the same time that their kids had been accounted for, they cranked their cars one by one to drive their children safely home. Dad wasn't ready to leave, so we sat silently in the car as everyone else flipped on their headlights and wheeled out of the parking lot. Dad hadn't accused me of any wrongdoing, but still I felt guilty, as if all of this had been my fault. A lapse in judgment is never plain until after it's made. It never even occurred to me until right then that Nathan hanging out in the square might not be safe.

Tap, tap, tap. We hadn't noticed the young deputy walk over to our car, but he was knocking lightly on Dad's window. Dad rolled it down to see what the deputy had to say.

"Sir, I know that you're worried, but you need to go home. We are doing everything possible to find the boy, but sitting out in this parking lot, you're going to attract the attention of every officer who passes by. Do you understand me, sir?" Dad nodded. "Good, then please take your son on home. We'll call you as soon as we have something."

Dad nodded again. He thanked the deputy, switched on the headlights, and pulled carefully out of the parking lot on to the street. Dad intentionally took the wrong turn and slowly drove around the square a couple of times before heading back out to the main road.

30

Fair Play Friday Night

A Fair Play Friday night never looked like this before. Usually the streets were full of teenagers driving up and down and filling the parking lot of the Tastee Freeze. The sidewalks would ordinarily be full of families or couples on dates making their way to the movie theatre or someplace to eat. The arcade should have been a hive of middle schoolers with kids spilling out through the front door waiting for a turn on the most popular machines. But tonight, Fair Play looked more like a post-apocalyptic movie, with its shops all closed, empty sidewalks, and only the infrequent car moving through the typically busy streets. There was no sign of life, yet the street lights and store signs still burned bright, as if someone had forgotten to turn them off before going to bed.

Dad drove very slowly through town, but instead of heading straight out to Cherry Field, he turned off and continued the slow cruise up to the dark Fair Play Middle School. He circled the school, stopping once to get out with his flashlight and look around the dumpsters.

I heard the grind of metal as he slid the side door of the big metal box open to peer inside. He said nothing at all as he climbed back in behind the wheel, and I didn't ask any questions.

Dad pulled down to the other end of the parking lot, letting the headlights from the car shine out over the athletic field. "Lock the doors and stay here, Chris, I'm going to go take a look at something." I nodded, but before Dad could open his door, our car was filled with a flood of lights. The blue and white strobes of two police cruisers that had rolled silently up behind us ignited the darkness. Startled, I turned to see, but was blinded by the brilliant flashes streaming in.

"You in the car; please step out with both hands on top of your head," the dark command came over a loudspeaker from behind the blind of lights.

"You stay here, Chris," Dad ordered and then added, "don't worry."

Dad opened his door and stepped out. I heard the rush and the shuffle of feet and a final hollow bang as my dad was slammed across the hood of the car hard enough to make the front end bounce. My door ripped open and before anything could register, I was grabbed by the shirt collar and yanked out too hard to keep my feet. I went to the pavement, but I wasn't allowed to stay down for long. I was pulled back to my feet and pushed back against the car. A heavy flashlight clicked on, stabbing my eyes. I turned my head in retreat.

"Lift your head. Let me see your face." I was grabbed beneath the chin and turned full face into the light. "What's your name, son?" a voice demanded from the dark. I couldn't answer right away. "What's your name?!" The grip tightened around my chin.

"Chris...Chris, my name is Chris," I stammered.

"That's my son," my dad groaned from the hood of the car.

The flashlight flipped from my face to my dad's, and I was released. The police officer who had jerked me from my seat waded through the headlights around the front of our car to where Dad was being held. He tapped one of his fellow deputies on the shoulder, "Alright, guys, let him up."

I could feel the fury begin to burn inside me as Dad eased up and I saw his bruised face and bloody nose.

"Okay, sir, I know you think you're helping, but I told you back at the church something like this would happen if you didn't take your son, go home, and stay home." I now recognized the young deputy from the church, but he wasn't nearly as amicable as he had been earlier in the evening. "Now do I have to use valuable resources to have you escorted home, sir, or will you go straight there without any fuss?"

"No, no," Dad answered, wiping his nose, "I understand; I'm sorry. It's just that Nathan doesn't really have a mother or a father, and my wife and I...well, he doesn't have a dad to look out for him...we *have* to find him. He *has* to be okay."

"I understand, sir, but there are three deputies here that should be someplace else. Now I need you to go home."

Dad nodded, but before he could fully agree with the young deputy, the police radio crackled to life over the loudspeaker.

All units, all units, please be advised that the missing boy has been located. Repeat, the missing boy has been located. We have two units with him now at Fair Play Memorial Hospital. Be advised if you are off shift you are to return to base immediately.

The three deputies cheered and clapped at the announcement like they had just scored the winning run. Dad reached down and hugged me tight, but I could tell that he wasn't relieved yet.

"Why is Nathan at the hospital, Dad?" I asked.

"I don't know, Chris."

"Do you think he's okay?"

"I don't know, Chris."

"Sir," the young deputy turned back to Dad, "would you like an escort to the hospital?"

Dad nodded.

"Then just follow me, sir…and sir, I'm glad that we found him."

Dad nodded again, still unsure of how reassured he should be.

The deputy whipped his cruiser around and waited for Dad to move up behind him. We followed our police escort out of the parking lot, down the empty streets of Fair Play, and up to the hospital. The deputy waved us off, leaving us to park the car and find Nathan inside the building by ourselves. We had no idea what had happened to Nathan or what kind of condition he would be in, and although I was relieved that he had been found, walking through the doors of the hospital,

I started to feel the embrace of a whole different kind of worry.

The big glass doors slid open directly across from a very stern-looking woman sitting behind a tall counter. Everything was so familiar, almost as if it had been frozen in time since Nathan's grandmother had been sick; the dirty antiseptic feel, the television on the wall with nothing on but news, and the same curt woman working her crossword puzzle behind the help desk. She looked extremely busy with important matters. Dad put his elbow on the counter and glared down at the woman, waiting for her attention.

"Can I help you, sir?" the woman finally asked without looking up. I could tell by her monotone voice that she was a little put-out by the interruption.

"I hope so," Dad said. "There is a boy here. He probably has the police with him, and I need to know what room he is in." The night had already been long, and Dad's impatience with the woman behind the desk started to bubble quickly.

The woman laid her pencil down and put her elbow on her desk to prop up her chin. She sighed, looking up at my father. "You mean the boy who has been coming here almost every afternoon for the last two or three weeks, sir?" she asked in the same monotone voice.

"What?" huffed my dad.

"Nathan, you're talking about Nathan, right, sir?" the woman behind the desk confirmed with dry irritation.

"Yes, I'm looking for Nathan," Dad nodded.

"You know, sir, it's really not a good idea to let kids his age go walking through town all on their own with all that's going on right now." If there had been any emotion in her voice, she would have been chastising my dad, but without normal animation, she came off as making a simple statement of fact. "He was about fifteen minutes late coming down tonight, so I wouldn't let him leave the hospital without a ride. He really pitched a fit and told me that he was catching a ride at the church, but I just couldn't be sure, so I told him that he would have to be picked up here instead. I thought he had used the phone, but when nobody came for him, I went ahead and called the sheriff. I can't wait with him all night, you know, but I couldn't let him leave by himself either, with the Crabapple stuff and all. He seems to be a nice boy."

As the woman half-scolded my father for not keeping better track of Nathan, I realized that Nathan had never come in to play practice so that he would be free to walk over here to the hospital. She said that he'd been coming here for two or three weeks. *But why?* He hadn't said anything to me at all. As a matter of fact, I never would have even known about Nathan's secret excursions if this woman behind the desk hadn't detained him on the final night of rehearsal. He was fifteen minutes late, but practice went late by forty, so he would have easily made it back before anyone noticed. This all seemed so strange, but Nathan's visits to the hospital didn't seem to pique my dad's curiosity at all.

"Please, where is he?" my father asked again.

The woman dropped her head back to her puzzle and, without looking up again, pointed over the counter with her pencil. We turned to see Nathan sitting between two deputies with his back to us watching cartoons way over in the kiddie section of the waiting room. Dad sighed heavy with relief and so did I. Dad explained the situation and showed the officers his identification before they would release Nathan from what he later called, *"His waiting room arrest."*

"I am so, so, so sorry," Nathan welled up to my father. "She wouldn't let me leave. Everything would have been fine, but she wouldn't let me leave. The police said that I caused a bunch of trouble tonight and that the whole state and everybody else is out looking for me." Nathan paused with an involuntary snort that crying sometimes causes. He started to sputter, barely coherent as he tried his best to explain to my father through wet, red eyes. "I didn't mean to…I'm sorry…she wouldn't let me… sir…I'm…"

My father kept silent, looking down on him as Nathan did his best to plead his case and beg forgiveness. I didn't really know what to expect from my dad as Nathan dangled out in front of him. Finally, when Dad felt that there had been enough apologizing, he leaned down and hugged Nathan tight.

"I'm sorry," Nathan whimpered through a snotty nose up against my dad's shirt.

"I know," Dad whispered back. Then he broke off and rubbed Nathan on his head. "Don't do that again. Do you understand me?" Nathan nodded that he understood. "This would probably be pretty upsetting for your grandmother, don't you think?"

"Yes, sir," Nathan sniffled, looking up at my dad.

"Then we probably shouldn't mention it to her. Okay?"

"Yes, sir," Nathan agreed, wiping his nose.

Dad left it at that, having nothing more to say about it to Nathan. He told Mom most of what had happened, but he left out a few details to spare her from being unduly upset with the Sheriff's Department. I understood about Mom, so I never mentioned anything about the dumpsters or the school parking lot either. My mother, of course, blamed herself for the entire ordeal.

31

The Hurried Anteater

By the time I arrived for the play the next day, wild rumors burned everywhere, fanned by both the youth and parents alike. Some were saying "*that Nathan kid*" had been killed while others said no, that he had been attacked and had dragged himself to the hospital. Some said that he had been abducted and never found, while others said that he had escaped his kidnapper, and a police sketch artist was standing by waiting for Nathan to come out of a coma.

I wondered if most of these people even knew who Nathan was or if they would recognize him when he showed up in a few hours to watch our production of Strozier's *Collage of the Bible.* They all jabbered with gleeful fright about the fate of poor Nathan as we continued to busy ourselves with the final preparations for the night. I wanted to set the story straight and tell them that everything was okay, but they were all having too much fun playing with their rumor to listen. So I kept my silence, learning more about people and myself than I wanted to know.

There was a brief rehearsal for only the speaking parts and then we said a blessing before attempting to eat our last pizza supper. Ms. Strozier thought it only fitting that Jesus should give the prayer over our final meal, so Bebe stood before us and offered a very theatrical blessing for the bounty. "*We just want to thank you, God, that this is the last time we have to eat cheap, cold pizza and orange soda for dinner*," would have been a more honest prayer, but I don't think that Bebe Jesus would ever say that in front of her mother.

Ms. Strozier and her assistants fussed with our costumes as people began filing into the church auditorium. Ms. Strozier was in charge of the stars, while Ms. Smith and Ms. Jones picked and tugged at the rest of us. They were dismayed when they finally noticed that the mate sewn to my side looked more like a deflated alien life form than a partner anteater. Ms. Jones attempted to lift my sagging sidekick by stuffing it with toilet paper, but all she succeeded in doing was wasting six rolls of paper and making my outfit more uncomfortable to wear. I was sweating bullets, and the toilet paper stuck to me like blue lilac-scented fly paper inside my costume.

I peeked through the curtain to see the room begin to fill. There were a smattering of empty seats, but they were being quickly filled by latecomers squeezing through the aisles past those who occupied the more premium spots. Mom and Dad were in the second row, fingering through the program to find my name and looking around for people they knew. I searched row by row, but the audience had yet to settle and all the bodies just seemed to blend together into one massive sea of alternate colors and indistinct conversations. The whole place buzzed like a giant beehive just before dark.

I looked again and again, row by row by row, getting a little more twisted every time I couldn't find who I was looking for. The cast behind the curtain was getting set up for Adam and Eve, and Ms. Strozier was about ready to walk out on center stage to make all of the appropriate introductions and *thank you's.* Ms. Jones tapped me on the head, calling me back to my place in the wings to wait for the Noah scene, when I finally spotted Nathan in the far back of the auditorium.

There, sitting beside him with a tired smile and her head on her father's shoulder was Halley Kate. It was great to see her, even though she hadn't noticed me watching over the sea of people. Ms. Jones grabbed me by the tail and yanked me away from the curtain to line up off stage with the other animals. I waited patiently for Ms. Strozier, Adam and Eve, and the Tower of Babel to finally conclude before I pulled on my anteater head and followed a pair of monkeys out to greet Noah at the ark.

The crowd roared with delight as soon as we stepped out. Through one of my anteater eyes, I could just see the unmistakable wave of amusement drawn by the adlibbing monkeys that preceded me. My head was floppy and hot, and I was having difficulty seeing through the sagging eyes of my costume, so I moved cautiously toward Noah with two squirrels right behind. The crowd's laughter had simmered into a rolling snicker as I continued moving slowly across the stage toward my mark.

Then I felt it, a tug at the cuff of one of my anteater legs. I thought a squirrel had stepped on my tail. Then I felt a long zip, kind of like line spinning off your reel when a big fish hits the bait. *That's weird,* I thought as I reached my mark and turned to take my place alongside Noah and the monkeys.

The crowd roared with laughter again. The monkeys were standing still now, so I had no idea what was still delighting everyone so much. I adjusted my head a little and looked down through one of my anteater eye holes to see that the toilet paper Ms. Jones had used to prop up my mate had fallen down through the cuff of my costume. One of the squirrels had stepped on the end of the paper, causing it to stream out of my pant leg and across the stage like a long, lilac-scented, light blue banner running right back up my pants. I'm sure it looked like the anteater had rushed off the commode to make sure he got a good seat on the ark before the rain started. Even through my mask, I could hear the mass flutter of programs as the audience searched for the actor playing the anteater.

For the rest of her life, Ms. Strozier never forgave me for becoming the accidental and terribly embarrassed star of her play. The hurried anteater with the toilet paper tail was all anyone wanted to talk about at the cast party later that night.

I manned the curtain after Act I, but by that time Nathan, Halley Kate, and her dad had gone, leaving their empty seats to be filled by others in the crowd. Mom gave me little chin waves from the second row anytime our eyes met and I smiled, but my mind stayed with Halley Kate. I hadn't realized how much I missed the red-stripe girl, and seeing her without being able to talk only made it worse. A terrible mix of longing and dread swirled in my stomach when I spotted strangers in their seats. I was eager for the evening to come to an end as I suffered through my responsibilities with the curtain under Ms. Strozier's disapproving eyes.

32

The Congo

Nathan wasn't in church the next day, and his grandmother said he wasn't feeling well when I went to his house later Sunday afternoon, so I didn't see Nathan again until he climbed in the back of Dad's car for a ride to school Monday morning. I had my posters and my papers all ready to deliver my report on Liberia in social studies, but Nathan piled into the back seat without any of these necessary materials.

"You know, we have to give our reports today in Ms. Baird's class," I said in my flat, early morning voice.

Nathan's hair looked like a cow had been licking his head all night long as he clutched his broken notebook crammed with papers against his lap. "Oh," he muttered and then turned to stare out the car window.

"Do you need to go back in and get something?" Dad asked, looking through the rearview mirror.

"No sir, I'm fine," Nathan piped up before returning eyes to the window. Dad started the car and we rolled down the driveway on our way to school.

There was never a lot for Nathan and me to say with Mom or Dad around. I guess it was too embarrassing to talk about the important stuff like we did in the woods or on the bus. I yawned and leaned my head up against the window, letting the road and news radio lull me into transient thought. My mind drifted around Halley Kate, our social studies project, and Aru, my fictional boy from Liberia. I wondered if anyone at school would talk about the anteater or would the rumors of Nathan's abduction fly among the students and faculty of Fair Play Middle.

I thought about the empty streets of town, Dad being slammed over the hood of the car, and the missing kid from Crabapple. I was uncomfortable with where I had let my mind drift, so I lifted my head to take a breath, looked around, and readjusted. Dad had been hypnotized by the news crackling over the radio, and Nathan seemed to be in a trance of his own as the road sped underneath the car. I leaned back against the window to ease my mind with thoughts of Halley Kate and Boulder Creek.

At school, the day passed with most of us still shackled to the weekend. There was a yawn or a blank stare in every desk as our teachers prodded and goaded an uninspired crowd. We shuffled from class to tedious class only to plop into our assigned seats and immediately look for any distraction that would help pass the time. Monday mornings were getting painfully difficult to endure. The weather was warm and the smell of summer vacation wafted through the outside air. The breezy promise of imminent freedom with all of its symptoms had grown highly contagious throughout the school, and the day passed as the year had, with most of us wanting to be somewhere else.

The only exception to our pervasive indifference was Ms. Baird's class. Today our projects were due, and we would all be making oral presentations and handing in our personal narratives. At first I was a little nervous about speaking in front of everyone, but my first few classmates seemed to set the bar pretty low by simply reading facts off their poster boards, so I relaxed and started to wonder if Ms. Baird would like the story I had written. When I turned it in, I did my very best to keep it at the top of the stack, but I could see now that after all the shuffling around, my paper lay buried amid all the others piled on her desk. If I could, I would have sifted through that whole mess, brought Aru to the surface, and placed him on top (*maybe second from the top*), but I was sure that Ms. Baird wouldn't tolerate me rifling through other students' work. So I just sat there and stared at the pile of papers as someone droned over facts about Kenya. Looking back on it now, I'd bet if I had asked Ms. Baird to read my story first, she would have.

"Chris, you're up." Ms. Baird popped from her desk, startling me back from my distraction.

"Yes, ma'am," I answered, picked up my poster board, and made my way to the front of the class. I had been excited about this project for nearly a month. I had a lot to say about life in Liberia and what a boy living there might think about all of us here in Fair Play. I welled with insights and commentary of what I had learned about our own community by contrasting it with an imaginary one on the west coast of Africa. There were some very interesting back stories about how the whole country got started, and I was eager to share. I was sure that I was thinking things that no one else ever had, or if they did, they had kept their thoughts to only to themselves. I stood in front of the class, brimming with possibilities, and then…I simply read the facts off my poster board just like everyone else.

"Okay, thank you, Chris," Ms. Baird sounded automatic from behind her desk as she put a check by my name. She paused over the roll. "Nathan, are you ready?" Ms. Baird called across the room.

"He forgot his poster board," Ms. Addler answered before Nathan had a chance to respond. A little snicker started to roll through the classroom, but it was immediately cut short by a disapproving glance from Ms. Baird.

Nathan shot Ms. Addler a nasty look. "Yes, ma'am, I'm ready."

"Are you sure, Nathan?" Ms. Baird asked.

"I'm sure," Nathan confirmed.

Ms. Addler shrugged her shoulders and took a seat at the back of the room to watch. Nathan tripped and knocked his way empty-handed up the aisle of desks. He stepped on purses and books as he climbed to the front of the room, bumping into Ms. Baird's little podium and toppling it to the floor. I could feel Ms. Addler roll her eyes behind me. Nathan's pants were too short, his clothes didn't really match, and that giant cowlick he had this morning had never receded. The class was ready to burst with laughter. I could feel a horrible disaster coming on that even the stern Ms. Baird would not be able to abate.

"My name is Nathan, and I am supposed to tell you about the Congo." He looked to Ms. Baird, who nodded for him to continue. "I didn't really do a poster," he stammered, "but I think I can remember the important stuff."

"Do you need to look at your paper, Nathan?" Ms. Baird interrupted.

"No, ma'am, I know what to say." Nathan's voice cracked, causing chuckles to surface from a few bright-eyed students who looked to each other in joyful anticipation of the coming spectacle. Nathan was clearly nervous and uncomfortable with all the eyes on him.

"My report is on the Congo," he stated. "My friend, my best friend from the Congo, she has a hard time breathing. We all walk around and we carry our books without too much trouble, unless they get accidently dropped, but when she carries too many books, it hurts her inside. Her lungs don't work right. She gets real tired real fast. She gets terrible headaches and has to go to the clinic a lot. She also gets infections inside, and she has to take a bunch of medicine and miss a lot of school. That's probably why some people don't know her or say that she's weird or stupid or something. My friend is really smart. She just gets sick a lot."

The snickering had stopped. The class went quiet as a cemetery with all its gravestones sitting up row by row, wondering what Nathan was going to say next. Ms. Addler started to stand, but Ms. Baird waved her down, allowing Nathan to continue with his report on the Congo. I was feeling nauseous and dropped my head into my hands as Nathan went on.

"You can't catch what my friend has; you have to be born with it. It only happens when two bad genes match up from your parents, so sometimes dads and moms feel guilty about the whole thing, even though it's not their fault. Some people want a lot of attention when they get sick, but my friend doesn't like to talk about it at all. She says that's the difference in just having the sniffles and having something serious, but I think that's the difference between her and the rest of us. She makes it easy for me to forget, but I know that she never really feels okay even when she seems to. I hate that my friend hurts all the time."

Nathan sniffled just a little. "I didn't even know what cystic fibrosis was until she told me that she had it. She tries to keep it a secret so that nobody treats her different or feels sorry for her. But people treat her different anyway. They say mean things or say that she has bad parents because she misses so much school. She says that it's hard to find a friend to talk to when so many people say things like that. She says that she doesn't need friends who just want to make a big drama out of her illness. I bet if she wanted, she could find plenty of people to do that."

I sat quietly as Nathan continued to pound on my feelings with his report. How long had he kept this secret, and why didn't he ever tell me? *I'm a good friend.*

"The Congo is a wild country, but even in America, people with cystic fibrosis don't live very long. If they get too many infections in their lungs, they can get really, really sick and..." he choked, "...their lungs just quit.

Sometimes the doctors run out of things that they can do, so all that's left is to sit in a hospital chapel and pray for God to fix it. I guess He could if he wanted to."

Nathan snorted a little and then collected himself. "When you're promised only a short life, my friend says that you have a choice: you can fret over silly popular things or you can roll up your pants and search for arrowheads in Boulder Creek. I'm not totally sure what she means by that." Nathan dropped his head. "But I like the way it sounds." He turned to Ms. Baird. "I guess that's my Congo report, ma'am."

Ms. Baird and Ms. Addler were silent, not fully knowing how to respond. The class started to murmur, but before I could be subjected to their adolescent critique of Nathan's report, I raised my hand and was excused to the clinic.

The nurse gave me some ice chips to suck on and put a wet rag on the back of my neck. She asked me what was wrong, but I was scared if I talked I might cry instead. I could feel that horrible pain building up behind my eyes as I fought to keep back my tears. I just shook my head at her question, and she let me lay down on the cot. If I was any place else besides the school clinic, I would have let myself fall asleep.

"Are you okay, Chris?" I opened my eyes to see Nathan standing over me. "Ms. Baird sent me down to check on you."

I stared at him blankly for a moment before understanding what he was saying. I sat up. "Why didn't you tell me about Halley Kate?"

"Well, I didn't really tell you anything about Halley Kate, did I? Every laughing hyena in social studies will tell you that I was only talking about a made-up friend from the Congo."

I paid no attention to his answer, "Nathan, how long have you known?"

Nathan sat down beside me as the nurse busied herself with some paperwork. "Ever since the very first day on the bus," he whispered.

"What? Why didn't you tell me?"

"Because she hadn't told me yet. I just kind of knew, like I could feel it in some weird sort of way. Later, when she did tell me, she asked me to keep it a secret…that was before you guys were friends, and after that, I guess I just forgot about it."

"You forgot about it? How could you ever forget about it?" I whispered in frustration.

"I didn't forget about Halley Kate; I just forgot about telling you, is all. Besides, it's her secret to tell, not mine."

"But why wouldn't she want me to know?" I whined, starting to feel more left out than anything else.

"I'm not sure, Chris, maybe because she likes you too much." He paused to let me consider his answer for a moment. "Hey, do you want to go see her after school?" I nodded. "Good, then can you get your dad to pick us up at the hospital later?" I nodded again. "Okay, visiting hours get over at eight o'clock."

"You seem to be doing a little bit better, young man," the nurse broke in. "Here, let me write you a pass so you two can get on with your schedules." She scrawled a couple of notes across some red paper and shooed both of us back out into the hall.

After school, I didn't even bother going out to the bus. I just called home from the office and told Mom that I was going to visit Halley Kate and asked if Dad would pick us up at the hospital. Mom made me promise not to go anywhere else and to stick with Nathan the entire time. She didn't want any more boys not being where they were supposed to be. I assured her that we were going straight to the hospital and that we would stay there until Dad came.

33

High Above Fair Play

I wasn't sure what to expect or even what to say to Nathan as we trudged over the school lawn, down the street, and across the hospital parking lot. I couldn't help thinking that I should feel different. I had it in my head this thing with Halley Kate was pretty serious, but I guess I was just too young or too inexperienced to really be scared…but I felt like I should be, so I pretended that I was.

Nathan gave the lady behind the tall counter a knowing wave as we walked past on the way to the elevators. He never stopped once for directions or a room number; he knew exactly where he was going. In the elevator my nerves started to catch up a little and I involuntarily shifted my weight from side to side as we rode up to Halley Kate's floor.

"Don't worry, Chris, she'll be glad to see you." Nathan put his hand on my shoulder trying to comfort me, but it didn't work. I just nodded and let go a deep breath. The doors slid open. I trailed Nathan past a nurse's station and around a couple of corners before arriving at a slightly ajar door with Halley Kate's name on it. My chest was pounding; I hadn't seen Halley Kate up close in a long time. Nathan tapped lightly on the door and stepped in. I followed.

Halley Kate's dad was slumped down in a chair with a book lying across his lap. He looked like a broken toy slung across the seat by an ill-mannered child. He wrestled to pull himself right as we came into the room. "Hey, boys," he yawned as he sat up and quickly put his finger to his nose signaling that Halley Kate was sleeping.

"It's okay, Dad, I'm awake. Would you mind opening the curtains just a little please? I'd like to catch a little of the sun before it goes down."

Halley Kate's dad stood to pull back the curtains as Nathan moved straight to her bedside. All of this seemed so personal, so familiar to everyone else, I felt like I was intruding on an incredibly private moment.

"Did you bring him along?" I heard Halley Kate ask Nathan in a dim, hollow voice just as the curtains slid back, letting the remainder of the day stream into the room.

There was Halley Kate tucked neatly in bed with tubes in her arm and an oxygen mask covering her face. She couldn't raise her hand for protection, so she turned her head to the side on her pillow to keep the sunlight from pouring into her eyes. Nathan stood over her like a loving brother, holding his hand up in an attempt to shield her face.

"Sorry, honey," her dad apologized.

Between the darkness and the light, Halley Kate had not yet realized I was in the room. I didn't know if I was welcome or not, so I waited for her to notice me and give consent for my visit. As Nathan hovered by the bed and Halley Kate's dad fidgeted with the curtains, I saw that the whole room was covered with paper. No, not just paper, they were sketches; they were pictures; they were Nathan's pictures taped up all over the room. Nathan's masterpieces covered the walls, the ceiling, and even the television set. His sketches and drawings were everywhere. They were all new. I had never seen any of them before! It must have taken Nathan weeks to do this many!

Nathan had always been good, but what was hanging in this room was better than that…they were…they were *magical.* I had come to see Halley Kate, but these drawings, these irresistible drawings, every one of them threatened to suck me away from this room and straight into whatever fantastic story it was telling.

"So, Chris, what do you think of my art gallery? Do you like it?" Halley Kate had recovered from the invading sunshine and was now sitting up in bed, smiling at me through her clear mask. "They won't let me take this thing off. Sorry, I know it makes me look like I should be trick-or-treating, but they won't let me have any candy either." She rolled her eyes trying to be funny, but her voice was weak and she sounded tired.

"Okay, guys." Halley Kate's dad stepped over to the bed. "I'm going to leave you three alone for a bit." He brushed the hair back out of Halley Kate's face. "She's had her medicine, so she shouldn't misbehave, but you boys will need to keep a close eye on her anyway. Nathan, you know the rules: don't let her get excited, don't let her get up, don't let her take off the mask, make sure that she doesn't pull on those needles, and if you need anything at all or she starts breaking any of the rules, push the nurse button. I'll be close by."

Nathan nodded that he understood and that he would take good care of Halley Kate. Her dad kissed her on the head, ordered her to behave, and closed the door as he left.

"I'm glad you're here, Chris," Halley Kate coughed a little under her mask. "You usually see flowers or balloons, but have you ever seen a hospital room decorated like this? These are all Nathan's." She was so pale and so thin that I couldn't believe this was the same girl who had climbed the bluff. Looking at her frightened me, and I was afraid if I spoke, she might know what I was really thinking, so I just shook my head and stayed on the far side of the room.

"I've been in this bed a long time, but somehow, with all of these pictures, I don't feel so trapped. It's like I can just look at any one of them and I'm there. Like that one, see that one." She motioned to a sketch taped to the back of the door. I didn't know what else to do, so I stepped up closer to take a look. I sniffed with amusement when I saw the anteater with toilet paper hanging from his pants as the monkeys bounced around Noah. I could see my parents sitting in the second row, and I could feel Ms. Strozier's scowl. I could hear the laughter of the audience and the flipping of the programs, and for a moment, I could taste pizza and orange soda.

"Chris," her hollow voice called me back, "I love that one, don't you? It's so much fun. It's almost like I was really there." I turned just in time to see her rub the sides of her forehead with her fingers. "Chris, come sit over here with us. I'm going to call the nurse for ice cream. What kind do you want?"

I heard her question plainly enough, but the drawings around the room weren't quite ready to let me go. There were superheroes battling all manner of evil foes and defending innocent children as crowds of bystanders helplessly looked on. I saw little Peter recognizing Nathan on the street in front of B & B Hardware, there was one of me in Ms. Baird's room and another of the three of us and Robert sitting at a table, laughing in art class. There were pictures of the cabin and the mine and of Halley Kate's adventure out at Boulder Creek. There were a whole lot of sunrises. I remember Halley Kate saying that she liked those. I could see why she loved this enchanted gallery with any of its pieces able to lift her and carry her far away from this room and her sickness.

Somewhere in the back of my mind, I knew it was time to tell Halley Kate that I wanted strawberry, but the sketch taped over the television screen caught me first. I saw a beautiful Halley Kate and a strong, solid Nathan sitting together in some smoky hills high above Fair Play. I could see the hospital, the school, the square, and all the shops along the main drag. The sun was just coming up, but people were bustling along the street already, and I could hear the rumble of the school bus making its last few stops. Halley Kate was so beautiful with a slight breeze flipping her hair and wisps of mist obscuring her smile. Her eyes were bright, and she was so happy. On top of the hill, I could feel myself looking at the red-stripe girl through Nathan's eyes, and I never wanted to see her any other way. I thought I might stay up here high above Fair Play for just a little longer.

"Chris! Earth to Chris, Earth to Chris, come in, Chris." Nathan's silly radio voice dragged me back into the room. He stepped over to me and leaned in to whisper so that Halley Kate couldn't hear, "Be careful, Chris, these drawings are for Halley Kate, not you."

"So," Halley Kate piped up, looking more like herself, "what did you decide, Chris, vanilla, chocolate, or strawberry?"

"Strawberry," I answered with a real smile as I stepped to the bedside.

Halley Kate was so frail, and her deep-set eyes and thinning hair made her look more like Nathan's grandmother than a young girl. The red stripe had faded, and the clear oxygen mask was unable to disguise the exhaustion in her face.

"Usually after a few days I get better. I don't know what's going on with me this time," she apologized as I moved closer.

"It's okay," I said, "you don't look that bad, a little bit like a fighter pilot, that's all."

She smiled at my joke. "I wanted to be better before you saw me, Chris, but I don't know what's happening this time, and I was afraid to wait anymore. So I asked Nathan…" She stopped. I could see a tear start to form in the corner of her eye.

"No, no, it's okay," was all I knew to say as the pain behind my own eyes started to grow. I put my hand on the bed, careful not to touch any part of her neatly tucked under the covers. She had more to say, but the tears rolling down into her mask wouldn't let her choke out the words.

"I have…" she coughed, "I have…"

My heart was breaking, stripping through all my fears as I watched Halley Kate struggle to speak. I was suddenly overcome by such honest sorrow that I could no longer contain myself. "I am so sorry, Halley Kate, I am so sorry," I wailed with monster tears and grabbed her up enough to hold her in my arms. "I have missed you. I'm so sorry. I didn't know. I would have…" I cried as I rocked her just a little.

"Okay, Chris." Nathan's hand fell heavy on my shoulder. "That's not good for her."

I let go, stood back away from the bed, and wiped my nose. I was terribly embarrassed as I watched Nathan adjust Halley Kate's mask and tuck the covers back around her. I was afraid I may have hurt her as Nathan fussed about, wiping the tear tracks from her face.

"I don't think Halley Kate's dad would like that," Nathan announced after finishing up with his patient, "so I think it would be best if we didn't mention it." Nathan sounded just like my dad, and we all agreed that nothing happened. I was terribly ashamed, and I apologized over and over, but Halley Kate said I shouldn't worry and she was glad it happened. Halley Kate and I smiled at each other a lot after that.

"Chris, before my dad gets back, I have something for you. Can you help me get my hand out from under these covers? They wrap me up like a mummy around here." I pulled some of her blankets away to help her free her hand.

"Hold out your hand," she ordered, "this is something that I want you to have. This is something from one of the best days of my life." She smiled up at Nathan. "I've always been sick, Chris, but I have also been lucky. All my life I never had any real friends, not like you and Nathan, but here you are now. I guess we were all meant to be together…like *destiny.*" She smiled weakly. "Chris, I want you to have this and think of me." Then she pressed the arrowhead that she found at the creek into my hand.

The door opened and Halley Kate's dad stepped in. "Well, boys, I think that's probably enough for today. Did you enjoy yourself, sweetie?" Halley Kate nodded to her father. "How'd she do, Nathan?"

"She was a good patient, sir," Nathan answered.

"Well, hopefully before too long you boys can come see Halley Cater out at the house, or maybe she can head out to Cherry Field and to that creek of yours."

"That would be great," I answered, and then we waved good-bye as a nurse came in to check Halley Kate's vitals.

Out in the hall, I had a sick feeling in my stomach. "You must have been coming here a lot," I noted to Nathan as we walked. He didn't respond. "She doesn't look too good, does she?" I tried again.

"No, she doesn't."

"What is it that she has?" I asked, having to hustle to keep up with Nathan's stride.

"She has a lung infection." He sounded angry over his shoulder.

"That's pretty bad, I guess."

We reached the elevator; he pushed the button and turned back to me. "Yeah, it's bad. She's had a lot of them, way more than usual. I heard the doctor talking to her dad. The antibiotics aren't working anymore."

"What does that mean?"

Nathan dropped his head, "I don't know, Chris. I don't know what that means."

The elevator door slid open, and Nathan stepped in. I put my arm out to prevent the door from sliding closed. "Where are you going, Nathan?"

"Downstairs to wait on your dad," he muttered as he pushed the button for the lobby over and over again.

"No, no, no, Nathan!" I didn't like his attitude, and I was losing my temper. "It is not eight o'clock yet!"

Nathan continued to push the button, but I held the elevator captive with my hand at the door. "We're going to the chapel! We're going to the chapel where God listens to you! We're going to the chapel where you begged for your grandmother, and now we're going to beg God for Halley Kate!"

I was yelling at Nathan as loud as I could. Doors up and down the hall began to click shut, and a nurse rounded the corner and headed straight for us as my shouting echoed along the corridor. I spotted the nurse on her way, so I stepped into the elevator and allowed the door to slide shut before she could arrive.

I was desperate. "Nathan, we have to go."

"What do you think I've been doing, Chris? I thought that God would listen to me after what happened with

Grandmom, but no matter what I say or what I do or how hard I plead, Halley Kate doesn't seem to get any better at all." A single tear rolled down the end of his nose. He was frustrated and tired. "Maybe if we went together, Chris, He might hear us better."

My father found Nathan and me in the chapel after visiting hours had long passed. This was the first time I had ever asked God for anything important, and the urgency and honesty of my prayers left me exhausted. When my father finally touched me on the shoulder, I felt much better about everything. I could see no reason in the world that God wouldn't do what I wanted and heal Halley Kate.

I slept well that night and looked forward to seeing my friend tomorrow after school.

34

Never Meant for Children

The sunrise was beautiful and orange. It almost looked like one of Nathan's drawings as the early sunshine streamed across an ocean of pink clouds with its individual rays piercing through to kiss the earth. It looked like the crown of the world, and I understood why Halley Kate loved the sunrise so much. Ms. Baird told me how much she had enjoyed my Liberian story and scrawled "*Chris, you are a wonderful writer,*" across the top of my paper.

She doesn't know it, but she changed the course of my whole life with that one comment. I couldn't wait for the school day to end so I could read my story to Halley Kate and show her what Ms. Baird had written.

The day was beautiful, and I was giddy all the way to the hospital. Nathan hardly said a word as I jibber-jabbered anxiously about anything that came to mind. I felt so much better that I had Halley Kate back and she kind of knew how I felt about her. I was light and hopeful as

I bounced up to the hospital with Nathan, running my mouth the entire time.

"Do you think she'll be feeling better today, Nathan? I hope she's feeling better. Does her dad usually stay in the room or does he always leave when company comes? I hope he leaves again so I can read my story. I guess he could hear it, though. Maybe he'll let us stay a little longer, you know, if she's feeling better. Do you think he may let us stay longer? I mean she likes us being there, so he'll probably let us stay since he knows it's okay. Do you think?"

I went on and on as Nathan marched along. I didn't shut up until we stepped onto the elevator, but even then I bounced on my toes and darted straight out as soon as the doors slid open on Halley Kate's floor. I knew where to go, so this time Nathan trailed behind me. I half jogged and half skipped right past the nurse's station and around the corner as Nathan quickened his pace to keep up. I couldn't wait. I knocked on the door and stepped in. I was quiet in case she was asleep.

The curtains were drawn back and the room was bright. Halley Kate's dad was nowhere to be seen, and all of Nathan's masterpieces had been pulled from the walls. The bed was empty and neatly made. *Oops,* I thought, *I guess I forgot which room.* I turned to see Nathan standing in the doorway. He had his forearm up over his face, and his stomach and chest were jerking uncontrollably.

"What? What's wrong with you? We just have the wrong room!"

Nathan fell back out of the door and crumpled down on the floor with his back up against the wall, starting to wail and sob like a wounded animal.

"It's okay, it's okay, it's just the wrong room!" I shouted at him, but he wouldn't shut up, and he wouldn't stop crying. "Stop it, Nathan! What's your problem? She's just in another room is all! She's just in another room!"

I stepped back into the hall yelling at Nathan, but I just couldn't get him to understand, and he wouldn't shut up. I kicked him in the legs as hard as I could to get him to stop, but he wouldn't, so I kicked him again and again. "They won't let us stay if you keep making all that noise, you idiot!" I screamed even louder than before.

Down the hall, I could see nurses charging around the corner. They were on us quickly, and one slid to the floor, putting her arm around Nathan as another tried to put her arm around me. I shirked it off.

"I'm sorry, ma'am. We didn't mean to be so loud. We just have the wrong room. We're looking for our friend Halley Kate, you know, the one with all the pictures." I could see the sorrow fall across the nurse's face as I tried to explain.

"I'm sorry," she said softly, "you shouldn't be back here right now. We were supposed to talk to you at the nurses' station. Someone wasn't supposed to let you go by." She glared over my shoulder at another nurse.

"Where is she? Where's Halley Kate?"

"I think we should call your parents."

I was getting frustrated, and Nathan was still whimpering on the floor refusing to shut up. "Call my parents, fine, just tell me where my friend is...*please*," I begged.

The nurse put her hands on my shoulders and looked me square in the face. I knew she didn't want to tell me, but I was making it clear that she had no choice. She drew herself closer. "She isn't here anymore," she whispered.

"What do you mean, she went home?"

"No, she didn't go home. She isn't here anymore." Then she put her arms around me and tried to hold me, but my knees buckled, and we both collapsed to the floor. I wailed in disbelief as this stranger dressed in white cradled me outside Halley Kate's empty room.

"Shhhh," she soothed as I sobbed on her shoulder. "Everything will be alright," she whispered into my ear. I hoped she was right, but I knew she was wrong.

Two orderlies put us in wheelchairs and rolled us down to the waiting room. They bought us sodas and peanuts, trying to make us as comfortable as possible until Dad arrived. I never opened either. I just stared blankly at the television fingering the arrowhead in my pocket, wondering how I could survive a sorrow never meant for children.

35

The Dirge of Boulder Creek

Mom didn't bother getting me up for school the next day. Every time she put her head in my room to check on me, I pretended to be asleep, but when she left, I opened my eyes and just stared at the ceiling. I didn't even know what death meant. All I knew was Halley Kate was here and then she wasn't. I kept telling myself if I had just known I wouldn't have saved anything up; I would have poured everything out for her to hear. If I had just known, I could have been a better friend. *This was all so unfair.* Fate was a cheat! Maybe that's why Halley Kate preferred destiny, maybe that's why Halley Kate was so different from the rest of us, and maybe I needed Halley Kate more than she ever needed me.

I twirled the arrowhead in my hand trying to soothe my tangled mind. I thought I was going crazy. *How could this be? How could this happen?* My insides screamed out, but my bedroom ceiling refused to answer.

A car drove up to the house. I could hear the door slam, footsteps on the porch, the doorbell, and a man's voice in the front room. I was curious, but I didn't get up until the doorbell rang a second time. I rolled out of bed and stepped into the hallway just in time to see Mom open the door to find Nathan standing there in his pajamas.

"I thought I saw Halley Kate's dad," he said meekly. Mom knelt down and hugged him tight. I walked over quietly and touched my mom on the shoulder. She turned and included me in her embrace. I saw that she had been crying.

"We have company," Mom finally whispered, and then she ushered Nathan and me back to the kitchen. As soon as Nathan saw Halley Kate's dad sitting at the table with my father, he bolted straight for him, almost tackling him off the chair. Nathan threw himself around Halley Kate's dad as tightly as a little boy afraid of drowning in the neighborhood pool. We watched silently as the two comforted each other without a word. My head hurt as I tried to hold back my own tears, so I reached for my mom, and she took me into her arms. I paid no attention to anyone else as I let go and wept into her dress. Nothing is as unashamed as grief.

We finally collected ourselves enough for Mom to pour coffee for the adults and orange juice for me and Nathan. We sat at the breakfast table as Halley Kate's dad told us that he was going to take her home. They had come to Fair Play after Halley Kate's mom went away and had only been here a few years. He had family up north and thought it was the best place for him to be. He was leaving that afternoon with Halley Kate, and the movers would be packing up the house next week. Halley Kate's dad told us he wouldn't be back.

"I can't tell you, Nathan, how much my daughter loved you. She loved to watch you draw, and she always felt better about everything when you were around. The nurses all talked about how good her vitals were after your visits. Nathan, I will always be indebted to you for making my baby girl so much more comfortable these last weeks. You did it like no one else." He patted Nathan on the arm.

"And, Chris, you know that Halley Kate was never one for middle of the road feelings, she never had the time. You were the one a dad worries about, because Halley Kate loved you something terrible. From the very first day you two met, she told me that there was something wonderful and special about you, and that when she got well, you were going to be her boyfriend. I don't think that she was going to give you much of a choice." He grinned. "She was nervous about seeing you at the hospital." He let out a deep sigh. "Anyway, I didn't want to leave any of her business unfinished, so thank you. Thank you all."

He paused again and gave Nathan a long stare across the table.

"Yes, sir," Nathan answered before a question was even asked. "You can have them all. The drawings belonged to Halley Kate and now they belong to you. And sir," Nathan added as an afterthought, "I did sign one of them...*just in case.*"

We walked Halley Kate's dad to the door, stood on the front porch, and watched as he wheeled his car down the driveway, heading back home and out of our lives forever.

Later that afternoon I went by Nathan's house, and we made a somber trek out to Flat Rock. The water seethed and hissed around the boulders, powerless to change its course no matter how hard it protested. The far bank was lush with near-summer and some stray wild flowers waved to us from the water's edge.

I stood next to Nathan on the big flat rock with the sound of rushing water filling my head. I turned Halley Kate's arrowhead over and over in my fingers. The creek wanted its treasure back, I know, and for a moment I thought about skipping it straight on across, but I just wasn't ready. The arrowhead was mine, and Boulder Creek would have to remember Halley Kate some other way.

I pushed the arrowhead back down deep in my pocket as a slow tear rolled off Nathan's chin. We never said a single word the whole time. We just stood there silently, lost in the dirge of Boulder Creek and wondering what would happen next.

36

Two Bored Boys

Nathan and I didn't go back to school for a couple of days, and then there was only one week left until summer. I didn't worry too much about school after Halley Kate left. I just rode the bus on in, warmed a desk in somebody's classroom, and then rode the bus home again. I didn't see much point in doing anything else. I was sent to the counselor's office a couple of times to listen to some lady I barely knew tell me how sorry she was. She asked me to tell her how I was feeling, but I don't think she really wanted to know, so I said I was feeling fine.

Nathan never did have to discuss his feelings with the counselor, even though he wasn't doing any of his school work either. Of course for Nathan that wasn't anything new. I guess they figured since the trauma hadn't impacted his behavior any, he was probably okay. Now if he'd started doing homework and paying attention in class, I bet somebody would have worried, but he didn't, so they left him alone.

School was coming to its last days, and no one seemed to mind being there as much. A general thrill and delight swept among the kids, and all the teachers seemed lighter and more tolerant of their playful students. It's usually the best time to be at school, but for me everything about it seemed tainted, almost like it was covered in a thin coat of dust. All the pre-vacation buzz left me cold, longing for Cherry Field and Boulder Creek. I did little more than put my name on my final tests, but as it turned out, my lack of effort didn't hurt my grades at all. I guess my teachers felt sorry for me.

Our last day at Fair Play Middle ended as our first had, with Bill hauling Nathan and me out to the middle of nowhere, having just survived another day at school. The bus hit the gravel turnaround at the side of the highway and hissed to a stop. Bill pulled on the lever, and the doors folded open to let us out. Mom was waiting on us as usual.

"Good-bye, Cherry Field, good-bye," Bill called after us joyfully, "I'll be back when the summer's over. Don't make me wait on you now. This big yellow thing will be rolling on up sooner than you think." We waved, and Bill swung the bus hard out onto the highway and headed back into town.

The weather got hot early that summer, and the neighbors' vegetable gardens burst to life, laden with fruit weeks before they were due. Like the beginning of every summer, Mom filled my mornings with odd jobs around the yard, and Dad brought home a pile of books for me to read in the afternoons. Dad was insistent that I do something intellectual while school was out. I always had the best intentions for diving right into my summer reading, but I usually did little more than thumb through any of the books until vacation was nearly over.

This year I decided to read them alphabetically, so I stacked them neatly over on my desk with one called *Awkward Grace* on top. Dad heard it was pretty good, but even so, that book would still have to wait with the others until more of my summer had seeped away. I mostly just milled around the house, both isolated and insulated by the confines of Cherry Field, until Mom threatened to find something for me to do; then I would go to my room and pretend to read or go sit with Nathan on his front porch. The beach was a full month away, but I wasn't even sure I wanted to go. A trip seemed like too much effort just to pull me from comfort of my misery.

Everybody was so obsessed with my lack of activity that when Ms. Hall came to the house accusing me and Nathan of stealing from her garden, Mom used it as an excuse to put me to work, gratis, helping a neighbor clear his yard. Of course I hadn't taken anything from Ms. Hall's garden. The charge of thieving cucumbers and squash—two vegetables I could barely look at, let alone eat—was so utterly ridiculous that I couldn't believe Dad didn't laugh Ms. Hall right off the front porch.

Even though Nathan and I hadn't been around her yard for weeks, she was sure that someone had been picking through her garden, and of course there are no suspects in the whole world better than two bored boys. In fairness, I don't think that my parents believed Ms. Hall's accusation, but still, it gave life to the notion that helping a neighbor was a good way for me to spend some of my extra time.

"Don't think of this as a punishment," Mom explained, "think of it as an experience, an opportunity to help others."

"Come on, Mom, don't make me go over there. It's not fair! Why do I have to go over there and work for free? It's just not fair," I complained bitterly.

"Here's the thing, Chris, you're not reading and you're not writing." She wanted me to keep a diary or write some stories this summer, but about what? "All you do is mope around and grumble about being bored, so I've decided to help you out a little. This has nothing to do with Ms. Hall. This only has to do with you."

"But, Mom," I started to protest again, but she held up her hand to silence me.

"I don't want to hear it, Chris. You need to be at Mr. Lewis's tomorrow at eight o'clock. If you're up early enough, I'll make you some breakfast, if not, you're on your own. You'll need to wear long pants and cover your arms, so get one of Dad's old long-sleeved work shirts. Mr. Lewis is clearing a few feet out of the woods, and he says there's poison ivy. He's old and he needs some help, Chris."

"What's an old man doing clearing the woods anyway?" I muttered to myself as I stomped back to my bedroom to sulk. I plunked down on my bed staring over at the stack of books waiting to be read, and then I got up and headed over to Nathan's house to talk him into helping me with Mr. Lewis.

The next morning, I woke to the sound of Mom rattling around in the kitchen. I thought that I might roll on over and go back to sleep or at least wait for her to wake me, but then I remembered I had work. I thought about staying in bed anyway, but decided it wouldn't be a good idea to provoke Mom this early in the morning, so I got up to brush my teeth. I heard Nathan arrive and Mom offer him some French toast, so I hurried to dress and slinked into the kitchen as Mom was pouring the milk. Mom made really good French toast, and if I was going to be pressed into indentured servitude at Mr. Lewis's for the day, I wanted to get my fill.

Between Mom's good cooking and work avoidance, I sat at the table and ate way more than I could hold. My stomach was tight as a tick, and the milk sloshed around my insides when Nathan and I finally pushed away from the table and walked over to Mr. Lewis's house. I moaned and groaned the whole way over, and as it turns out, the few extra moments of freedom sitting at my mom's table eating wasn't worth feeling like an overblown tire. I let go a belch in the cool morning air that sounded more like a moose than an overstuffed middle school boy and probably had our neighbors scrambling for their deer rifles. Nathan groaned in disgust, saying that he could smell my syrup burp from where he was standing and thought he might barf if I did it again. It was funny, and if I hadn't been so uncomfortable, I might have laughed.

We didn't go by Mr. Lewis's much; he wasn't on the way to the bus or the woods, so our dealings with him were limited to a wave from the porch. We didn't bother stopping at the door; we walked straight on around the house to an unfamiliar back yard. The flower beds and small vegetable garden were neatly kept. The grass was cut low, and I didn't see a weed in the entire yard. Mr. Lewis obviously spent a lot of time fussing around back here, and from the look of things, I could tell that he was "*a place for everything and everything in its place*" kind of man. I'm sure the big red and yellow limb grinder he had rented in town and which now sat in the middle of his lawn was making him crazy. I had a feeling he would want to finish the job as quickly as possible and return the interloping eyesore to wherever it came from.

"Good morning, boys. Thanks for coming," he called cheerfully from his back porch as we came around the house. "Can I fix you some breakfast?" The thought of eating anything else made me sweat.

"No thank you, sir," Nathan laughed back to Mr. Lewis as he watched my reaction to the idea of another breakfast. "We already had French toast this morning."

"Suit yourself then." He took a final sip of coffee and stepped down into the back yard. "I see you have your long sleeves and long pants," he said to me, noting my jeans and my dad's floppy old work shirt, "but what about you, young man?" he asked Nathan. Nathan was wearing white shorts and a white tee shirt. He looked like he had just shown up in his underwear. "You know we'll be pulling out some briars and poison ivy today. Do you want to go put something else on?"

Nathan thought for a second. "No sir, I think I'll be okay, as long as I can borrow some gloves. I'm not really all that allergic to poison ivy, and I'll make sure I wash off good this afternoon. Besides, it's going to be pretty hot today."

"Alright then, suit yourself." Mr. Lewis was old and walked with a slight hobble, but even though he was a little broken down, I still got the sense that he was a strong man who knew the value of experience as a teacher. "Come on, boys, I'll show you the job."

We followed him to the back edge of his yard where his neat, well-kept lawn ended and a thick mat of heavy underbrush began. His yard wasn't very big by Cherry Field standards, and the woods that bordered Mr. Lewis's place seemed a little less friendly than what I was used to. Mr. Lewis laid a stick down at the corner of his yard and then hobbled along the wood's edge another thirty feet and laid another stick down.

"Okay, boys, you see the sticks? That's how wide we go. We're going to clear everything in between and five feet deep." He said "we," but looking at the old man move, I couldn't imagine that "we" meant anything other than me and Nathan. The job looked big, and I wanted to go home.

"We're going to pull all these vines and all this scrub and throw it into this big grinder I have. When you shove the stuff in, be careful not to get too close. That big ol' thing doesn't know the difference between scrub brush and young boys, if you know what I mean."

Nathan and I both nodded that we understood. Mr. Lewis walked us over to his tool shed to arm us with gloves, pruning shears, machetes, scythes, and whatever else we thought we might need to start hacking away at the underbrush. "When you boys get a big enough pile, I'll crank up the grinder and we'll mulch up the whole mess."

"So, Mr. Lewis, are you planning on a bigger garden next year?" Nathan asked as we emerged from the tool shed.

"No, I think I'm too old for that. I just need a little more separation between the woods and garden I already have. I need to do something to keep the danged old rabbits out of my vegetables."

Mr. Lewis stood behind Nathan and me to supervise as we started to tug and whack at the underbrush. But the morning was heating up, so it wasn't long before Mr. Lewis retreated to his back porch to watch us work from there. I was disgusted with the whole set up.

"Danged ol' rabbits," I repeated to Nathan as we struggled with dull tools, "I'm not sure if I'm working for Elmer Fudd or Yosemite Sam." Nathan snorted hard at my observation, which coaxed a snicker from me as well. That was the first we laughed together in a very long time.

Nathan and I worked the whole morning just like we were working for free, so I don't think Mr. Lewis was very happy with our progress. The day was hot, and wearing my dad's floppy shirt made it worse. I was sweaty, I was tired, and I had only a small pile of debris to show for the morning's effort. Looking at the woods, Nathan and I seemed to be getting nowhere.

Mr. Lewis insisted that we have lunch at his house, which was wise on his part, because I wouldn't have been back for hours if I had been allowed to go home. This whole thing was way more miserable than sitting in a cool house reading a book or writing in a diary. *Lesson learned, Mom.*

Our pile of debris didn't grow much faster after lunch, but Mr. Lewis grew impatient enough to come down off his back porch and crank up the grinder anyway. The machine coughed and sputtered to life and then settled into a heavy, low growl like a big red and yellow mechanical beast. Its mouth was wide, and at the bottom was a powerful grinding wheel with big metal rotating teeth. Mr. Lewis showed me how to feed the limbs and vines into the machine as the mechanical monster chewed it all to bits and spit it out the top in a fine spray of fresh mulch. He stood by, watching me closely for a minute or two before returning to his perch out of the sun. I was now in charge of grinding, while Nathan was still cutting away at the underbrush. I guess Mr. Lewis thought we might work faster if he separated us.

As it turned out, he was right. Nathan was dragging armfuls of vines and limbs, adding them to the pile faster than I was able to stuff them into the machine. I thought I had the easy job, but I found that I had to feed the grinder in just the right way for its metal teeth to take hold and suck the debris into the mulcher. So by the time I filled up the mouth and reached in to position the stuff at the bottom for the wheel to catch it, Nathan had already brought another load. I was tired, and I was getting frustrated.

"Slow down, Nathan," I complained on his next trip to the pile, "this stupid machine isn't working right."

"You want me to try, Chris?" Nathan offered, but I wasn't ready to give up the cushy job.

"No, no, I got it. I just wish the stupid thing would work right. I'm tired of being here with Elmer Fudd. I know one thing—I'm not coming back tomorrow."

Nathan nodded and headed back for another load. I reached in again to adjust the debris to get the overstuffed machine to do its job. I fiddled with some privet limbs at the very bottom, taking care not to get fingers caught in the grinder. The wheel grabbed hold and slowly sucked its throat clear of everything I had crammed in. The contraption whined as it spit everything out the top in a flurry of dust and chips. I reached down to collect another armload before Nathan got back. I seemed to have the hang of this thing now, and I wanted to gain a little ground before Nathan added more to the pile. I shoved everything I could hold down into the mouth and reached in to adjust the load for the temperamental monster. I knew what I was doing now, so the machine's teeth grabbed the debris more easily as the mouthful of limbs and vines were slowly pulled into the grinding wheel at the bottom.

I went to retrieve another load for the grinder, but this time I wasn't able to move away. I yanked hard, but still I couldn't pull my arm out of the chute. I yanked again and again, but a long privet branch being slowing dragged deeper into the grinder had fish-hooked the sleeve of my father's work shirt and refused to set me free. I couldn't slip out! The shirt was sweaty and wet, holding on to my arm like a pair of Chinese handcuffs. The monster had me by the wrist, hauling me down into its jaws along with the other chaff. Nothing else made sense but to pull away!

I yanked and I tugged like a fish on a line, but the machine only tightened its grip as I struggled to pull back. It whined loudly as the first chips of this load spewed from the top. Mr. Lewis, sipping tea on his back porch, couldn't hear me screaming over the roar of the big machine, and Nathan was still at the wood line providing more separation between the vegetable garden and the rabbits.

Everything I had never considered about tragedy and pain reeled within me as I realized that my arm was about to be spit out across Mr. Lewis's beautifully manicured lawn. I wailed and begged God as the machine pulled me to my toes, dragging me down its throat with the rest of the debris and lawn trash. No one heard. The red and yellow beast was too big and too loud. It pulled me steadily deeper and whined again in a flurry of chips.

"Hey!" I could barely hear Mr. Lewis call from his porch. Then I realized Nathan was lying on top of me in the mouth of the machine. He had come sprinting across the grass and dived right into the throat of the grinder. His weight pressed my face deeper into the brush as we slid closer to the whirring metal blades waiting for us at the bottom. I could feel him reaching past me, down deep into the machine, struggling to free my shirt sleeve as the beast spewed again from the top. I writhed and twisted, not knowing what he was doing as he fought to pull my sleeve forward just enough to unhook it from the branch!

"No! Stop!" I screamed into a face full of thorns as I tried to kick Nathan off me. And then slack, I was free! Someone grabbed my legs, pulling Nathan and me out of the machine to collapse on the lawn. I lay on my back staring up at the blue sky, panting like a dog. The clouds were rolling over the trees like sea foam on a breezeless summer day.

"Go get help!" Mr. Lewis appeared over me.

"What?" I didn't understand what he wanted.

"GO GET HELP, NOW!" he yelled and then disappeared.

I rolled to my feet to see Nathan lying quietly in the grass. He was weeping softly with big silent tears as Mr. Lewis knelt beside him, telling him that everything would be okay. Mr. Lewis kept saying how sorry he was as Nathan mustered an occasional tearful nod. I saw that Mr. Lewis had stripped off his shirt and had wrapped it around Nathan's whole hand. It was bright red and full of blood.

"GO-GET-HELP!" he commanded me once again. This time I understood. I launched to my feet and ran straight home to my parents.

37

Familiar Little Waiting Room

I bolted through the door breathless to explain as best I could what had happened. Dad ordered me to go get Nathan's grandmother as Mom rifled the hall closet for the first aid kit. They jumped in the car, tearing off across the grass and around the house into Mr. Lewis's neatly kept back yard. I explained to Nathan's grandmother on her front porch, but I didn't wait for her to get her purse from inside the house. As soon as her back was turned, I leapt from the stairs and ran straight back to Nathan and the scene of the accident.

Mom had removed Mr. Lewis's shirt from Nathan's hand and had wrapped it up in enough gauze to weave a catcher's mitt...but it still wasn't enough. Bright blood soaked the bandages all the way through. I felt myself start to swoon at the sight and had to lean over on Dad's car parked at the edge of the flower garden. Through fading eyes and ringing ears, I saw my dad lift Nathan's limp body and slide him into the back seat. My mother followed him in. I don't even remember climbing into the front seat or picking up Nathan's grandmother as she was walking over from her house. I remember the two women cradling an unconscious Nathan in the back of the car, praying and reassuring one another as they worked to catch his blood on their own clothes.

As we sped toward town, I felt like I was watching some terrible scene cut right from a movie I would never want to see. I admit at that moment I felt relieved Nathan was lying there across my mom's lap instead of me. But that feeling didn't last forever, and I'm not sure if it is a matter of time or perspective that makes me wish now the situation had been different.

Dad carried Nathan into the hospital through the emergency entrance. Nathan's friend behind the counter took one look and had him immediately whisked away in a blur of nurses. Dad helped Nathan's grandmother give the lady behind the counter some information, and we were shown to our familiar little waiting room. This place was beginning to be my home away from home. One of the nurses took Mom and Nathan's grandmother down the hall somewhere to get cleaned up and to change from their bloody clothes into some doctor's scrubs. Mom looked good, just like a real doctor, when she came back, sat down, and leaned against my father.

When Nathan's shriveled old grandmother showed back up in her scrubs, though, she looked more like something straight out of a comedy skit. I don't know why she thought that she had to wear the cap. In other circumstances I would have laughed out loud, but I slouched down into my chair instead, to do what you always do at hospitals…*wait.*

I watched the clock tick every single second away as we sat in silence. Nathan's grandmother was the only one who bothered to look through any of the ancient magazines, tattered and lying on the little end tables around the room. Mom lifted her head from Dad's shoulder.

"Chris," she said softly, "can you tell me what happened?"

I felt a sudden flood of emotion threaten to burst from my eyes when she asked. The whole accident started to replay in my mind. The whine of the machine, the smell of fresh mulch, the beautiful blue sky, and the terror of helplessness all swirled inside me. I didn't realize that I was so upset. "I got…I got," I snorted and choked. "I got…" I couldn't get the words out as my eyes began to water.

Mom raised her arm, inviting me to her embrace. I went to her immediately, just like a little baby without any shame. "I got, I got caught," I finally stammered out on to her shoulder. "He, he, he…" The words still wouldn't come.

"Just relax, just relax, Chris," Mom soothed as she patted my back, "it's okay. Everything is okay."

"He, he, he….saved me," I choked.

"Mr. Lewis?"

I pulled away and shook my head. My ears were ringing and my nose was all stopped up. Everything I was feeling, everything that I needed to say was all rushing for the exit, causing such a jam up that nothing was getting out. "No, no, no, ma'am," I stammered again, "it was Nath,

Nath…" I closed my eyes, took a deep breath. *"Nathan saved me."*

"Knock, knock." We were interrupted by a light-hearted doctor entering the room dressed just like Nathan's grandmother. I turned my head and wiped my face. "Well," the light-hearted doctor announced, "it looks like he's going to be fine…but there will be some permanent damage. He's lost about an inch from the tips of three fingers on that right hand, and unfortunately, there's nothing that can be done about that. They were severed pretty clean, bone and all. He'll be better with physical therapy, but if he plays an instrument or does anything much with that right hand that requires any fine dexterity… well, he won't be able to do it anymore. I'm sorry. Any questions?"

We didn't have any right then.

"I'm going to ask that," the doctor looked down at his clipboard for the name, "*Nathan,* stay here over night so we can keep an eye on him. We're going to dose him up with some heavy antibiotics so that he doesn't develop any infections, and you can take him home tomorrow. The nurse will be down to talk to you shortly. One of you can stay the night if you want, just ask the nurse. Alright then, folks, I'll talk with you tomorrow." We thanked the doctor as he backed out of the door and disappeared down the hall.

38

Already Been Told

The day had been too much for Nathan's grandmother, so after we all peeked in on a sleeping Nathan, it was my mom who stayed the night with him. The next morning Nathan's grandmother wasn't feeling well enough to make the trip into town, so Dad and I rode in alone to collect Nathan and Mom from the hospital. Mom still looked surprisingly good in her scrubs, and Nathan was awake and sitting up in his bed when we walked into his room. Cartoons were on the television, but Mom didn't seem to mind. She stood up and hugged us both and then asked Dad out into the hall to talk about something private and adult. Nathan just stared up at the television as if I wasn't even there. I didn't know what to say, but I couldn't stand not saying anything at all.

"How are you doing, Nathan?" It was a stupid question, but it was all I could think of.

"I've been better," he answered in a flat tone, not taking his eyes off his cartoon.

"How does that feel?" I nodded at his right hand wrapped in white bandages lying across his lap.

"Numb," was his short answer.

Nathan obviously had no interest in talking, but standing there in silent guilt, pretending to watch *Mighty Mouse,* was even worse for me than Nathan's curt responses.

"Did the doctors tell you anything about your hand?"

"Well," he broke his attention from the television to look over at me, "they told me I would never play trumpet or accordion again. Apparently the bugle *is* still an option, so I guess I have that going for me." He shot me a weak smirk.

"You're probably still good for the cymbals too, I guess."

"Yeah, Chris," he smiled a little bigger this time, "I hadn't thought of that, and probably the cowbell. I hear a good cowbell player can go far these days."

He seemed better, so I took the opportunity to take the conversation where it had always been headed. "And of course you'll be drawing again in no time, so you have that going for you too."

As soon as the words left my mouth, I knew that it would have been better left unsaid. The smile fled from Nathan's face as he lifted his hand to examine it. He turned it slightly back and forth to get a better look. "I don't have enough fingers left to hold a pencil the way I like to, Chris," he said, still staring at his hand. A tear rolled down his cheek.

"I'm so sorry, Nathan," was all I knew to say now.

"Oh, don't feel bad about it. I did it to myself. It was my choice."

But I did feel bad about it, and I still do, so I wasn't ready to let it go just yet. "Come on, man, don't talk like that, you're the best in the world. I really mean that, and I'm sure that you'll be drawing again in no time at all."

Nathan was still staring into his hand, answering me from somewhere else in his head. "It would have been nice to have kept it just a little longer, but after Halley Kate left…I really didn't need it anymore."

He was acting really weird. "What are you talking about, Nathan? You'll be able to draw again just like before."

He dropped his bandaged hand back to the bed and smiled over at me. "I don't think so, Chris, but it's okay. That part of the story has already been told."

39

Watching

For the next two weeks the summer dragged by even more painfully than usual in Cherry Field. There wasn't much to do other than help Mom in the yard, ignore the books stacked alphabetically on my desk, and wait for Nathan to heal. My parents had invited Nathan on our beach trip, which was still a week away, so Nathan and I sat on his porch for hours, talking about catching sharks and finding gold coins in the surf. Dad had an argument with Ms. Hall about us stealing her tomatoes, so he told us to steer clear of her yard. It seemed like everybody was going crazy, or maybe they always were and I was just now starting to notice. It didn't matter anyway, because Nathan was in no shape to make the trip out to Flat Rock and to our usual distractions, so staying out of Ms. Hall's yard was no problem.

My bedroom was hot when I woke up, and I lay there under the fan listening to my parents stir through the house. The day was early for me, but I'm sure that Mom and Dad had been up for hours listening to the news over coffee and preparing for their daily chores and errands.

"Honey," I heard my mom call to my dad from the front porch, "do you know where that little camping spade is? I need it to do a little work between the shrubs and the house, and that's about the only shovel we have that will work in such a tight spot."

"It was out in the garage the last I saw," my dad called back from the kitchen.

"No, it's not there. I've looked. Where in the world could that thing have gotten off to?"

As I lay there in my bed listening to their conversation through the house, I realized that her spade lay neatly hidden in the underbrush along with a bucket, a rope, and a pulley at the edge of a clearing by an old, decaying cabin. I had been punished before for leaving tools in the woods, so if she had asked me about it, I'm sure I would have lied. The summer was hard enough without being shackled by some parental restriction for a crime I had committed months and months earlier. That wouldn't be fair. I took a deep breath and wondered how I could avoid being questioned about the missing tool when I heard my father greet Nathan at the door.

"Well, hey, buddy, how are you feeling?"

"Much better, sir, thanks. See how small my bandages are now? Grandmom says that everything is healing nicely, but gosh, it sure does itch."

"That means it's healing," I heard my mom interject as she walked in from outside.

"That's what Grandmom says too," Nathan answered.

"So what can we do for you this fine morning, young man?" my dad asked, using his good-natured jovial voice.

"Well, I've been cooped up so bad I just came over to see if Chris wanted to go down to the creek with me. We haven't been in a long, long time…ever since…well… Halley Kate left. I thought that it might do me some good to get out, you know, with my fingers and all."

There was a pause in their conversation as my parents considered his request. I'm sure that Mom had plenty of chores for me this morning, but Nathan had mentioned both Halley Kate and his fingers, so I felt sure that she would let me go. Now I could go get the spade and hide it somewhere in the garage where Mom would be sure to find it. Trouble avoided. How lucky was this?

"Okay then, Nathan, how long are you guys going to be gone?" I heard Mom ask.

"I think all day, ma'am."

"Well, I guess I had better make you boys some sandwiches."

I smiled to myself and walked into the room stretching and yawning. I acted surprised to see Nathan.

I got dressed and gulped down some cereal as Mom packed our lunches. I was relieved about the spade, but I was also eager to see the creek again. We hadn't been in a long while. Flat Rock had always been my sanctuary, but it was the first thing I had abandoned after Halley Kate left and Nathan had his accident. I had only made one silent trip back since either, but still, I couldn't help feeling that the creek already knew about everything that had happened.

"Chris, you and Nathan go way, way around Ms. Hall's yard," my dad ordered as we headed out the door. "I'm sure she'll be over here as soon as she lays eyes on you two anywhere near that garden of hers, so let's not aggravate that old lady any more than we have to."

"Yes sir," we answered in unison as we leapt down off the bottom step, giddy about our overdue trip out to Flat Rock.

We rounded Ms. Hall's yard and slipped into the woods undetected. The canopy was full and the shadows were deep. Nathan and I paused for the trees to recognize us as we stepped in and allowed our eyes to adjust to the new light. Our usual path was thin with lack of wear, and the heavy summer growth crowded in, threatening to reclaim our beaten way if we didn't pay more attention. Prickly vines and underbrush nipped at our ankles as we passed along, and I couldn't help feeling like I was getting the cold shoulder from a long-neglected friend. Even so, I was glad to be back, and I was certain everything would warm up again before the day's end.

Looking around at all the new growth and weedy flowers, I wondered what had really kept us away, and I was sorry that Nathan and I hadn't come back sooner. I could hear the rush of water up ahead as Nathan traipsed along behind me. I quickened my gait, and before much longer, Nathan and I were standing shoulder to shoulder at the edge of the bluff peering down at Boulder Creek. There wasn't as much water as usual, maybe with the summer drought, and Flat Rock seemed a little bigger and the climb down more menacing.

Everything was the same but at the same time everything was different too. You couldn't really see the difference as much as you could feel it. This year we hadn't been present for the changes of summer, but I figured as soon we reacquainted ourselves with our old stomping grounds, everything would be back to normal. We'd be digging for gold and hunting arrowheads in no time. I slid over the side for the climb down, and Nathan followed me without any problem. We planted our feet on Flat Rock, taking a solemn moment to stare out over the water.

"It was a sad day the last time we were here, eh, Chris?" Nathan and I were both thinking the same thing.

"Yeah," I responded without breaking my gaze out over the creek.

"You know what's weird, Chris?" Nathan was looking down at the water flowing by. "It might look like it, but this isn't the same water as the last time we were here."

"What do you mean?" I was still looking out over the boulders.

"I mean the water is always passing by on its way to somewhere else."

"Yeah," I sighed, considering his thought, "but look around, Nathan, these are still the same rocks. They're always left behind."

"Yeah," Nathan agreed.

"Hey," I broke the moment, "I don't want to just stand around here all day. Let's head over to the beach and see if we can find another arrowhead or maybe a gold nugget or something. We both know you couldn't skip a rock before, but now that you're *No Fingers Nathan,* who knows what you can do!"

Nathan smiled wide. I hadn't searched for treasures on the far bank with him in a long, long time. Usually I just judged what he found, but today was different, and I was feeling grateful. We slid off Flat Rock and waded to the other side to spend the day looking for arrowheads and catching salamanders. The rocks and the bluff echoed hearty laughter as Nathan and I reminisced above the sound of water. We talked about my clay bomb, Ms. Flitty Art Teacher using his fried egg in the front case, and the time when Jimmy and Brett got poison ivy. We made all sorts of jokes about Mr. Butler and Ms. Strozier. We laughed loud, but the woods didn't mind.

"I couldn't believe it when you told Mr. Butler that you were paying attention, just not to him." I chuckled at the memory.

"What about you, walking out on stage in front of the whole town with toilet paper coming out of your costume! That was the best!"

"You're crazy; it was way better when you had to go to school smelling like a skunk and they sent you to the nurse. Ha ha ha!" I laughed so hard that I slipped and fell over into the water, soaking all my clothes. There was no point in getting up, so I just sat with the cool water washing around me.

"How about on the bus, and you fell out of the seat on the very first day when Bill pulled the Cherry Field turnaround? That was great…on the first day, Chris. That was funny!"

"No, no, no! On the first day, it was better when you stepped on Halley Kate's purse and Ms. Addler thought someone was chewing grape bubble gum. I can just see her sniffing and walking up and down the aisle like a bubble-gum police dog! "

Our tit-for-tat game was over with the mention of Halley Kate, and Nathan sat down in the water next to me. The year had been better than I thought, but at the same time, it had also been harder than I wanted to remember. The creek gurgled by.

"Where do you think she is, Chris?"

"Her dad said they were headed back up north."

"No, Chris, I mean where do you really think she is?"

I knew how I was supposed to answer, or at least I thought I knew what Nathan wanted to hear. But Halley Kate really loved the sunrise, so I thought she might be somewhere with her pants rolled up wading in that or maybe searching for treasure along its rays. I liked the way that felt. But it sounded stupid, and maybe even a little sacrilegious, so I kept it to myself.

"Watching," I answered, "I think she's watching."

"Me too," Nathan agreed.

I paused a long while to find courage for my next words. "Nathan, I'm sorry about tipping your books in the hall."

"I know."

"And for the butterflies too."

"I know, Chris, but thanks for saying so."

We stood up out of the water to skip a few stones. As it turns out, the wet bandage and three missing fingertips didn't help Nathan's skipping ability at all. Everything he threw plunked straight into the water. Mine, as usual, skimmed all the way across.

40

A Great Day

We had eaten our lunches and spent the whole day free of our cares…in absolute freedom. This was a great day. I felt good for the first time in months and thought maybe I could finally write a few things in that journal my mom had given me. Ms. Baird said I was a good writer, so maybe I should at least try. Next year would be different for me and Nathan. It would be a second chance to be a real friend. We had been through far too much together now for me to ever go back to being such a jerk. Nathan and I spent the day soaking wet, talking about all the important things boys do and throwing rocks as Boulder Creek carried away the time.

"Oh gosh! Look how late it's getting, Nathan! Mom and Dad are going to kill me! We got to get home." The sun was just now dropping into the trees, signaling that we had dallied here too long. I plunged into the creek to wade back over to Flat Rock, make the climb, and head back to the house.

"What about your mom's spade, Chris?" Nathan called after me.

Shoot! He was right. I was already in enough trouble for being late, but if Mom didn't have that spade in the morning, well, it would all be a lot worse. I turned and made my way back over to Nathan. We climbed up on the far bank and pushed our way up to the hidden path that led back to the cabin. Nathan moved nimbly down the little path ahead of me. I was in a hurry, but it was impossible not to notice the overwhelming scent of honeysuckle all around. All the time we were working on the mine, these vines had been flowerless, but now they were in full, leafy bloom, called to duty as first guardian of the hidden cabin. The summer underbrush was so much thicker than before that it was almost like we were discovering this place for the first time.

Nathan broke into the clearing at the cabin ahead of me, but I was close behind. I had almost forgotten how bottled up this little clearing was with only one way in or out. With summer growth, the woods had tightened its viney grip on this secret place, and now that the sun was sitting low, it felt more like a trap than the friendly place where we used to play. Automatically Nathan crossed straight over, brushed away some leaves, and slid the cover off the mine.

"What are you doing?" I asked.

"I don't know, Chris," Nathan admitted, stepping back in my direction. "I guess it's just force of habit."

"Yeah, well, we're in a hurry, okay. So let's get Mom's spade and get on home." I started for the tools when I noticed the ashes of a cold campfire. There was a blanket lying beside it.

"Nathan, come over here," I muttered.

"I know, Chris, look."

Nathan pointed up into the brush where the woods had tightly woven its perimeter around the cabin yard. There, hanging from the vines right above all of my hidden dirt, were a pair of pants and a shirt that had been set out to dry. The remaining sun was starting to sputter and the air grew gray.

"Someone's been here," Nathan shuddered.

I breathed deep, forgetting about the spade. "I think we had better get out of here, Nathan."

He nodded and we both moved to retreat down the path…but it was too late. Someone was coming! We could hear him moving through the honeysuckle. I thought to hide in the cabin, but there was no time! The feeling of being sucked into Mr. Lewis's machine stirred through my stomach. Someone was coming, and all Nathan and I could do was step back and let him come. The underbrush rustled closer, and he emerged.

41

The Gingerbread Man

The sandy-haired man with an arm full of vegetables and a pack of hotdogs didn't notice us right away. He was still trying to untangle his foot from a vine he'd picked up while carrying his goods down the tight little path. Nathan and I stood still and quiet. I thought about bolting right past the man while he fiddled with the vine, but I hesitated, and when he looked up and saw us watching, it was too late. He seemed immediately at ease with our presence, almost as if he was glad to see us.

"Why, hi, guys, what a surprise," he said lightly, meaning to rhyme. "I don't get many visitors. My name is Donnie, what's yours?" His voice was a little whiny and high pitched, but his manner was friendly and inviting.

Nathan grabbed my arm to silence me, but I couldn't help myself. "I'm Chris," I answered, trying to sound confident, "and this is Nathan."

"Well, it's good to meet you, Chris and Nathan. You sure came at a good time. I've just been shopping. You know that old lady who lives up the way? Well, she grows the absolute best vegetables I have ever eaten. *And, and, and, and...*she keeps a little meat in that freezer out in the garage, so tonight we have hotdogs! I'm sure you guys are going to want to stay for dinner. Am I right or am I right? *I-have-plenty*!"

"Well," I stammered, "maybe, but I'll have to ask my mom first." I took Nathan's arm. "Come on, Nathan, let's go ask."

"Nooo, you don't need to go and do that, Chris. I'm sure your pretty little mom and that big ol' dad of yours will say it's just fine," Donnie grinned as he placed his vegetables and hotdogs neatly on the ground. "I think what we really *need*...is to get us a fire going so we can cook up this beautiful bounty that I have so graciously provided. Whata ya say, Chris?"

Donnie stood up, blocking our way to the path. In the remaining sunlight, I could see that he was youngish and slightly built. He wasn't much taller than I was, and if I had just two more years, I don't think he could have stopped me from leaving.

"Ah, Chris, you really don't want to stay? That hurts my feelings. What about you, Nathan? Do you want to stay and have supper with your new friend Donnie?" He moved away from the path to sit down on the log where Nathan used to rest while waiting for me to close up the mine.

Donnie waited, but Nathan didn't answer. He just stood frozen and mute, so Donnie turned his attention back to me.

"Well, Chris, there have been a few others that didn't want to hang out with ol' Donnie either. I guess we're all entitled to our own opinion of who is and who isn't fit to eat alongside. Ordinarily I don't even make this offer until everybody is found and accounted for, but the cops around here are so dang stupid, I don't think they'll ever find my little friend over in Crabapple. Besides, it's not like I'm out here fishin'. I'm just out here coolin', but what am I supposed to do if they just jump on in the boat? I guess I'll do like anybody else would, and go ahead and fry 'em on up." He smirked like a devious little weasel.

I had no idea what he was talking about, which unnerved me even more. His tone had remained light and cordial. This all felt like a dream as the sun dipped down a little further. I couldn't wrap my mind around all that was happening. I hadn't yet put it all together—*the boogey man that Fair Play had worried about all year and this stringy little ferret sitting on the log insisting that I stay for dinner.* Sometimes it's hard to recognize the devil face to face.

Nathan stood silent, and I was growing more uneasy.

"If I don't go ask, though, my parents will come looking for me," I protested weakly.

"That is *sooo* funny, Chris! You know as well as I do that nobody will ever, ever, ever find this place. I'll bet the three of us are the only ones in the big wide world that even know it exists. The whole FBI could walk right on along here and never see a thing. Look at those trees, look at those vines. This place is like my very own 'Fortress of Solitude.' Nobody, and I mean nobody, will ever find me here, and *they-won't-find-you-either.* I can do whatever I want as long as I have this place to hole up. SO, SIT DOWN AND SHUT UP, CHRIS!" He lost his temper and it surprised me, so I dropped to the ground immediately where I stood.

"No, no, I'm sorry, Chris. I didn't mean to yell." His tone was light and friendly again. "Come on over here and sit next to me. It's alright. I won't get mad again."

I stood, not knowing what else to do, and walked slowly over to Donnie. He patted the log, inviting me to sit down next to him. So I did.

"What's wrong with your friend Nathan over there? Does he usually stand around frozen like a dumb statue? Hey, Nathan, what's wrong with you, boy?!" Donnie hooted across the little clearing and laughed.

The light had really fallen off now, and without Donnie's campfire, I could barely make out Nathan's outline in the gray. Between now and the moonrise, I thought, Nathan might be able to simply disappear down the path for help.

"Hey, Chris, I got an idea." Donnie's attention was back to me. "If you don't want to stay for dinner, that's okay, but before you go, why don't we at least play the choke game like me and Daddy used to. I didn't like the game much when I was little, but I got better at it. Daddy used to say that it helps a boy grow up strong and tough. He was real good at it too, God rest his soul. He died in prison a few years back, and I haven't been able to find a good game since.

"Here, let me teach you how to play just like Daddy taught me. Problem is, you can't be scared, okay, Chris? Daddy always used to say 'They don't make boys like they used to,' but I don't think that's true, so let me show you how, and we'll just see how good you are. Who knows, you might be a natural." He let go another weasel's snicker.

"I don't think I want to play."

"NONSENSE, BOY!" He grabbed me by the back of the neck and shoved me forward off the log. "EVERBODY PLAYS!" I went to my hands and knees. "NOW GET UP SO WE CAN GET TO IT, CHRIS!"

Donnie stood over me waiting for me to pick myself up and face him. The moon was just starting to rise, peeking through the trees and making Donnie look much bigger and more menacing in its shadows.

"Come on, Chris, let me show you. There's nothing to be scared of." Donnie was back to being friendly again. "Here we go," he said as I pushed up to my feet. "I'm going to grab you around the throat and I'm going to start squeezing. You bang down on my arms with yours as hard as you can, and if you're able to break my grip... well, then you win. *But, but, but, but,*" he wagged his finger at me, "if you don't...well, then you lose. I guess that will leave me and Nathan, but he doesn't look like he has too much game in him."

I could see Nathan better now in the moonlight. He stood, still frozen, and I wasn't sure if he was in shock or just waiting his turn to play the choke game with Donnie. I wished Dad would come, but Donnie was right, nobody would ever find this place. Nobody would ever find us.

"Good luck, Chris, but just so you know, I *am* the undefeated choke game champion of the world with a standing record of twenty-one and zero." He cupped his hands over his mouth to make a fake crowd roar and then raised his arms and spun around like an arrogant prize fighter.

"After tonight I'll be twenty-three and zero and on my way to a *new-world-record* of fifty consecutive victories… maybe more, if I'm careful and take good care of myself. I'm the scariest thing they've never seen, and no one even has a clue who I am! That is *so* cool! I'm invincible! I'm like some kind of shadow scout or the gingerbread man or something, right, Chris?"

Donnie was the kind of crazy that you only see in movies, and watching him beam in the shadows about all of his victories at the choke game, I knew Nathan and I wouldn't be going home. I swallowed hard and my head began to swim. I was sure I couldn't defend myself from Donnie any more than I could defend myself from Mr. Lewis's limb grinder. I couldn't move and I couldn't speak as I watched Donnie dance around bragging on himself in the pale air.

A slight breeze came through the trees, and the moonlight danced all around, making everything seem to move in slow motion. I could smell the honeysuckle, and I could feel the dark audience of vine-covered trees moving in closer to watch. If anyone was looking for us, they would be too late. The beast of my parent's fairytale was here to claim his next prize, and Nathan and I were too weak to stop him.

"Here we go!" Donnie was back up in my face. "Ready or not!" His eyes locked into mine, and a big, slow smile crept across his face. He paused briefly, waiting for some internal signal and then, quick as a whisper, his hands sprang up from the shadows and caught me around the throat. He was fast and he was strong, and I could feel his fingernails dig in like barbs on the back of my neck.

I struggled to break his grip, writhing and flailing and beating down on his wrists trying to pull free, but his arms were like baseball bats and his hands like steel. This must be what drowning feels like. The fight in me waned, and all the strength began to fade out of my body. I was already exhausted, and I was surprised that everything would be over so quickly.

"Too easy! Too easy!" I heard Donnie laughing somewhere in the distance. "Ha, ha, ha! You should see your face, Chris!"

My dry eyes felt like they would burst from my skull as fluid streamed from their corners. They began to darken and fail. I wanted to go home. I was so late, and I was going to be in so much trouble. I needed to start reading those books on my desk before too much more of the summer got by. I held on to Donnie's wrists loosely to prop myself up as I tried to stay awake.

"Ha, ha, ha," I could faintly hear Donnie laugh again, "I wish I had a mirror!"

I hadn't taken a breath in forever, and the moonlight and the shadows around me began running together into a single blur. *It's just about over,* I thought.

Over Donnie's shoulder, I could see Nathan's face slowly floating in the gray light. I could hear nothing but Donnie laugh and a faint rustle at my feet as my sleepy legs thrashed involuntarily through the leaves. My ears were ringing, and it seemed like I might not really even be here. Nathan's face floated closer. *What about my reading books?* My mother's spade, I could almost see it hovering in the shadows. *She's going to need that tomorrow. I have to take it home before she finds out.*

Thud! I heard the sound of the metal slap bone as Nathan swung the spade heavy in the dark, catching Donnie in the side of the face. He released me, and I fell to the ground gasping for breath. Everything was spinning as I lay there gulping for air.

"OOOO, OUCH! DANG IT, NATHAN, THAT'S CHEATING! THAT DOESN'T COUNT! YOU'RE NOT SUPPOSED TO HIT IN THE FACE!" Donnie leaned way over, holding the side of his face like he had been stung by a giant bee. Nathan went to take another swing, but Donnie took the spade away from Nathan easily and flung it somewhere into the bushes. I lay on the ground trying to collect myself, but my strength wasn't coming back quickly enough.

"THAT HURT, YOU STUPID LITTLE TURD! YOU'RE A CHEATER, YOU KNOW THAT!" Donnie moaned, cupping his cheek. "AND CHEATERS NEVER WIN, NATHAN! CHEATERS NEVER WIN!"

"Run, Nathan!" I rasped from the ground.

"Shut up, Chris!" Donnie kicked at me with his foot. "You know that doesn't count."

Donnie stood at the head of the path blocking Nathan's only escape. It didn't matter, though, Donnie wasn't hurt all that bad, and he would have caught Nathan easily if he had somehow managed to get by. The moon shone through the trees, and long, dark shadows licked through the cabin yard. The passing clouds threw us into intermittent darkness, but in between we could see everything that the moonlight and the trees would allow. Nathan stood and watched quietly from the far end of the clearing.

"So I guess you want your turn now, huh, Nathan? It isn't going to be fun like me and Chris," Donnie sneered and touched his sore cheek. "There's no place to run either, so don't make me chase you, 'cause you'll only make things worse if you do."

Donnie crept toward Nathan carefully like he was approaching a skittish rabbit. "Now don't you move, Nathan," Donnie coaxed in his friendly voice, "and everything is going to work out *just* fine."

Nathan stood silently in the darkness and obeyed.

Donnie moved slowly over to Nathan, expecting him to break and run for the path, but Nathan never moved. Donnie slithered closer, until he and Nathan were face to face.

"You popped me pretty good, Nathan, but that was cheating, so now we're going to play for real." Donnie smiled and went to put his hands on Nathan's throat, but Nathan slapped them away. "Ooooo, aren't you the tough little guy," Donnie cooed with a big grin.

I slid my hand along the ground and found a stick about the size of a souvenir baseball bat. If I could just pick myself up, I was sure I could hit Donnie a lot harder than Nathan had.

"I'm not worried about you, Donnie." Nathan spoke for the first time. "You're nothing but a skunk. I'll bet my grandmother can choke harder than you...and she's like a thousand years old."

I thought Nathan would be stalling this lunatic, not trying to antagonize him. Donnie smiled big and let out a whiny little laugh. "You shouldn't talk to me like that, Nathan." He sighed deeply like he was considering his next move, and then quick as a serpent, he shot his hands up around Nathan's throat. I heard Nathan gag and choke for air; the strength would be gone from him soon.

I pulled myself to my feet, club in hand, without any thought of my own escape. Donnie's grip tightened, wringing the life from Nathan like a wet sponge. I staggered closer. Nathan held on to Donnie's wrists, writhing in a futile attempt to break free. Donnie laughed with delight.

A breeze whispered through the honeysuckle, bathing the three of us in its perfume as I moved closer. Donnie gritted his teeth and groaned, forcing more strength into his hands. He gasped as he squeezed the life from Nathan. Nathan dug his nails in tight on Donnie's wrists, twisting like a hooked fish ready to make its final run for deeper water. He held fast and lurched back with all of his remaining might, pulling Donnie one step forward over the edge of the mine.

Donnie screamed trying to catch his balance, but Nathan didn't let go, and together they plummeted into the pit that had been conspiring with Nathan before we even knew about Donnie. Instantly they were gone!

There was silence. A breeze kicked up through the vines. The woods had swallowed them up like they had never even been there.

42

The Hiding Spot of a Secret Place

Everything was suddenly quiet, and a new terror ran up my spine. I was alone with the gaping black pit watching me and waiting for me to do something. I knew that I could run for help now, but Nathan was in the hole and help was a long way off. I only had a second to decide. Donnie was down there too, waiting, and I was sure that he would be even more dangerous than before. *Should I run for help?*

Trembling, I shuffled through the moonlight toward the mine. I dropped to my hands and knees, sliding up to the edge on my belly. I hung my head over the side and peered down into the deep blackness.

"Nathan, Nathan," I whispered into the hole. "Can you hear me? Are you okay? Nathan, Nathan!" No answer, only the smell of damp dirt and clay. "Nathan, please, *please* answer me," I begged. But still there was only earthy silence.

I sat up, not knowing what to do. I beat my head into my hands and started to cry for the first time since Halley Kate. I rocked back and forth, feeling myself slipping away to a place where I wouldn't have to move, to a place where I didn't have to do anything at all. I wanted to go back in time so none of this would have happened. I wanted to disappear, to fade away, to have never existed. I rocked and hummed to myself at the rim of the mine. I needed something. I needed something familiar, something routine, something predictable!

I felt like a ghost as I floated to my feet and drifted to the edge of the underbrush. I reached deep into an old hiding place and pulled out our bucket, pulley, and both ropes. The light was dim, but it didn't matter, my hands knew what to do. I had done this a hundred times before. I strapped the pulley to the limb and threaded the rope through without even thinking.

"Nathan, Nathan," I whispered down into the hole, but I got no answer. I hoisted his backup rope to my shoulder. I felt like I was watching someone else as I stepped into the loop, swung out over the mine, and started to lower myself in.

The pulley creaked under my weight, and I swayed gently from side to side as I let the rope run through my fingers. I wasn't thinking anymore, I was just moving along frame by frame like some hapless victim in a bad horror movie. It didn't matter, because this wasn't really happening to me anyway.

I watched myself descend deeper into the pit. I could hear my breath and the strain of the rope on the pulley, but nothing else. The mine had always been stingy with noise. I was a universe away, suspended alone in total darkness with only my heart beat and the sound of my breath to let me know I was still alive. Time passed so slowly that if not for memories of Halley Kate, I would have guessed I had been lowering myself into this abyss for my entire life. *Why did we to dig this thing so deep? This is taking too long. This is not right.*

My bearings were lost. I had no idea how far I had descended or how much further I had to go. The rope creaked and I swayed. Thoughts of what waited for me at the bottom preyed on me until I changed my mind and decided to pull myself up and run for help instead. I stopped. I listened. I swayed gently.

Then right as I was ready to change course, my foot brushed somebody lying quietly on the bottom. I recoiled and held my breath. My heart was beating up through my throat. I closed my eyes tight as I hung there, waiting to feel the hands around my throat again…*but nothing.*

Donnie was either dead, unconscious, or playing another game. I took a deep breath to collect myself. I stepped down off the rope on top of the two tangled bodies lying in the dirt. I knelt down among them. The darkness was oppressive, and I had to search like a blind man looking for his cane to find Nathan. I was too afraid to whisper, and when my hand ran over the back of Donnie's head, I pulled back and froze, praying not to wake him. But again, nothing; he didn't move.

I went back to work, and feeling around, my hands told me that Donnie had fallen on top of Nathan and they were all mashed up together. But even blind, it was easy to tell Nathan from Donnie. I had lost all track of time, but I sensed that it was running out. There was no time to be afraid. I had wasted too much of it already. So at the risk of waking Donnie, I reached into the dark and tugged and pulled at his arms and legs, untangling him from Nathan. Finally I rolled his limp body to the side. I slid the backup rope off my shoulder and looped it around Nathan's chest up under his arms. I patted his shoulder, but he still lay quiet. I reached around, found my rope, and hoisted myself to the surface.

The moon was bright as dusk now and the smell of honeysuckle blew through. I whipped my rope off the pulley and threaded the end of the backup rope over the top. It was untested and a little smaller than our regular rope, so I prayed that it would be strong enough to pull Nathan up. I took in the slack until the rope went taut with Nathan's weight.

I had hauled Nathan out of this hole a hundred times, but tonight, somehow, he felt heavier. I pulled and I pulled, but this rope was more of a clothesline, and it stretched with the load. The elasticity of the line made everything more difficult. I panted heavy in the moonlight. Exhausted, I could feel myself starting to panic. Hauling Nathan up had never been like this before. A terrible thought sprang to mind. *Was it really Nathan I was pulling out of the mine?* I paused.

"Nathan, Nathan," I whispered as loud as I dared, but no response came back. "Nathan, Nathan," I tried again, but still no answer. I was tired, my hands hurt, and I was suddenly afraid that I might be bringing Donnie up from the pit. For an instant I thought about letting go of the rope and dropping the whole load back to the bottom…but I didn't, and I started to pull again.

One more pull, two more pulls, three more pulls… there he was—I could see his head! Another pull and another, and he dangled limply above the mouth of the well. I held on to the rope, working my way over and finally hoisting Nathan safely to the surface. In the moonlight I could see that the fall into the mine had crushed him up pretty good.

Without thinking, I automatically unstrapped the pulley and started to wind it up in the rope. I heard Nathan stir. *Thank God,* I thought and knelt down beside him. A moon beam meant just for him pierced the canopy above to light his face. He shot me a weak, smirky little grin.

"Ahhhh crud, Chris," he groaned, "I guess…" He paused to draw a breath, "I guess…I guess…this means six more weeks of winter."

I shook my head and laughed a little through my nose. "You're going to be okay, Nathan. I'm going to get you home."

He took a deep, labored breath. "I know, Chris. I know you will. Thank you, Chris. Thank you for getting me out. Thank you for not leaving me." Then Nathan closed his eyes and went to sleep.

"Hey, Chriiiiis, hey, Naaathan," the pit called sweetly. "I know you're up there."

Even though I was standing at the edge of the mine collecting the gear to hide it in the underbrush, I could just barely hear Donnie's faint voice from the bottom of the hole. *The mine was stingy with noise.* Donnie sounded sweet and healthy. "You really got me good, boys. I admit it, you win, game's over, now it's time to help me out of here."

I continued to put away the tools as Nathan lay silent. I shoved our gear into its usual place in the underbrush where no one would ever notice. I walked back to the edge of the mine and stared down into the black pit. It was a long way down, and Nathan and I had killed a lot of time digging it out looking for imaginary gold. I had a feeling that we wouldn't be coming back. I had a feeling that nobody would be coming back.

"Hey, fellas, I was just foolin'. You know how I am; I wasn't really going to hurt you guys, you boys aren't like all the others." Donnie's syrupy voice faintly echoed from the bottom of the pit. "Oooo, Chris, I think I may need a doctor. I think I may have twisted my ankle a little bit. Please, come on now, pull me out. I need a doctor for my foot."

I listened from the top as Donnie went from coaxing to pleading to yelling. "GET ME OUT OF HERE NOW OR I'LL START WITH YOU, CHRIS, AND FINISH WITH EVERY KID IN FAIR PLAY! IT WILL ALL BE ON YOUR HEAD! DO YOU HEAR ME, CHRIS? IT WILL ALL BE ON YOUR HEAD!" He screamed as loud as he could, but the mine only gave up a whisper of his threats.

Nathan lay unconscious, so the cabin was the only witness as I dragged the cover over the top of the mine. I couldn't hear Donnie anymore. Then, just like Nathan had always insisted, I spread leaves across the top to camouflage our claim. It was indeed the hiding spot of a secret place that not even Halley Kate knew existed.

43

Boulder Creek Always Keeps Its Secrets

Nathan was hurt bad, and I had to get him home. I tried to lift him, but I couldn't manage his weight, so I took him by the wrists and dragged him away. His foot got tangled once or twice in the honeysuckle as I pulled him down the narrow cabin path to the creek bank.

"Nathan, Nathan," I shook him gently trying to wake him up. I needed him to walk so we could cross the creek, but he wouldn't move. Boulder Creek was loud, keeping the rest of the world away as I knelt beside my friend. Its white waters showed like teeth in the moonlight. "Nathan, Nathan," I tried again…but nothing.

I grabbed his wrists again and pulled him down into the water. I hoped that the creek would revive him, but Nathan floated limply as I dragged him over the rocks. "I'm sorry, I'm sorry," I apologized as I pulled him over the rocky creek bed, but he didn't complain. I reached down and took Nathan by his shirt collar to keep his head above the surface as we moved into deeper, swifter water. I slipped and fell, but I wrapped my arms around Nathan, holding him close, to keep Boulder Creek from taking him away from me.

"Help! Help!" I yelled, but only the rocks and the trees on the far bank heard me. I sat clinging to Nathan, trying to regain my footing as the water rushed around us, licking away all evidence of the mine from our bodies. I slipped again, gulping water and almost losing Nathan to the creek.

Why won't he help? Why won't he wake up?

I was holding Nathan tightly around his chest now, in a tug of war with Boulder Creek, trying to keep his head up and from being swept away myself. With all my strength, I struggled against the relentless rush of water. I was exhausted and breathing heavy when I finally stood waist deep leaning up against Flat Rock.

"We made it. We made it, buddy." I patted Nathan across his shoulder. I held him there, resting for a few minutes, and then I reached down, taking him around the waist, and rolled him up onto the rock out of the creek. I climbed up after him, panting and wondering how I would get him up the bluff.

"Come on, Nathan, quit fooling around now. Get up so we can get home. Please, Nathan," I begged, *"please wake up."* I sat down to rest.

"CHRIS! THANK GOD! CHRIS!" Flat Rock was suddenly bathed in light from above. "Chris, are you okay?" my father called from behind the flashlight beam.

A radio crackled. "This is Deputy White; we have located the missing boys," I heard another man's voice report. "Are you boys okay?" Deputy White called down from the bluff.

"He…he fell!" I yelled up. "Nathan's hurt, Dad. Nathan's really hurt!" I went to my knees and started to cry.

The radio crackled again. "Cindy, we need an ambulance and a rescue squad out in Cherry Field right now. Tell them this is a rescue, and they will need rappelling gear on site. Tell them to get here now! We have a boy down. Repeat, we need rescue now! We have a boy down!"

"He fell, Dad, he fell!" I wailed up the side of the bluff. "And he's not waking up!" I convulsed into sobs.

"It's going to be okay," Deputy White called down from behind the light, "help is coming. I don't think I can make it down to you, son, so just try to relax and stay with your friend."

"You're going to be fine, Chris. Everything is going to be just fine, now that we found you boys. Help will be here soon." Dad tried to comfort me as my tears rolled off Flat Rock and into Boulder Creek.

I don't know how long I was there before I heard other voices above. Flat Rock was suddenly doused in a light as bright as day, and firemen came crashing over the side of the bluff. They zipped down in their rappelling equipment as easily as stepping off a curb. They examined Nathan briefly and then strapped him into a flat sled and hauled him straight up. They buckled a rope around me and pulled me up as well, but by the time I got to the top, they had already taken Nathan away.

Dad hugged me, radios buzzed, lights flashed, and a paramedic looked me over. I could hear the fireman stomping back through the woods carrying Nathan to safety. A summer breeze picked up, carrying honeysuckle from the far bank. I heard the trees sway and the creek rushing by to somewhere else, but only the mine could hear Donnie's screams for help. I walked home with my dad and Deputy White without saying a word.

I had nothing left by the time we were shown to our little waiting room at the hospital that night. The doctor said that Nathan had ruptured his spleen in the fall and was gone before he ever arrived at the emergency room. I wondered if he had even made it out of the cabin yard or if Boulder Creek had pulled him away from me after all.

Mom and Dad never asked anything more about the accident or why Nathan and I had been so late that night. I guess they were afraid to. Everyone assumed that Nathan had fallen from the bluff, and I just let them believe it. Besides, the cabin was never going to tell, and Boulder Creek always keeps its secrets.

44

The Bones of Boulder Creek

That ended the worst string of serial killings this country has ever seen. You may remember the press calling these the Black Jack Child Murders because they stayed at twenty-one. Of course the FBI kept looking, but without any more victims, their investigation ran into a dead end. So after a while they boxed up all their evidence and filed it behind a cage somewhere in the unsolved mysteries section of a government records room.

People eventually began feeling safe again, and all the small towns that had been plagued by the boogeyman were finally able to relax. No one ever knew, or even seemed to care, what had happened or who had saved them.

Nathan's grandmother had his body cremated and then she packed up everything lock, stock, and barrel to move to Florida. She couldn't sell her house, so Mom and Dad dipped into their savings and bought it from her. Then we had to move too. I guess that was my fault, though, because after Nathan left, I didn't talk for a while. Dad's passed away now, and Mom lives with us. She is having a hard time remembering things these days. Just yesterday she asked me if I ever keep in touch with my old friend Nathan. I didn't tell her that I talk to him every single day.

I write a little column in our local paper, and I teach social studies at the middle school. My wife is a health consultant working from the house so she can be home when Nathan, Christopher, and Katie get off the bus. Their bus ride is only about five minutes long, and we live in your basic neighborhood with lots of houses and other kids for them to play with. There are some days I lament cheating my children out of the magic that a creek and the woods have to offer. I guess every decision has its price.

Many years ago, I promised Nathan that I wouldn't tell anyone about the cabin or the gold mine, but Nathan always saw me better than I am, and since there's no time limit on a promise, I guess I'm breaking my word now. Sitting under the fried egg on the edge of my desk are the settlement papers I received last week for the sale of our properties out in Cherry Field. They have already bulldozed the houses and are clearing the land on the far bank for the factory they're building.

Anyway, I saw on the news that all work has been halted with the discovery of some human remains. The conjecture in the press is the bones of Boulder Creek belong to a squatter of "unknown origins," but the authorities are saying at this point they simply don't know. Well, now they do know, and the FBI can go ahead and move the Black Jack Murder files to the solved side of the records room.

I've turned this arrowhead over in my fingers a million times, agonizing over what to do if they found Donnie in the construction. I tried to honor my promise and say nothing, but I've decided now that I would rather honor my friend with our story instead. As Donnie said...*It is all on my head.* If I did wrong, well, there is a reason genies are bottled. As self-serving as it sounds, I don't think everything is so easily judged, even in hindsight. In the end, you have to look carefully to find meaning; if not, you will find only history. There is much more to truth than fact, and there's more to destiny than fate.

I spent so much of our relationship being ashamed of him, but as it turns out, Nathan is the kind of person I wish I had always been and I wish to always be. My heart aches for the things I can never undo and for those I have left undone. I wish that I had been kinder. I wish that I had been a better friend.

"Thank you, Nathan, thank you for everything...and please say 'Hi' to Halley Kate for me."

The End

Made in the USA
Columbia, SC
27 January 2020